TED TAYLER

RED HERRING SEASON

BOOKS

TED TAYLER

RED
HERRING
SEASON

vinci
books

By Ted Tayler

The Freeman Files

Fatal Decision

Last Orders

Pressure Point

Deadly Formula

Final Deal

Barking Mad

Creature Discomforts

Silent Terror

Night Train

All Things Bright

Buried Secrets

A Genuine Mistake

Strange Beginnings

Dead Reckoning

A Normal November

Into the Sunlight

Tame the Storm

One True Friend

Whispered Truths

A Morning Murder

Quick to Anger

Red Herring Season
Gathering Clouds
Still Standing

Vinci Books

vinci-books.com

Published by Vinci Books Ltd in 2025

1

Copyright © Ted Tayler 2022

Chapter One

THE ELUSIVE SCOOP

Tuesday, 6 November 2018

THERE HAD BEEN few days since he became Chief Constable where Kenneth Truelove had wished he could have stayed in bed. Every day brought a fresh challenge, especially when the Police and Crime Commissioner was on the warpath. The phone call he'd received from the current PCC late last night had put the proverbial cat amongst the pigeons.

As he stood by his office window, gazing across the car park, Kenneth knew his planned itinerary was disappearing over the horizon. Should he have asked Vera Butler to call Gus Freeman to tell him their morning meeting would have to be postponed? He wasn't looking forward to informing Gus that, sooner rather than later, he was losing four team members.

Kenneth prayed the enforced disruption would only be temporary.

According to the PCC, a new group of activists

announced they were launching a concerted civil disobedience campaign. In addition, intelligence gathered by the Metropolitan Police suggested the minor outbreaks they'd monitored over the past two weeks would escalate from the seventeenth. As a result, they sought additional regional officers to bolster their already stretched resources.

"The Met need boots on the ground, Mercer," he'd told his right-hand-man as soon as he arrived at London Road this morning. He repeated the PCC's words.

"We don't often hear the words intelligence and the Met in the same sentence, Sir," said Geoff. "Why don't they tell the Premier League they can't have police boots around the football grounds next weekend?"

"The PCC stressed that Extinction Rebellion is calling on the government to reduce carbon emissions to zero by 2025," Kenneth had continued. "They want to establish a citizens assembly to devise an emergency plan of action similar to that seen during WWII."

"I remember reading about that crowd a couple of weeks ago," said Geoff. "One hundred academics, including a former Archbishop of Canterbury, hit the headlines by backing the cause. Given the scale of the ecological crisis, they believe it's an appropriate scale of expansion. More than sixty people have already been arrested for glueing themselves to government buildings and blocking major roads in the capital. I hope it doesn't catch on and spread to the streets of Devizes."

"Groups similar to this have come and gone," said Kenneth. "Extinction Rebellion hope their campaign of respectful disruption will change the debate around climate breakdown and signal to those in power that the present course of action will lead to disaster."

"Good luck with that, Sir," said Geoff. "We've seen what

happens when large groups of people hit the streets in London. All sorts of extremists come out of the woodwork to join in the fun. It's never a good time to be a copper in uniform, even if you've got a riot shield and bulletproof vest. Respectful disruption won't last five minutes if someone like the Anarchist Federation gets wind of what's happening."

"They emerged from the Miner's Strike in the mid-Eighties, didn't they?" asked Kenneth.

"Yes, Sir, and came to prominence during the Poll Tax riots five years later," said Geoff. "They've been under the Met's watchful eye ever since, along with several other unsavoury organisations."

"The PCC wants a list of names from me by the end of today," said Kenneth. "I know it's going to be unpopular, but to reach the numbers he quoted last night, we'll need Grace Packenham and the three serving officers working with the Crime Review Team to travel to the capital."

"What, and leave Gus and Lydia Logan Barre to soldier on alone?" said Geoff. "How long will we lose the others?"

"They'll have to leave immediately," said Kenneth. "The Met has sufficient trained personnel to cope with a moderate influx of protesters, so I don't envisage all four getting sent to the Specialist Training Centre in Gravesend. Freeman's people aren't up to speed with current crowd control techniques, so I foresee their role filling gaps in other less confrontational situations. How long for is another matter altogether. The PCC wasn't prepared to commit himself on that score."

"I wouldn't want to face DI Packenham in full riot gear, Sir," said Geoff. "However, DC Umeh would probably be best behind the counter at the police station at Paddington Green."

"Quite," said the Chief Constable. "Horses for courses. Hardy and Davis might find themselves at the Emirates or Stamford Bridge watching the crowd."

"What will you do with the civilians on the Crime Review Team, Sir?" asked Geoff. "I imagine Wiltshire will be losing personnel from other sections across the county."

"I'm sure Ms Logan Barre will appreciate a change of scenery," said Kenneth. "It will be another credit on her CV when the time comes for her to move up the ladder."

"You'd like me to find Lydia a special project she can handle with minimal supervision," said Geoff.

"You read my mind, Mercer," said Kenneth. "Something to occupy her for ten days."

"Did you cross your fingers then, Sir? Does that mean you're concerned this civil disobedience business will be an ongoing thorn in the Met's side?"

"If it is, and spreads countrywide, every region providing support next weekend will need their people back. Then they'll have to start hunting for additional boots on their own patch," said Kenneth. "I don't think anyone can predict how long this will last. Ours not to reason why, Mercer, we must adapt to whatever the government and the people throw in our direction. Our opinions are irrelevant."

"Message received, Sir, though I haven't got a clue what Gus will think about it all."

"I've been wracking my brains all night trying to think of the best way to break the news to him," said Kenneth.

"Don't look at me, Sir," said Geoff.

"Typical," said Kenneth. "I suppose I'd better stick to the planned meeting over lunch and tell him he's not getting another case to review until this rebellion business quietens. I don't want you sneaking off, Mercer. Is that clear?"

"Crystal, Sir," said Geoff.

DS Mercer had left the office, and Kenneth took up his position by the window. A light tap on the door told him Vera was outside.

"Come in," he called.

"Everything's ordered for your lunch, Sir," said Vera. "I spoke to Gus just after he arrived in the Old Police Station office. He'll be here at noon with another completed case file to present."

"He never ceases to amaze me, Vera," said Kenneth.

"Gus enjoys doing what he loves, Sir. After his superiors in Salisbury decided they could dispense with his services, he thought he'd never get another opportunity."

"I hope he can pick up where he left off," said Kenneth.

Vera looked puzzled.

"Don't worry, Vera," said Kenneth. "Events in the capital have forced me to hit the pause button on the work Gus and his team are doing so ably. Yet, somehow, I must find a way to break the news to him gently."

"Oh dear," said Vera, "rather you than me."

"Not you too, Vera," groaned Kenneth.

"You're paid to make the tough decisions, Sir," said Vera. "I've every confidence you'll make the right one on this occasion too. You haven't let us down so far."

Vera crept out of the office and closed the door. She sensed the Chief Constable would be standing by that window for a while. Time to find Kassie Trotter to tell her the news.

IN THE OLD Police Station office, Gus and the team were working hard on the housekeeping. They were otherwise engaged at the custody suite yesterday, so there hadn't been enough time to update the Freeman files when they returned to their desks after lunch.

Almost as soon as Gus had sat at his desk at nine o'clock this morning, Vera Butler had called from London Road. He'd gone out on a limb and promised her everything would be ready to hand the completed Millie Clark case files to her boss by noon. When the call ended, Gus looked to see whether an early frost had struck the mood in the office. He needn't have worried.

"I should be finished before ten, guv," said Lydia. "I can either do the coffee run or remove street maps and crime scene photos from the walls. Which comes first?"

"I won't be far behind Lydia, guv," said Blessing. "We'll make short work of both jobs if we work together."

"That works for me," said Gus. "Grace and I had more to update this morning due to our involvement in the interview with the Clark sisters. Does anyone think we'll struggle to make the eleven-thirty deadline I recklessly agreed to?"

"We'll be ready, guv," said Alex. Neil nodded.

Gus glanced towards Amazing Grace, but she continued typing at an impressive speed without responding. He checked his notebook and calculated how long it would take him to finish his report. It wouldn't pay to slack.

By ten o'clock, Lydia and Blessing were heading for the restroom. Neil was first to break the silence after the drinks had been delivered.

"I reckon we should keep searching for Tyler Rowe, Alex. What do you think?"

"If we can prove he was guilty of the assault on Viv Whitaker," said Alex. "When we listened to what Jeanette and Monique had to say yesterday, it was hard to distinguish fact from fiction. They misled the police on so many occasions."

"Nobody could recall seeing Tyler Rowe in Bristol after he left that flat," said Neil. "My guess is he *did* move to Westbury or Warminster. Because, although the sisters convinced the police that Tyler contacted Micah Harvey, there were good reasons for him to disappear."

"Cameron Keel recognised Tyler as a guy he'd often seen around the city," said Alex. "But Harvey and Coombs had dozens of men on their books, and Keel didn't know his name or role in the gang. Coombs just needed numbers to help search properties in Withywood. Keel made sure someone reported the Whitaker incident to cover his backside. That attack brought unwanted attention to the gang's business affairs. Thanks to Jeanette and Monique's misdirection, all five gang members ended up in court on trial for Millie's murder."

"The sisters couldn't have foreseen what would happen next," said Neil. "If everything had gone to plan at the first trial, they would have been home free. Jeanette and Monique would have pinned the blame for Millie's death on the drug gang. Nobody would have queried the result. The sisters could have waited for the dust to settle, then sold the watch. Nobody would have been any the wiser."

Lydia had been listening while she helped Blessing clear the decks ready for the next case.

"I wonder if Tyler Rowe ever did go to Warminster," she said. "Monique told Gus that Tyler went to the flat in Weymouth Street, not to get Jeanette back, but to see whether he could persuade Millie to buy her drugs from him."

"I thought Tyler told the gang where Millie was because she was one woman he couldn't get into bed," said Blessing. "I was wrong about that, but Neil's right. We should start looking for Tyler Rowe. He deserves to go to prison for what he did to that poor man."

"I agree," said Lydia. "We could start by asking any unmarried mothers with kids under five if they're chasing a boyfriend for unpaid maintenance. Tyler Rowe will be among the names we hear. I'd bet on it."

"Of course, he may have moved again," said Blessing. "Nathan Harvey told Gus he and Craig Coombs could wait. They would find Tyler Rowe in time and deal with him."

As Lydia and Blessing were busy cleaning the whiteboards while they still chatted about the case, Alex collected the empty cups to return them to the restroom.

"You were quieter than usual yesterday, Neil," said Alex. "Did that have anything to do with Jake Latimer and Rick Chalmers?"

"Don't remind me," said Neil. "Melody was not a happy bunny when I arrived home on Sunday."

"What time did the taxi drop you off?" asked Alex.

"Just before lunch," said Neil. "Rick had suggested I jump into a taxi with him when he left the club in Swindon Old Town at two o'clock. I wish I'd gone with him, but Jake persuaded me to go back to his place. Janina wasn't asleep when we arrived. She realised we needed plenty of coffee, but Jake topped our mugs with rum once her back was turned. According to Jake, I fell asleep at four."

"Did Jake keep drinking?" asked Alex.

"I didn't believe it was possible to drink yourself sober," said Neil. "When I surfaced at around half-past ten, feeling like death, Jake still had a glass in his hand and was as bright as a button. He asked if I wanted a fried breakfast. That finished me. When I finally left the bathroom, I rang for a taxi and crawled through my front door at a quarter to one. Safe to say, I'm grounded until after the baby's born. Melody's mother stood beside her as I crept into the kitchen to get myself a black coffee."

"It was a good night, though, apart from that?" asked Alex.

"A cracking night," said Neil. "Young Travers was a lightweight. Two pints and he was giggling like a schoolgirl. We lost track of Travers early doors. Jake and Rick know a lot of coppers who enjoy a drink, as you can imagine. Several pubs in Swindon, and the club in Old Town, probably had their best takings of the year. Apart from Christmas Eve and New Year's Eve."

Alex disappeared to the restroom. When he returned to his desk, Lydia and Blessing had just finished getting the office ship-shape.

"Is there anything the three of us can do, guv?" he asked.

"The biggest help you can offer will be to keep the noise down while Gus and I finish our reports," said Grace.

"That's us told," said Neil as he leaned back in his chair. "My contribution is ready to go, Alex. So who's in charge of collating everything?"

"Forward your files to me, and I'll do it," said Grace.

Lydia and Blessing escaped to the restroom.

"Someone's touchy this morning," said Lydia.

"I don't think Grace has got used to sleeping at the farmhouse," said Blessing. "John and Jackie Ferris are up at the crack of dawn, and there are more bird and animal noises in the countryside than Grace is used to."

"You've never complained since you moved there," said Lydia.

"I'm a heavy sleeper," said Blessing. "My alarm went off

three times before I was awake enough to silence it this morning. Grace will become acclimatised in time."

"Should we risk going back to our desks?" asked Lydia.

"If we don't, she'll only have more ammunition to throw at us after Gus drives to Devizes."

Lydia could see sense in that, so they made their way quietly back to their desks.

Gus closed his notebook and read through his final summary. It had been an odd case throughout. Perhaps there were instances where Tom Brewer could have chosen a different path to follow, and he might have uncovered the truth. But it was several days before Gus realised the main characters were being orchestrated by a hidden hand. It never ceased to amaze Gus what families could do to one another.

He forwarded his file to Amazing Grace and checked the clock on the far wall. Unless Grace was struggling, he should make his noon appointment with the Chief Constable even if there were traffic delays in Seend.

"Almost there, Gus," said Grace.

"Uncanny," said Gus. "I hadn't said a word."

Grace spent a further five minutes editing and polishing her report. Then she gathered the contributions the rest of the team had provided and sent the completed file to the printer.

"I always enjoy that sound, guv," said Blessing. "It means that later this afternoon, we'll learn where in the county we're off to next. Another week, another new destination."

At twenty past eleven, Grace handed Gus the case folder.

"We'll see you later then, Gus," she said. "Have fun."

Gus slipped on his jacket, grabbed the folder, said farewell to the team. and made for the lift.

No two trips were ever the same between the Old Police Station and London Road. Gus left Church Street and headed out of town. He negotiated the first two round-abouts without needing to stop, and then he spotted a new sign as he approached the roundabout leading to the custody suite on Crook's Way.

"That wasn't there yesterday," said Gus.

He caught the gist of the message as the line of traffic drove past at a sedate thirty. Six hundred and fifty new houses were due to be built in the field on his left. Bob, the House Builder, apologised in advance for any inconvenience this would cause over the next two years.

Gus wondered whether he'd still be making this trip when the two, three, and four-bedroomed townhouses were scarring the landscape. Yet, one of the few pleasures on this stretch of road was the rolling pastures and uninterrupted view of Bowden Hill and Caen Hill.

The journey through Seend and onwards to Devizes passed without incident, but Gus was still concerned with the poor souls who would enjoy the views he cherished while struggling to find school places for their children or get registered for a doctor or dentist. So, perhaps, Bob, the House Builder, should reserve his apologies for the town's newcomers.

Gus parked in the visitor's car park at London Road, rescued the case folder from the passenger seat, and trotted up the steps of the main building. Once inside, he gave the desk sergeant in Reception a broad smile and a wink. Gus knew that would unnerve someone who spent most of his working life facing people who sneered or snarled as soon as they set eyes on them. Gus liked to do his bit to even the score.

Vera met him at the top of the stairs.

"Geoff Mercer will join you in a minute," she said. "The boss is waiting for you. Kassie will deliver your lunch within the next five minutes. I hope you're well. How's Suzie?"

"That's more words than you've shared with me for months, Vera," said Gus. "Have I missed a balloon going up somewhere? I can only assume you've heard bad news. What is it?"

"Kenneth will explain," said Vera. "He hasn't given me the full details. Kassie has her new set of wheels today, by the way. You won't hear her trolley coming across the mezzanine."

"A rapid change of subject doesn't fool me, Vera. I smell trouble."

Vera gave Gus a sympathetic look and returned to her desk. Gus spotted Geoff Mercer emerging from his office and crossed the mezzanine to join him.

"I would have appreciated a heads-up, Geoff," he said as he fell into step beside him.

"It's only temporary, Gus," said Geoff. "As far as I can tell."

Geoff knocked on Kenneth's door. They waited for a grunt from inside and then entered. The Chief Constable had completed his car park survey and sat at his desk.

"Good morning, Freeman," he said. "I see you have brought the fruits of your labours from last week with you. Another successful cold case review. Well done. I must admit it was a surprise to learn the killer was someone nobody suspected. My money was on one of the gang members. I can't wait to read your report. Perhaps you could give me the headlines?"

"I thought I was here for some kind of announcement, " Gus said. "When Vera met me at the top of the stairs, I half expected her to say she was sorry for my loss."

"All in good time, Freeman," said Kenneth. "Did Tom Brewer emerge unscathed from your investigations? I have fond memories of working with him many years ago."

"Several opportunities were missed by detectives in Bristol and Warminster, Sir," said Gus. "The distance between Withywood and your old stamping ground might be low in mileage terms, but they were light years apart in how they were policed. Mick Budd and his team worked under a Chief Constable with a very different approach to how things were run here by the man in your chair five years ago."

"I was that man's Assistant Chief Constable, Freeman," said Kenneth. "He had his faults, but I think DS Mercer will agree; we were singing from the same hymn sheet. Barry Knee was in charge in Bristol between 2012 and 2015. Unfortunately, he left under a cloud, and although I don't expect to see a written report on the matter, it's safe to say the IOPC has held a series of interviews with senior officers working in Bristol during that period."

"A rough translation of which is that Knee's pension's safe," said Gus. "If anyone asks an awkward question, they'll get told there's nothing to see. Move along, please."

"I couldn't possibly comment, Freeman," said Kenneth. "So, the inference from what you've uncovered is that Harvey and Coombs got an easy ride from DI Budd and his team. The gang may have had someone on the inside protecting their interests. Maybe financial inducements were offered and accepted. If the Bristol team had been more diligent, they could have provided Tom Brewer with more pertinent information."

"That's a fair analysis, Sir," said Gus. "However, Monique Clark was the person pulling the strings. Her younger sister, Jeanette, was weak and easily manipulated. I learned just how much the sisters were involved on Saturday night. That's when the pieces of the jigsaw fell into place."

"I hadn't realised you were working on the case over the weekend, Gus," said Geoff. "You didn't clear any overtime for the team with me."

"I suppose I'd better come clean," said Gus. "Nathan Harvey sent his thugs to collect me. I was enjoying a nightcap in the Lamb with a friend, Brett Penman, and after he left me in the lane outside my bungalow, I was grabbed and taken to a remote spot where Harvey told me how we'd all been duped by Monique and Jeanette Clark."

"You could have been killed, Gus," said Geoff. "Why are we hearing about this now?"

"I was perfectly safe," said Gus. "Harvey would never have accepted the offer of a friendly chat, and we needed a lot more to get him into an interview room with his solicitor. So, I decided to listen to what he had to say."

Gus thought a little white lie was permitted, just this once.

"It doesn't sound like you had much choice," said Geoff. "Were they armed?"

"Of course," said Gus. "But with three of them in the car, I would have had to go to meet Harvey whether they were carrying a gun or not. Harvey insisted he and Craig were never near the churchyard. They stayed in the flat until Keel and Thatcher returned. Micah Harvey had gone with them and confirmed Millie Clark had been punished for her part in the robbery. They left the girl alive, as instructed, lying by a gravestone. The five men then made their separate ways back to Bristol. Harvey said someone attacked and stabbed Millie after they'd left."

"Very convenient," said Kenneth. "That was their defence at the first trial, but why should you believe a word he says?"

"I reminded him that Keel and Thatcher claimed they weren't responsible," said Gus. "Those two assumed, instead of heading straight for Bristol, that someone went to the churchyard and killed Millie. Micah had driven to Warminster alone, and Nathan and Craig travelled by car together. Keel believed one of those three could have done it. Nathan pointed out that Micah is left-handed, so, as Henry Ash swore the attacker was right-handed, that ruled him out. At that point, Nathan Harvey told me about his gold watch."

"DI Budd told Tom Brewer that Millie had sold the valuables stolen from Harvey's property to buy drugs," said Geoff Mercer. "I hadn't realised Millie Clark still had anything to sell."

"Millie hid several items at her home in Withywood," said Gus. "Jeanette found the gold watch. Monique realised it could help them escape from Withywood, and that's when they hatched the plan to move to Warminster. Millie had been a thorn in her mother's side for almost fifteen years. Monique convinced Jeanette she would always have to get her out of trouble. The best they could hope for was an overdose. That's when Monique started sowing the seeds which would confuse the investigation and offer an opportunity to murder Millie and put the blame on the drug gang members."

"A tangled web," said Kenneth. "I look forward to reading the report in full."

Gus hoped he was about to hear the real reason behind this lunchtime session.

There was a knock at the door.

"Come," called Kenneth.

Curses, foiled again, thought Gus. Kassie Trotter breezed into the room, pushing her shiny new trolley. She was still suited and booted, with numerous tattoos hidden beneath a crisp, white shirt.

"Good morning, gents," she trilled. "Luncheon is served."

"Someone's full of the joys of spring," said Geoff.

"I have your favourite baps today, bacon and sausage, Mr Mercer," said Kassie. "Plus, a cream horn for later if you have room for it. "

"He'll find the room, Kassie," said Gus. She handed him his chicken wrap and a black coffee.

"Thank you, Kassie. How's Noah?" he asked.

"Oh, everything's going fine, Mr Freeman," she replied. "There's just one dark cloud on the horizon. Noah wants to meet my parents."

"Quite right, too," said Geoff. "I remember doing something similar when I was ready to ask Christine to marry me. I wanted to check with her father first, to see whether he was happy for his only daughter to marry a young police officer."

"He must have said yes," said Kassie. "You're still together, despite everything."

"Quite," said Kenneth. "What do you propose to do, Kassie?"

"Perhaps I should come back later when you're not busy," said Kassie.

Gus knew why Kassie was concerned about Noah's wish to meet her family. Kassie had left home at sixteen. The bright lights of London enticed her, as they did so many others.

Kassie had returned eighteen months later, stayed with school friends, sleeping on their sofas, and then when the hospitality ran out, she slept rough for two months. Kassie had once told Gus they were the longest eight weeks of her life, and she had resigned herself to the fact there was only one way for her to earn money to live.

Kenneth and his wife had spotted a wet and bedraggled Kassie on the side of the road one night when they were on their way home from church. They had taken Kassie home and helped get her back on her feet. Kenneth promised her a job if she got herself together and stuck to it. Look at her now.

"Strike while the iron is hot, Kassie," said Gus. "The Chief Constable is tucking into his favourite lunchtime snack. There won't be a better time."

"You've been like a father to me, Mr Truelove," said Kassie. "I don't remember my Dad because he left us when I was still in nappies. I admit I was a handful in my early teens, and no doubt my mother was glad to see the back of me. My stepfather was a creep, and as far as I know, they're still together, so I'm not keen to return. I don't feel a connection to that life anymore. Ever since I've worked at London Road, the people I work with have become my family. It's still early days, but if I did get married to Noah, I'd like you to give me away."

"I'd be honoured, Kassie," said Kenneth. "Does that mean you and Noah might call on us this weekend?"

"You'll have to remind me what time you'll be at that church of yours, Mr Truelove," said Kassie hugging the Chief Constable. "I remember where you live. Noah will play rugby on Saturday, so we can pop round on Sunday afternoon if he doesn't get injured again. I'll be baking in the morning. Please let me know if you and your wife want anything."

"Sunday afternoon, three o'clock," said Kenneth. "We'll look forward to it. I know Betty enjoys a Battenberg, but to be safe, I'll check with her tonight and confirm things tomorrow."

"Brilliant," said Kassie. "That's taken a load off my mind. I'd better finish my rounds."

With that, Kassie wheeled her trolley to the door and silently slipped away.

Geoff Mercer was eyeing his cream horn.

"I ought to leave that until this afternoon," he said.

"We need to get on, Mercer," said Kenneth.

"Fair enough," said Geoff, wrapping his cake in a napkin. "I'll keep it for Ron."

"Back to business then," said Gus. "Where are we off to next?"

Kenneth Truelove stood and walked to the window.

"There won't be a new cold case today, Freeman," he said. "I had a call from the PCC last night. The Met are desperate for help next weekend to cope with a likely invasion from a group of protestors."

"They weren't too inconvenienced while I was on that enforced holiday last month," said Gus. "If the media didn't inflate the reported numbers, three-quarters of a million people demanded a second referendum. So how does this affect our team, anyway?"

The Chief Constable explained that the PCC had told him to supply a list of names before he went home today. He wanted Wiltshire to be seen to be helping to keep the peace.

"What he means is," said Gus, "he hopes if our people

are seen on the streets of London, enabling these people to carry out a peaceful protest, we might avoid having them glueing themselves to the railings on the stairs leading to this office in a few weeks."

"I've added four names to the list," said Kenneth. "Packenham, Umeh, Davis, and Hardy. I can't control what they'll be tasked with for the ten days they'll be away from their desks. However, unless the main event on the seventeenth goes pear-shaped, you'll have everyone back in one piece for Monday the nineteenth. I'll see you at the usual time, and that's when I'll hand over your next murder file."

"What about Lydia and me?" asked Gus. Was there a light at the end of this tunnel?

"Lydia will be working with Suzie, Gus," said Geoff.

"On the corruption investigation that she won't tell me about," said Gus.

"I'm glad to hear it," said Geoff. "Lydia will have to keep everything she learns under her hat, too."

"At least her time will be spent on something positive," said Gus. "And who will I be working with?"

"DS Mercer and I decided the best option was to book you for a diversity and inclusion training course," Kenneth said.

Gus groaned. It wasn't a light. Yet again, it was an oncoming train.

Chapter Two

THE CHIEF CONSTABLE showed no signs of shifting his position, either from gazing into the car park or subjecting Gus to his worst nightmare. So, Geoff Mercer picked up his afternoon treat and nodded towards the door. The meeting was over; it was time to leave.

Gus followed Geoff across the mezzanine to his office.

"Who complained?" he asked when they were seated.

"Nobody, as far as I know," said Geoff. "Kenneth had to find something to occupy your time next week and wouldn't accept my argument that it might do more harm than good. So we have arranged for you to receive the training in-house at London Road, Monday to Friday next week. The hours are nine to five, which means you'll be home sooner than you often are when working on a case."

"You can stress the positives as much as you like," said Gus. "But it won't wash. I should return to the office to let my team hear the bad news."

"Ah," said Geoff. "There's no need, Gus. Kenneth sent one of the ACCs to put them in the picture. Your team are

20

already on their way home for the rest of the day. Tomorrow they'll transfer to wherever the Met feels they will be the best fit."

"I can't help feeling this is the beginning of the end," said Gus.

"Don't be such a drama queen," said Geoff. "You've been around long enough to have faced minor inconveniences like this a dozen times. Of course, it's not ideal, but after the protestors go home and brag to their friends they were part of a world-changing event, things will return to normal."

"The more things change, the more they stay the same," said Gus. "I've heard that somewhere before. Unfortunately, it feels less relevant with each passing year."

"Look, you have to face facts, Gus," said Geoff. "Kenneth won't be around for more than a year. He's under pressure from Betty to retire, and she's more powerful than any PCC or up-and-coming ACC who fancies the top job. I could be gone by then, or I'll follow him out of the door. So it's inevitable a new face from another regional force will be in Kenneth's office."

"I understand. While you two are in your current roles, I have a degree of protection," said Gus. "Suzie keeps trying to convince me of that, too."

"Naturally, you worry about the team you've built," said Geoff. "You want them to move into better jobs when the time comes."

"I don't want their careers to suffer because the new regime believes their reputations have been tarnished by working with a dinosaur."

"The new regime is some way off, Gus," said Geoff. "This is a temporary blip, nothing more. You have ample time to improve the skills and reputations of your team, and although there are senior officers who think the current model for modern policing is the answer to society's ills, nothing beats successful detective work that removes hardened criminals from our streets. We may not be around to see the switch in emphasis, but it will happen."

"If I'm not seeing my team until Monday week, I might as well go home," said Gus. "Typical that the PCC forces Kenneth to put me on garden leave when there's very little chance I will be able to step outside the door. This wet and windy weather isn't forecast to move on until early next week."

"Cheer up," said Geoff. "Tell you what. You didn't have a cake when Kassie offered it. Why not pop outside to see if she has anything left on her trolley? I'll put the coffee on. I'm thick, and I know I could wait until Kenneth passes the folder to me, but can you explain the final steps in the Millie Clark case?"

"I've got nothing else to do, I suppose," said Gus.

Geoff shook his head. It would take more than a black coffee and a cream horn to get Gus out of the doldrums.

Gus returned with the last slice of Victoria sponge and sat down.

"My day just gets better and better," he said.

Geoff brought two coffees to his desk and unwrapped his cream horn.

"You didn't tell us the whole story in Kenneth's office, did you? That midnight tryst with Nathan Harvey was dangerous. You should have told me about it on Sunday morning."

"Suzie said much the same thing, Geoff," said Gus. "I recognised my dangerous position, but sometimes you need a short, sharp shock to get the little grey cells moving. Everything he told me helped debunk much of what we'd accepted as gospel, and I could see a possible solution. Harvey and Coombs only employed people who followed orders and had created a solid outfit the police couldn't crack. Nothing has changed. Nobody will speak out against that gang even five years later. What happened in the churchyard didn't fit with how they had always operated. Keel and Thatcher were told to hurt Millie Clark. So why would they suddenly go rogue? What did Harvey and Coombs have to gain by treating Millie differently to Cannings and Munro?"

"It's all about respect with criminals like them, isn't it?" said Geoff. "The public might view them differently, but among their peers, they would lose respect by committing a murder than shone a spotlight on every criminal in the city. I question whether there's honour among thieves, but I accept the conclusion you drew that you could eliminate the likelihood one of the five men in the flat with Millie had killed her."

"It was the first positive step we'd made all week," said Geoff. "It started me thinking about what the sisters had said about Millie and Tyler Rowe. Monique told us Millie had seen him in Warminster and was scared he would contact the gang. Two days later, according to Monique, Jeanette had a visit from Tyler, who told her he wanted to find Millie. Everyone assumed Tyler had followed Millie to the flat, hoping to continue supplying her with drugs. What if he wasn't in Warminster that first day? How would he know where Jeanette lived? The story didn't unravel immediately, but I started having doubts. The sisters reckoned Tyler passed the message to Harvey and Coombs. When she told us that, I noticed a brief smile."

"Was that unusual?" asked Geoff.

"You know what it's like, Geoff," said Gus. "Little things

stick in your mind during an interview. One day you write a comment in your notebook; the next, an anomaly doesn't strike you until the middle of the night when you're suddenly wide awake. Monique is a cold, hard woman, for whom a smile is a rarity, and I realised she was congratulating herself on having pulled the wool over another copper's eyes, just as she had five years earlier."

"So, they concocted a story about Tyler Rowe being in Warminster, so he could be fingered for bringing the gang's hatchet men to the town. Clever."

"That played into Monique and Jeanette's scheme without them realising it. Coombs wouldn't offer anything except 'no comment' before, during, or after the trials because he didn't wish to incriminate himself. Tyler Rowe was responsible for the savage attack that almost killed Viv Whitaker. While he was at the Warminster flat that afternoon, Craig saw an opportunity to deal with Rowe plus confuse Tom Brewer and his detectives. He knew Tyler Rowe and Millie Clark would never have talked to the police about their beatings."

"It all ties in, doesn't it?" said Geoff. "Easy, once you understand who was responsible."

"The tipping point was that the sisters didn't know Nathan Harvey had a sentimental attachment for the gold watch stolen in the robbery," said Gus. "Once he saw the watch advertised on eBay, Nathan knew who had killed Millie and why. He already knew a woman had called the gang, telling them where Millie had gone. Nathan paid thirty thousand pounds for a watch he could have taken by force. As he told me on Saturday night, he and Craig regretted Millie's death. They wanted to put things right in some way."

"The sisters had no idea things would go pear-shaped at

trial," said Geoff. "Those two women needed the patience of a saint to sit on that watch as long as they did. If they hadn't made it so obvious by putting it on eBay, they could have sold it for less under the counter somewhere, and Harvey would have been none the wiser."

"Nathan Harvey paid thirty thousand for his own watch because he felt guilty over Millie's death," said Gus. "But when he learned who was selling the watch, he realised he'd been taken for a mug."

"No matter how you got the final pieces of the jigsaw, you can chalk it up as a win," said Geoff. "Maybe, whoever's in charge in Bristol these days will find a weak link in the gang, and they'll get Harvey and Coombs in front of a jury that will put them away for a long stretch."

"We live in hope," said Gus.

"Do me a favour, Gus," said Geoff. "Avoid late-night meetings with gangsters in the future. You have too much to live for."

"After hearing what Kenneth has in store for me next week, I'm not so sure," said Gus.

"It could be worse, Gus," said Geoff, wiping pastry crumbs from his jacket front. "He only had a few hours to get something organised. The training people are working on a tailor-made course with modules that will keep you out of mischief for five days. Recruits breeze through an initial one-day seminar, while the professional course occupies high-flyers for up to six weeks. Nobody else will have the same experience as you."

"For which I'm supposed to be thankful," said Gus.

"Kenneth thought this was the option that would leave you the least annoyed," said Geoff.

"All I want to do is get stuck into a new case. Roll on Monday week."

With that, Gus left Geoff's office and went downstairs to the car park without visiting the admin area. Gus wasn't in the mood for a friendly chat with Vera or anyone else. At times like this, Gus found it best to be alone. He needed to let his anger and frustration dissipate before speaking with someone. He didn't want to risk saying something he would regret until the red mist had passed.

Gus sat in the Focus for several minutes before driving to the bungalow. Once he had parked under the rambling roses and opened the front door, he calculated he had four hours to kill before Suzie would be home.

A year ago, before the Crime Review Team was a possibility, his first thought would have been to visit the allotment if something had annoyed him. One of the books in his garden shed would have contained a few words of wisdom to help weather the storm.

He would sit outside the shed on dry, sunny days and let Soren Kierkegaard help calm his mood. As he gazed through the kitchen window today, Gus wondered whether he could sit inside the shed to avoid getting soaked. There was nothing for it. He had to stay indoors.

A glance at the available reading material showed that since Suzie had moved in, fewer books he returned to on dark days were available. So they were safely tucked away in his shed. His next thought was that music soothed the savage breast, and as most of their near neighbours were at work, he could delve into his vinyl collection for help.

Three hours later, Gus reduced the volume on the stereo to a more modest level and thanked Black Sabbath, The Stooges, and a large glass of Malbec for their contribution. Then, he returned the albums to the lower end of their shared listening so that Suzie's more middle-of-the-road albums were easily visible.

Gus walked through the hallway to the kitchen and started to prepare an evening meal.

Everything was progressing nicely when Suzie's Golf arrived outside.

"I thought I'd find you here," she called as she breezed through the front door. "Are you alright, darling?"

"I'm better now than I was at lunchtime," said Gus. "I'm quite enjoying the free time. It's next week and this blessed training course that scares me."

Suzie dropped her bag and coat in the hallway.

"Geoff called me mid-morning with the news," she said as she joined Gus in the kitchen and threw her arms around him. "It came out of the blue, didn't it? Don't take it personally. These protestors don't know you from Adam."

"I do know that, sweetheart," said Gus. "I'm not stupid. They have a bee in their bonnet about climate change and don't believe anyone's listening. I wish the Met had the same number of officers available as they did when I was on the force. Kenneth wouldn't have had to consider moving people from valuable roles to fulfil a quota. Other teams in the county will be stretched to breaking point next week while our people keep the capital's streets protected. What makes Londoners so special?"

"Even if the protestors' message falls on deaf ears, some good should come of it," said Suzie. "One, I get to see if Lydia is as good as you say she is, and two, I'll make progress on my special project."

"Geoff warned me Lydia will need to sign the Official Secrets Act," said Gus.

"I wouldn't go that far, sweetheart," said Suzie, "but the less anyone outside my office knows, the better."

"I get it," said Gus. "All will be revealed in time."

"We might even get it wrapped up by the end of next

27

week," said Suzie. "Of course, I was forgetting the third possible benefit of the upheaval. Your training course might give you a better appreciation of how we should operate in these enlightened times."

"Anyone would think I retired before the Equality Duty came into force seven years ago," said Gus. "If I remember correctly, it had three aims. First, to eliminate unlawful discrimination, harassment, and victimisation. The other two aims required us to advance equality of opportunity and foster good relations between people who share a protected characteristic and those who do not."

"I don't recall you telling me you'd ever been on a diversity course," said Suzie.

"I haven't," said Gus. "My superiors at Salisbury kept inviting me to attend, but I said I would do so when I wasn't rushed off my feet. I was never sitting around looking for something to do, and before I knew it, they offered me the chance to hand in my warrant card. That didn't mean I hadn't read the memo that came around four years earlier. Tess told me I should have seen it coming. The top brass knew I'd dig my heels in and treat the courses as an unnecessary intrusion. That allowed them to brand me a dinosaur and get rid of me. The benefit of not having to conform to the new mindset almost cancelled out the pain of not chasing villains every day."

"Hmm, who are you trying to kid?" said Suzie. "Anyway, it's only for a week, and living with me might have softened some of your rough edges. You might even enjoy it. A change is as good as a rest. I don't suppose you can remember the list of protected characteristics?"

"Dinner will be ready in fifteen minutes," said Gus. "If you'd like to shower and change. We can think of another topic of conversation for later."

"You won't get away with it that easily, darling," said Suzie. "If you let me coach you, five days will fly past before you know it."

Gus wasn't convinced, but after they'd eaten, Suzie dug out notes she'd made seven years earlier, and instead of suffering another evening watching a mindless reality programme on TV, they discussed the equality information Wiltshire Police was required to hold.

"That's enough for tonight," said Suzie at ten o'clock.

"I suspect you have a list of jobs you'd like me to do before Friday," said Gus. "An early night will mean I can get cracking as soon as you've left for London Road."

"True, this wet weather will rule out a trip to the allotment," said Suzie. "But, I have an ulterior motive."

Gus tidied the sheets of paper on the coffee table and followed Suzie to the bedroom.

Wednesday, 7 November 2018

"RISE AND SHINE, SLEEPYHEAD," said Suzie.

Gus risked one eye and studied the clock on the bedside table. It was a quarter to eight.

"Just as well that you don't have to get to work this morning," said Suzie. "If you're quick, we can have breakfast together."

Gus rolled out of bed, showered, and made it to the kitchen within five minutes.

"Very fetching," said Suzie when she spotted his dressing gown.

"I was cold," said Gus, "and yours was closest to hand.

Anyway, I didn't know what to wear until I learned what I was doing today

"Coffee and cereals first," said Suzie. "I've left a list on the hall table. Don't try to do everything at once. We're meeting Brett and Clemency in the Lamb this evening. I don't want you yawning while they tell us about their wedding arrangements."

"Wedding arrangements? They've only just got engaged. Does this mean….?

"Don't be daft," said Suzie. "The Reverend told us they planned a short engagement. Bert's not going to last forever. Brett wants his grandfather to know he's settled."

"Well, I hope Bert sticks around until this weather improves," said Gus. "I've got a few questions I need to ask him yet."

Suzie finished her breakfast and was getting ready to leave. Gus lingered over his second coffee. He didn't know when he'd have time for another. Suzie could be a hard taskmaster, although he hadn't complained last night.

"I'll see you tonight, darling," said Suzie at twenty-five past eight. "Lydia should be waiting for me when I reach London Road. I'm looking forward to working with her."

"Don't remind me," groaned Gus. "Geoff is convinced I'll get my full team back in the office on Monday week, but seeing is believing."

Suzie kissed him goodbye.

"Stay," she said when Gus started to get out of his chair. "Don't even think of standing in the porch to wave me off."

Gus listened as the Golf dashed to the gateway with its usual spray of gravel and then made its way into the lane. Time to check what was on his to-do list. He put his breakfast things in the dishwasher and walked to the hallway.

The first item was to refresh his memory on the information held on hate crime, violent crime, stop and search, and how the London Road teams used the various statistical data they gathered. Suzie had unearthed another set of study notes from 2011.

Gus remembered they were eating out tonight and returned to the kitchen to hand wash the breakfast things. He'd always been a fan of equal opportunity.

MEANWHILE, Suzie was making her way slowly towards the Wiltshire Police HQ. The volume of traffic never seemed to vary, nor did the minor delays that irked Gus so much. Progress by the gas board on the roadworks was marginal, but Suzie had to admit that access to the London Road car park was less awkward than it had been a week ago. She eased her Golf into its designated bay and was about to climb the steps to the front door when she heard a familiar voice.

"Hi, Suzie," said Lydia Logan Barre. "Or should I call you ma'am?"

Suzie did a double take. Was this the same Lydia that Gus spoke about? The one he had to continually warn not to give criminals a heart attack with her short skirts and four-inch heels.

Lydia spotted the raised eyebrows.

"Soberer than you expected?" she asked. "Alex told me to tone down the colours and suggested I wore my dark grey trouser suit with flat shoes."

"You won't look out of place when we reach the mezzanine," said Suzie. "You're taller and thinner than Kassie Trotter, but you've both sold out. Of course, I need to wear a uniform, but I don't see why the others working here should abandon their individuality."

"Gus tells me Kassie decided to don more suitable office wear when searching for a partner," said Suzie. "I've heard about Noah. Kassie seems to have ended her search. Perhaps the piercings and tattoos will reappear in due course. As for me, I don't want to antagonise the Chief Constable or DS Mercer. It might damage my prospects. So I'll still risk the colourful tops and leather skirts in the Old Police Station office on the right occasions."

"I'm glad to hear it, Lydia," said Suzie. "For the next three months, I expect to be wearing comfortable clothing outside work, and I've already got permission to modify my uniform to compensate for my expanding waistline."

After Lydia had signed in at Reception, they climbed the stairs to the administration area.

"You didn't answer my question, Suzie," said Lydia.

"Call me Suzie while we're working together in my office," said Suzie. "If we spend time with other officers of my level or above, that's a different kettle of fish. Some will demand you use the correct form of address; others are more lax. Just follow my lead. My office is in the opposite corner to the Chief Constable, but we can't avoid walking past Geoff Mercer's door, I'm afraid."

"I've spotted Vera Butler just coming out of the restroom," said Lydia.

"Eyes like a hawk, that one," said Suzie. "Nobody makes it onto the mezzanine without Vera noticing. If security downstairs ever had a mishap and an eco-terrorist found their way up here, the alarm would be raised in seconds."

"And here was I thinking I would miss out on the excitement next week," said Lydia. "How's Gus? We were worried about how he'd react when Alex saw a stranger appear on the camera outside the lift yesterday morning.

When she arrived on the first floor, her insignia showed her to be one of your Assistant Chief Constables. Grace did all the talking, as you can imagine, but even she was surprised to hear what was in store for us."

"Gus has had to come to terms with it," said Suzie. "He thinks I didn't see the vinyl albums had been re-shuffled when I was in the lounge last night. I imagine any pigeons on the bungalow roof yesterday afternoon would have been hopping around like mad things. Not just our roof but several houses on either side. He'll moan throughout next week, but he'll benefit from it, and it might extend his stay with the Crime Review Team if he knows the right things to say in a tricky situation. Let's get into my office. My door isn't closed that often, but when it is, people usually accept I want peace and quiet."

"I need to be brought up to speed," said Lydia when they were safely inside the corner office. "Geoff Mercer told me I had to keep whatever I learned under my hat. I know it's an investigation into possible corruption, but whatever background you can give me will be useful. Gus is the only person I've worked for, and we've concentrated on solving murder mysteries, not checking whether detectives involved in the earlier investigations were using devious tactics, accepting bribes, or something of that nature."

Suzie retrieved a folder from a locked drawer in her filing cabinet. She selected a file near the top and handed it to Lydia.

"It's rare for Wiltshire to need an investigation of this nature," she said. "The combination of rural settings and low crime figures has meant the opportunity, or perhaps the need, for corruption has been lacking. Sadly, Chief Constables across the country have reported a deterioration in the situation over the past few years and highlighted it as a cause for concern. They cited drug crimes, bribery, theft, fraud, sexual misconduct, and unauthorised disclosure of information. The latter has become the most frequently reported issue."

"What have they been doing about it?" asked Lydia. "I thought the Police and Crime Commissioners would have got wind of this worrying trend and wanted it reversed."

"The report in your hands shows an apparent reluctance to engage in the matter. Chief Constables from Bournemouth to Blackpool blame a lack of resources for not being able to pursue inquiries into malpractice claims."

"Surely, our superiors should prioritise checking their officers don't break the law?" asked Lydia. "As for resources, they didn't have any problem finding funds to pursue ancient sex abuse allegations a few years back, with little to show for their efforts."

"Fair comment," said Suzie, "and Wiltshire didn't escape criticism on that score, but the vast majority of our fellow officers do what can be a tough job with honesty, skill, and good humour. Alex and Neil are prime examples."

"You make it sound as if corruption is the sole prerogative of male officers," said Suzie. "You could have died when Sandra Plunkett was in the Chief Constable's chair. She was far from blameless."

"As if I'd forget," said Suzie. "Sandra was the exception that proves the rule, I guess. She couldn't face the humiliation of the court case that would have followed when the truth came out and committed suicide."

"We're not talking about uniformed female officers or detectives in this instance, are we?" asked Lydia. "Can we move on to the specifics now?"

"You'll be familiar with the places and people involved," said Suzie. "Geoff Mercer told me these accusations started eighteen months to two years before Millie Clark's murder. Flats in Warminster town centre were said to have been used for various criminal activities, including prostitution and domestic slavery. However, officers at all levels were said to be content to allow these activities to continue unchecked."

"I remember Gus telling us about posters in the town calling for a full investigation by the Police Complaints Authority," said Lydia. "He also told us that we should disregard any suggestion there was a connection to the murder case we were reviewing. Nobody discussed it in the office after that, but Alex and I discussed it at home. We wondered whether the Chief Constable was covering for his old colleague, DI Tom Brewer. He wasn't prepared to accept that the straight arrow he'd worked alongside twenty years earlier was a crooked copper. However, after I'd visited Tom and his wife with Gus, I was inclined to agree with the Chief Constable. Tom seemed a genuine man who loved his wife dearly. I'd hate to find out that he'd fooled me."

"Those campaign posters accused Warminster officers of failing to investigate the background of key witnesses in the Clark case. The case was in its infancy when the campaign gathered strength, and the people the campaigners were referring to on those posters were supposedly linked to the businesses housed in a handful of town centre buildings."

"So, it was convenient to attempt to link a high-profile murder case to their campaign," said Lydia. "The media would jump on it and give the campaign plenty of coverage. They never care who they smear with their accusations. The whole matter could have been incompetence rather than a criminal act."

"The campaign claimed to have uncovered evidence

linking Millie's murder to the people running the criminal enterprises in those buildings," said Suzie. "They further claimed that their allegation was never properly investigated."

"Gus mentioned that but warned us it mustn't alter how we approached the murder case," said Lydia. "Justice for Millie Clark was our priority. He mentioned that DS Mercer had asked you to check everything had been above board."

"Geoff Mercer tasked me with speaking to senior officers from London Road responsible for dealing with complaints of that nature," said Suzie. "We had a different Chief Constable, and only two of the ACCS still work here. Mark Colbourne has been at London Road since 2011, as has the person you met yesterday morning, Melanie Sloper. I've interviewed both, and they remember the poster campaign but weren't directly involved in investigating the possible failure to act on information received."

"Did either of them have an opinion about whether there could have been any truth in these allegations?" asked Lydia.

"Melanie Sloper is all business, as you would have noticed yesterday, but Mark Colbourne has retained a sense of humour. He shrugged his shoulders and told me this sort of spurious complaint comes to the surface from time to time. He termed it red herring season."

Chapter Three

"RED HERRING SEASON? I've not heard that one," said Lydia, "How would the original complaint have been investigated, anyway? Who would have carried it out?"

"We have to refer serious complaints to the IOPC," said Suzie. "They're an independent body that handles complaints about a death, an injury, an assault, a sexual offence, or corruption. But the emphasis is on whether an action or lack of action that led to the complaint had a serious outcome. So a complaint won't be sent up the line if it's not reasonable and proportionate for the IOPC to get involved."

"I want to understand why the unwillingness of the local police to act on information received wasn't serious enough to contact the IOPC."

"Most complaints are dealt with by the relevant police force, Lydia," said Suzie. "We have a Professional Standards Department that oversees complaints. After logging a complaint, we assess its nature and seriousness," said Suzie. "A complaint handler not directly connected to the complaint would have looked into it. They contact the complainant to clarify missing details and answer questions. Often, that's as far as it needs to go. A resolution to the problem is found, and everyone can move on. For some more serious complaints, we carry out a full investigation. The person who made the complaint is told how their complaint will be investigated and how a decision will be reached. We keep them informed on progress, and they are informed after the outcome has been reached. As for who would have handled a complaint of this nature, it would have been an Inspector, at least."

"Have you found a paper trail for the original complaint?" asked Lydia.

"Not yet," said Suzie. "At first, I thought I was onto something. I even told Gus that I feared the investigation had legs. But the deeper I've dug, the more I realised there could be several reasons for the lack of paperwork. First, the paperwork was probably destroyed after three years if the complaint didn't come to anything. If we kept every scrap of paper for centuries, we'd need another site as big as this one to house it all. Then there are the people involved in the complaint at various stages. You've met DI Tom Brewer, but what do you know about his successor?"

"Amazing Grace spoke with Clare Edwards on the phone," said Lydia. "She's an ACC in Norfolk these days. Did you ever meet her?"

"I was still a Detective Sergeant in 2015," said Suzie. "Clare was a DI on a fast-track to the top, like *Detective Inspector* Packenham."

"Sorry," said Lydia. "We never use her nickname when she's in earshot. So, Clare Edwards was parachuted into Tom Brewer's position in Warminster, but everyone here soon recognised that she wouldn't put down roots."

"Nicely put, Lydia," said Suzie. "Our paths crossed on the odd occasion, but as I understood it, Clare made no attempt to get to know anyone well, not just me. She didn't intend to stay in Wiltshire for long. Tom Brewer had retired at the end of 2015, and in an ideal world, he and Clare would have had a reasonable handover period for her to learn the ropes."

"Grace told us what happened there," said Lydia. "Clare's transfer was delayed because her old bosses in Hertfordshire didn't want to lose her. As a result, she only had seven days with Tom Brewer before he disappeared on a cruise to celebrate his retirement, and she had to rely on DI Budd in Bristol to prepare her for the retrial at Bristol Crown Court in April 2016."

"Tom Brewer attended the retrial as a private individual," said Suzie. "He wanted to see the Millie Clark case reach a satisfactory conclusion. Clare also sat beside him in the courthouse, but she reckoned they barely spoke after the non-appearance of the prosecution's main witnesses abruptly ended proceedings."

"That must have knocked Tom sideways," said Lydia. "All his efforts for nothing. Gus reckoned DI Edwards would have been kept busy in Warminster with an ongoing case-load and wouldn't have looked into any past crimes recorded in the town. How long before she got her next promotion?"

"Clare moved to Norfolk as a Detective Inspector in November 2016," said Suzie. "The promotion to Assistant Chief Constable came early in 2017. I've asked how she handled the complaint relating to the poster campaign. She told me she questioned the officers named on the posters, who all pleaded ignorance, and they said they knew nothing about any dodgy addresses in the town centre. They claimed the complainant was a fantasist. According to them, it was common knowledge in that part of the county that Sid Selman had a vivid imagination. The poster campaign wasn't his first attempt to make a mountain out of a molehill. Clare tried to contact Sid Selman to get his side of the story, but the last time anyone remembered seeing him was about six weeks after Millie Clark's murder."

"So, if this Selman character was behind the poster campaign," said Lydia, "he inferred that whatever was going on in the town centre was connected to the murder and then disappeared. Doesn't that sound sinister to you?"

"Just because Selman wasn't contactable when Clare Edwards tried to get hold of him in 2016 doesn't mean he isn't alive and well," said Suzie. "We'll look for him."

"I guess because nobody had died, and there were no assaults reported in or near those addresses, DI Edwards decided there was insufficient evidence to show any serious misconduct and kept the investigation in-house."

"That's not unusual, Lydia," said Suzie. "I'd like to take a closer look at whether I believe Sid Selman was the fantasist Mark Colbourne and others described. Selman claimed to be an eyewitness to the illegal activities in the town centre and reckoned the police would never take a statement from him. He had photographic evidence available, but the police refused to look at it. Why would they do that? Why not humour him, look it over to be sure, and then threaten to charge him with wasting police time? That would have had him running for cover. We wouldn't have heard from him again."

"We haven't," said Lydia.

"I can see Gus has trained you well," laughed Suzie. "The conspiracy theory is alive and well in the Old Police Station office. Sid Selman had every right to go wherever he chose, and we'll start looking for him in earnest now I have an extra pair of hands on this task."

"I don't believe the evidence Selman had available was relevant to the Clark murder case," said Lydia. "But, what about its relevance to the criminality in those flats? The people behind that could have silenced him. They couldn't risk a new broom in the Warminster office suddenly believing Selman's fanciful suggestions that one or more police officers were turning a blind eye to domestic slavery and prostitution."

"Geoff Mercer gave me chapter and verse on Sid Selman when he briefed me on this investigation," said Suzie. "He was an elderly freelance journalist who had spent two decades in Fleet Street. His best days were already behind him before some newspapers moved to Wapping towards the end of the Eighties. Sid Selman enjoyed a drink in Fleet Street's famous watering holes and became unreliable during the Nineties. The freelance work dried up, and at the turn of the century, Sid moved to Wiltshire and offered his services to regional newspapers."

"Did he find much work?" asked Lydia.

"Enough to keep the wolf from the door," said Suzie. "There weren't the same pressures for meeting deadlines here. Sid had a talent for writing and supplied articles popular with readers, but when you've dined at the top table, a weekly by-line in the Hedger & Ditcher doesn't fill you with pride. So after Sid had a few whiskies, Geoff thought he would describe himself as an investigative reporter to anyone who'd listen to him in the pubs in town."

"Sid Selman told them he could have been a contender, you mean," said Lydia. "He couldn't accept he was washed-up."

"That was certainly how Geoff saw things," said Suzie.

"He reckoned Sid started hunting for a scoop to get him back in the big-time."

"Perhaps there *was* the odd bit of criminal activity in the town centre," Lydia said. "Sid Selman inflated it until it resembled a national scandal. Why use a poster campaign, though? Was he working alone, or were other residents aware of what was happening?"

"There was never any record of a complaint," said Suzie. "Several independent businesses operating in the area, five to seven years ago, are boarded up or have changed hands. It could be tough finding people to contribute genuine sightings of wrongdoing. Unless it directly affected them, those business owners had too much on their mind trying to earn a crust, to keep watch and record comings and goings from certain addresses."

"I imagine we would get loads of rumours but few hard facts," said Lydia. "Gus always tells us to ask different questions to the ones asked in the initial investigation. That approach would be impossible if we don't have the paperwork to know what was asked."

"Our first task must be to trace Sid Selman," said Suzie. "He claimed the officers he named on those posters harassed and intimidated him. Geoff thinks Selman believed the whole force was corrupt, which deterred him from letting us examine his evidence. He didn't trust us."

"Don't we need to talk to the officers he accused?" asked Lydia. "Are any of them still working in Warminster?"

"Don't forget Clare Edwards has interviewed them already," said Suzie. "We'd need new evidence to get them to speak with us again five years later. They would call their Federation rep, and things could get tricky."

"Where do we start the search for Sid Selman?" asked Lydia.

"His last known address was a bungalow on Avon Road, Warminster. Why don't you drive over there, ask around, and see if the neighbours can remember him? Maybe, whoever bought his place has a forwarding address."

"I wonder why nobody made this trip before?" asked Lydia.

"Human nature," said Suzie. "Gus is always bemoaning the fact that matters which should be investigated get swept under the carpet."

"Nothing to see here. Move along, please," said Lydia.

"Tom Brewer had retired, and Clare was trying to make her mark in a new role," said Suzie. "Sid Selman had stirred up a hornets' nest over the eighteen months before she arrived, and then, suddenly, he stopped. Why on earth would she chase after him to see why? Any Detective Inspector would have done the same. We have enough ongoing cases to deal with without looking for work."

"I blame the Chief Constable," said Lydia. "If he hadn't selected the Millie Clark murder case for Gus to review, this Selman character's story would never have seen the light of day."

Lydia picked up her handbag, searched for her car keys, and prepared to leave.

Suzie was deep in thought.

"What?" asked Lydia.

"You've got me at it now," said Suzie. "I blame Gus, not Kenneth. Gus and his blessed conspiracy theories. Now I'm wondering whether Kenneth chose this case for review because he knew the Sid Selman poster campaign would pose questions and offer the opportunity for it to be put under the microscope one last time before he retires. That's the way he works. Did you ever wonder why he gets Geoff Mercer and your boss to join him in his office for lunch?

Why not get Vera Butler to call your office whenever a new file folder is ready for collection? Gus or Neil could have dropped in to see her on their way to work over the past six months. No, Kenneth gets his favoured team around the table, helps them relax with coffee and grub, then drip-feeds them highlights of a new cold case, taking great care to downplay items he wants Gus to concentrate on."

"Could the Chief Constable be that devious?" asked Lydia.

"I'll see you when you return from Avon Road," said Suzie. "I'll visit the Hub and see whether Divya Yadav can provide us with a detailed breakdown of which businesses occupied premises in the town centre between 2011 and 2016."

Lydia crossed the mezzanine and headed for the stairs. She heard, rather than saw, Kassie Trotter on the far side, wheeling her trolley of goodies. Suzie was right. They *were* dressed alike, but she hoped she didn't talk quite as much or so loudly.

"Good morning, Lydia. Are you settling into your new job?"

Lydia spotted Vera Butler standing behind a filing cabinet and stopped for a second.

"It's temporary, Vera," she said.

"That's what they always say," said Vera.

Lydia decided not to bite. Two minutes later, she was in her red Mini and easing into traffic on London Road. The drive to Warminster took her under forty minutes, and she parked outside the first row of detached bungalows on the left-hand side of Avon Road.

She sat and looked around for a few moments before getting out of the car. There wasn't a For Sale sign in sight, and each driveway held a modest saloon car. Car ports had been provided when these houses were built in the Seventies, and many were still in evidence. Every small front garden looked as if someone who lived there cared.

Lydia walked to the nearest house, fully expecting an answer when she rang the doorbell.

"Hello, dear," said the white-haired lady who opened the door. "What brings you here today? We weren't expecting visitors."

"Nothing to worry about," said Lydia. "I'm not selling anything. Do you remember a Mr Selman who lived here?"

"We bought this place from him five years ago, dear. Why are you asking?"

"My name is Lydia Logan Barre," said Lydia. "I work for Wiltshire Police. Could I come in and chat with you and your husband? Sorry, what was your name?"

"Mrs Cotton, dear. I'm Bernice, but everyone calls me Bernie. Yes, come inside, dear. It's nippy out there on the doorstep. My Will's sat in the lounge; he was only reading the newspaper. The police, you say? Oh dear, how can we help you? Will, put that paper down. There's a young lady from the police here."

The white-haired gentleman folded his newspaper over the arm of his chair and slowly stood. Lydia thought it looked painful.

"Will Cotton," he said. "Is this a visit to remind us about crime prevention? We have locks on every window and chains on both the front and back doors. We bought an answering machine and recorded a message. Now we never answer the landline, which keeps the scammers off our backs. I get fed up hearing that the other person has cleared, but they won't get money from Bernie and me."

"No, this isn't about crime prevention, Mr Cotton," said

Lydia. "Your wife told me you bought this bungalow five years ago from a Mr Sid Selman. Is that correct?"

"Our neighbours still refer to us as newcomers," said Will. "Bernie, why don't you get this young lady tea or coffee? We don't get many visitors, and if we aren't sociable with the ones we do get, we'll get even fewer."

"Coffee, black, one sugar, please," said Lydia.

Bernie scuttled away to the kitchen.

"This little estate is full of people our age," said Will. "Nobody has moved out since Mr Selman left. No doubt there will be a queue of people wanting to downsize when the next place on this street becomes vacant."

"I noticed everyone had a car," said Lydia.

"It's the only way we can get around," said Will. "We're too far from town to walk, and although we've got our bus passes, they don't always run at convenient times. No bus stop on this estate, and we'd catch our death carrying the shopping home on a cold, wet day like today."

Bernie returned with a tray containing three cups of coffee.

"Black with one sugar, dear," said Bernie turning the tray towards Lydia.

"Thank you," said Lydia. "So, Mr Selman left then? He wasn't carried out in a box."

"Oh, he was alive and kicking, but we didn't have any dealings with him," said Will. "The lady from the estate agents showed us round. Sid wanted to live closer to Bristol, she told us. He was a journalist and hoped to write articles for the Bath Chronicle and Bristol Evening Post. He was semi-retired, I believe."

"She told us he'd had a big job in London," said Bernie sipping her milky coffee.

"If he wasn't working full-time, where was he when you viewed the property?" asked Lydia.

"Sid Selman didn't drive, dear," said Bernie. "He had travelled to Bath by train on the day we arranged to view the place."

"We took one look and realised it was just what we were looking for," said Will. "There were a few issues that needed sorting. Mr Selman wasn't the tidiest of people."

"We understand he liked a drink," said Lydia. "I imagine there were some maintenance issues."

"Nothing I couldn't tackle," said Will. "He wouldn't have recognised the place if he'd come back six months later."

"Did the estate agency give you a forwarding address?" asked Lydia. "In case any mail arrived after he moved out."

"They told us he was after a flat on Bathwick Hill," said Bernie. "We never learned whether he got it or not. So, no, we never had an address for him."

"We had his mobile number, though," said Will. "That young woman who showed us around gave me his card. The landline was the old one for this place. We could transfer our number from our home in Longbridge Deverill, but that mobile number might still be valid. We never needed to use it, as Sid had nothing delivered here that needed sending on."

"Would you still have that card, Mr Cotton?" asked Lydia.

"It might take me a minute to find it," said Will. "I don't remember throwing it away."

"Check the drawer in the kitchen first, love," said Bernie.

Will made his way slowly into the hallway.

"He's slowed up a lot this past year or so, dear," said

Bernie tapping the side of the head. "Up here, he's still the same. He'll find it if he doesn't remember getting rid of it."

"Did you live in Longbridge Deverill long?" asked Lydia.

"Ever since we married, dear," said Bernie. "Forty-eight years in the same house near Manor Farm."

"Had you ever heard about Mr Selman before you moved here? What about your neighbours? They were here when Sid was active in the town. What did they have to say about him?"

"Will's not one to listen to gossip, nor am I," said Bernie. "Mr Selman had his name in the newspapers quite often. I used to enjoy his weekly pieces, but I didn't take much notice of the other nonsense."

"What do you mean by nonsense?" asked Lydia.

"He complained in the 'Letters To the Editor' section that there were people in Warminster living off immoral earnings. Well, I ask you. That sort of thing might go on in the big cities, but here in the countryside, it doesn't seem possible, does it?"

"You'd be surprised," said Lydia.

"Well, I suppose you're in a better position than me to know," said Bernie. "How would Will and I know what goes on in town after dark? We never set foot outside the door."

"Got it," cried Will.

He made his way back into the lounge and handed Lydia a card.

"It was on the telephone table in the hallway, under a pile of trade directories."

"Thank you," said Lydia. "It will give us something to go on. Which estate agency handled the sale?"

"I've got their card in the kitchen," said Will. "It was the first thing I laid my hand on in the drawer."

"I'll get it," said Bernie. "I'll take these coffee cups back. You can ask Will the questions you asked me."

Will Cotton sat down and looked at Lydia.

"What did I miss?"

"I just wondered what you knew about Mr Selman before moving here, " Lydia said. "How did the others on the estate get on with him?"

"We didn't take much notice of what he was up to when we lived in the village," said Will. "We were only three miles out of town, but apart from the weekly shop or to visit the doctors, we didn't need to come here. Bernie would mention that Selman had another letter in the newspaper, complaining the police didn't seem interested in what was happening under their noses. I couldn't say whether he was talking rubbish or not. The last time I spent an evening in town, people had long hair and wore flared trousers. After we moved in, several neighbours told me they were glad to see the back of him. They told me he was a troublemaker with a high opinion of himself."

"He'd worked in London for one of the national daily papers," said Lydia.

"Not something to be proud of," said Will. "Certainly not based on the standard of journalist they have today."

"Did anyone believe his claims that the police knew about a brothel in the town centre but turned a blind eye?" asked Lydia.

"Keep your voice down," said Will, "Bernie's lived a sheltered life. I did my National Service and was among the last to join. I left the local Battlesbury Barracks for Civvy Street in 1962. I'd already met Bernie here in town and found a job locally. We got married in 1965 and moved into a house in Longbridge Deverill. She'd have a fit if she knew what us squaddies got up to when we were in Singapore."

"Your secret's safe with me," whispered Lydia.

"It's not unheard of for a woman to be available in a small town like Warminster if you get my drift, but Sid Selman seemed to think this was a far more organised affair."

"What did your neighbours think?" asked Lydia. "Or was anyone familiar with the inside of one of these properties?"

"If they were, they didn't let on," said Will. "But then, they wouldn't, would they?"

Bernie returned from the kitchen.

"Here's that card you wanted, dear," she said.

Lydia placed it behind Sid Selman's business card in her purse.

"I should get back to Devizes," she said, "thanks for the coffee. You've both been very helpful."

Will stayed in his chair and picked up his newspaper as Bernie led Lydia to the front door.

"I'm glad we could help the police with their enquiries," said Bernie. "It will be something to tell the girls when I visit the hairdressers. They think we lead such boring lives."

Lydia smiled, then remembered Gus's appreciation of a Columbo moment.

"Where do you get your hair done, Bernie? Is it in the town centre?"

"Yes, dear. Please don't take offence, but it might not be the right place for you. The girls are in their late fifties or early sixties, and the clientele is my age. Most of the ladies I chat to when we're under the drier are only a decade older than the staff, but they're girls to us. Odd, isn't it? When you get old, you look at other people and think they look ancient. It's a shock when you find they're a couple of years younger than you, but you never consider yourself to look the way other people see you. Not that you need to worry on that score for ages yet."

"Did you ever talk to your salon friends about Sid Selman's posters?" asked Lydia.

"Not right from the start, dear," said Bernie. "We had a mobile hairdresser visit us in the village. She gave Will a trim before she permed mine, so I was only aware of it through the local weekly newspaper. When we moved here, I discovered Marjorie's and booked a regular weekly visit. The social side of the trip to the salon is more important than anything else at my age. The posters were mentioned for a while just after we moved here."

"I wondered whether any staff had seen Sid putting his posters up," said Lydia. "Was he alone, or did he have anyone helping him?"

"Nobody knew," said Bernie. "The girls told us they closed up and went home one Saturday evening, and when they returned on Monday morning, there they were, on lamp posts and windows of boarded-up shops. Some were torn down over time, but a new set would appear now and then. Sid Selman could have had help, but they were put up overnight or early on a Sunday morning when the town centre is quiet."

"Never mind," said Lydia. "When will you next visit Marjorie's?"

"Friday morning, dear, at half-past seven. Four girls with four old biddies getting prettified for the weekend, even though none of us will be going anywhere exciting."

"An early start," said Lydia. "Just the four girls, no teenage trainee or someone to sweep up the trimmings and fetch and carry things?"

"They haven't needed anyone to do that job for a while, dear," said Bernie. "Fewer customers need Marjorie's services yearly, for obvious reasons, and the girls cope with the extra chores. In a couple of years, one of the girls will become a client, and then there will be three girls and three chairs available. That's life. When I first visited the salon, I remember a foreign girl flitting between chairs doing odd jobs. She wasn't there long, maybe a month or two. When I asked what had happened to her, one of the girls told me she had to go home."

"Back to Europe?" asked Lydia.

"A lot further than that, dear. Thailand or the Philippines, I would have thought."

"That's it then, Bernie," said Lydia. "I might bump into you again when we visit some of the businesses in the town. Bye now."

Bernie Cotton stood holding her front door as Lydia walked to her red Mini. Lydia gave her a wave and was pleased to see Bernie reach for the chain as she drove away. On the return journey, traffic was a little heavier on the A361, but Lydia turned into the London Road car park forty minutes later. She tapped on Suzie's door and entered.

"Any joy?" asked Suzie.

"I have business cards for Sid Selman and the estate agent that handled the sale of his property," said Lydia. "He told the estate agent he was looking for a place in Bath, on Bathwick Hill. She might be able to help trace him if the mobile number on his card is no longer in service. The current owners are a lovely couple, who knew nothing about the seamier side of Sid's accusations, but the wife did mention an Asian girl who worked at a hair salon in the town. She disappeared soon after Sid left the area. The staff at the salon thought she had had to return home."

"We can check whether she was an overstayer or an illegal," said Suzie. "I'll ask Divya to do the necessary digging. So this was at the end of 2013?"

"Bernie, the wife, said the girl was there for a month after she and her husband, Will, moved from Longbridge Deverill."

"It doesn't sound like an organised example of domestic slavery, does it?" said Suzie.

"Is Divya working on the other things we needed?" asked Lydia.

"We won't get anything from the Hub this week, I'm afraid. They're rushed off their feet. Let's chase this mobile number for Sid Selman."

Lydia's fears were realised. The number was no longer in service.

"On to the next one," she sighed.

The estate agency was still in business, but the woman who handled the Avon Road sale had left the company. When Lydia asked whether they had a contact number, the manager said they couldn't divulge personal information without a warrant. As they didn't suspect the woman of any criminal offence, that proved to be another dead end.

"We're not having much luck, are we?" said Lydia.

"Let's do what you did this morning," said Suzie. "Take a trip to Bathwick Hill, knock on a few doors, and see if anyone has heard of Sid Selman. We'll take your car. It can be a devil to find a parking space in Bath."

"While we're in Bath, we could visit the offices of the Chronicle first," said Lydia. "Bernie Cotton reckoned Sid Selman wanted to be closer to the Chronicle and the Bristol Evening Post. If they took any articles from him, they would have an address and phone number."

"Doh! Why didn't I think of that," said Suzie. "Come on. The game's afoot."

Chapter Four

LYDIA REMEMBERED to keep to the speed limit with a Detective Inspector in the passenger seat. They reached Bath in thirty minutes, and Suzie directed her to Green Park car park.

"There was a Green Park railway station at this end of town at one time," she said. "We can walk to the Westpoint building on James Street in two minutes once we've found a parking space."

Five minutes later, they set off on foot for the Chronicle offices. After explaining to the young receptionist they were police officers looking for a person of interest, they found themselves in a light, airy office on the third floor, where a press officer met them.

"Is this some kind of joke?" she asked.

Suzie handed over her warrant card.

"Far from it," she said. "We're looking for a Mr Sid Selman, who moved to Bath five years ago. He had been a journalist for over forty years and was contributing articles to various weekly and monthly publications in Wiltshire. We understood he proposed doing something similar for you and the Bristol Evening Post."

"Oh, I'll check whether we've had him on our books. We received an announcement recently that we're leaving this building at the end of November and moving into premises belonging to Bath University. They've got a site just across the road. History doesn't count for much these days. The Chronicle has been around for two hundred and fifty years in one form or another, and we've been in this building since the early Eighties. To be reduced to a space within a University building is tough to take, but when the police arrived on our doorstep, I feared the worst."

"We don't believe Mr Selman has broken the law," said Suzie. "We're simply doing a follow-up. All we need from you is an address or a phone number."

"Wait here," said the press officer, whose name badge revealed she was Fiona Marsh.

"Perhaps I shouldn't have referred to Sid Selman as a person of interest," said Suzie. "It was the first thing that came into my head. I wanted to give away as little as possible."

"To avoid a reporter and cameraman following us when we leave," said Lydia. "I get it."

Fiona Marsh returned after two minutes looking even more stressed than when she left.

"We did have Sid Selman write a handful of articles during 2014 and 2015. He was a more than competent wordsmith, and readers enjoyed his whimsical musings. Mr Selman lived in a flat off Bathwick Hill at the time. Whether he's still there, I wouldn't know. Here's the address. We did have a mobile phone number for him, but our records show it went out of service in 2015, and the address doesn't appear to have a landline. Do you know how to get to Bathwick Hill?"

"If we get lost, we'll ask a policeman," said Suzie.

They left Westpoint and walked back to the car park.

"I've visited Bath a few times," said Lydia. "Can't we walk?"

"It would take us half an hour on foot," said Suzie. "I don't fancy it in this rain. We won't know how far up the hill we must walk to find this address."

Lydia joined the heavy lunchtime traffic on Lower Bristol Road and skirted around the city centre until they reached the roundabout that would take them up Bathwick Hill.

"The third exit on your left," said Suzie checking the map on her phone.

"The buildings are impressive, aren't they," said Lydia. "Gus and I visited Combe Down on the Mark Malone case. His mother's place was a modern version of these Georgian townhouses, and Gus reckoned you wouldn't get change from three-quarters of a million."

"Many of these houses in this part of the city have been converted into flats," said Suzie. "What was the address again?"

"Sydney Buildings," said Lydia.

"We should have taken the first right when we turned onto Bathwick Hill."

Suzie closed her eyes as Lydia slammed on the brakes, executed a perfect u-turn, and headed down the steep hill a few yards ahead of an oncoming vehicle.

What the bus driver and his passengers thought Suzie couldn't imagine.

"Odd numbers on the right," said Lydia. "So we're

starting from the beginning. Here we are. We want the basement flat. I wouldn't want to climb down this staircase late at night after a few whiskies. Perhaps, Sid Selman does most of his drinking at home."

"If he does, there aren't many empty bottles in his recycling box," said Suzie.

She rang the doorbell.

An elderly lady, who reminded Lydia of one of her drama professors, opened the door with a flourish.

"Yes?"

"Police, ma'am," said Suzie, brandishing her warrant card. "Can I ask who you are?"

"Ms Denise Blanchard, ex-actress. I retired before it became fashionable to refer to myself as an actor."

"Did you purchase this flat from a Mr Selman?" asked Suzie.

"In December 2015, yes, I did. Why?" asked Ms Blanchard.

"We'd very much like to catch up with him, but he keeps moving. Do you have a forwarding address?"

"I had nothing to do with the man. Everything was done through the agency. He wanted a quick sale, and I could save myself one hundred thousand for a typical flat on this street. So I grabbed it like a drowning person grabs a lifebelt."

"Blocked at every turn," Suzie said to Lydia. "Did you learn why he was in such a hurry to sell, Ms Blanchard?"

"My neighbours told me he had blotted his copybook at the Chronicle. I wasn't interested in the details; I was too busy making this place habitable."

"A single man living alone," said Lydia. "I imagine housekeeping was low on his priorities."

"Oh, the place was clean enough," said Denise. "I enjoy

clutter and need my books and nick-nacks surrounding me. I have dozens of photographs to remind me of the years I trod the boards. My Ophelia was well-received, you know. I'm a cat person too, so I'm never lonely. Perhaps Mr Selman had a cleaner who came in and kept the place tidy because I had no complaints on that score."

"We understand Sid Selman enjoyed a drink," said Lydia. "Would any of your neighbours have mentioned any bar where he was a regular visitor?"

"The Raven was mentioned once or twice. Easy to get to from here via North Parade."

"Thank you," said Suzie. "We'll drop in to see whether anyone remembers him."

Denise Blanchard closed the door without a word, and Suzie and Lydia climbed the steps to the pavement. The rain had eased, so they set off to see what The Raven had to offer.

"Three years is a long time in the pub trade," said Lydia. "The chances of finding the same landlord's name over the door are slim. No wonder Fiona Marsh was keen to get us on our way earlier. I wonder what Sid Selman did to cause the parting of the ways with the Chronicle?"

"We might find out at The Raven," said Suzie. "Failing that, although Denise Blanchard didn't grill her neighbours on the matter, there's nothing to prevent us from trying it. There were plenty of flats in that building for us to call on."

There were only a handful of customers in The Raven when they walked into the main bar.

"I've often wondered how many people find the time to have a drink in the middle of the afternoon," said Lydia. "By the looks of this place, not many."

"Why don't they close as they did in the old days," said Suzie.

"Perhaps they will when climate change gets a tighter grip," said Lydia. "English folk will be having their siesta between two and five."

"The downside would be that bars would stay open until two in the morning every day of the week, not just at the weekend."

"What can I get you?" the young girl behind the bar asked.

"Two coffees, please," said Suzie. "Both black, one sugar."

"Is the landlord around?" asked Lydia. "Could you tell him it's the police?"

The young girl's face gave the game away. Her accent sounded Eastern European to Suzie, possibly Romanian. It was tough for the Bath police when many international students and tourists flocked to the Roman city. No wonder some youngsters' visas had long since expired.

"Relax," said Suzie. "We're after information, not checking up on his staff."

The girl disappeared through the beaded curtains at the end of the bar. When she returned, she was followed by a stout, middle-aged man in a red-and-white striped shirt and red bowtie. A wide, red leather belt held up his black trousers. Any ambitions for a six-pack had long been forgotten, and Suzie remembered her grandfather describing one of the local farmers as 'carrying all before him'.

"Frank Wooding," he said. "Adriana reckons you're police officers. What's this about?"

Suzie and Lydia waved the necessary proof in Frank Wooding's direction.

"Detective Inspector Ferris, Wiltshire Police," said Suzie. "Were you here in 2015, Mr Wooding?"

"For my sins, yes," he replied.

"Was Sid Selman, the journalist, a regular of yours?" asked Suzie.

"Sid? Yes, he dropped in most days. We kept an eye on him."

"You stopped serving him if he became a nuisance. Is that what you mean?" asked Lydia.

"He was never enough trouble for me to have to bar him," said Frank. "When I spoke to other landlords at our monthly meetings, his other haunts told a similar tale. Sid could keep an audience entertained with stories about his time in London. If you hadn't heard them before, they were fun, but we had heard every one of them. We have a high turnover of customers in the city, so Sid found plenty of fresh faces to latch onto. Now and then, we'd encourage him to toddle off home. Nobody loves a pub bore, especially on this side of the counter."

"He wrote articles for the Chronicle, didn't he?" asked Lydia.

"So I believe," said Frank. "Several of my regulars reckoned he must have been an editor's dream when he was in his prime. Sid had a weakness, though. He kept searching for an exclusive, a scandal that would make everyone in Bath sit up and take notice. Sid didn't drink during the day. According to my colleagues, he spent hours researching in the library."

"His neighbours suggested Sid had a falling out with his employers at the Chronicle," said Suzie. "Any idea what that could have been over?"

"I can't help you there, I'm afraid. Sid had stopped drinking here by then."

"He sold up in a hurry and moved away," said Lydia. "Did that seem odd to you?"

"It wasn't something he would have discussed with me,"

said Frank. "People come here for a drink, chat with friends, and enjoy a meal. I haven't got enough time in the day to hear everyone's life story."

"Did Sid have any friends here that might know where he went next?" asked Suzie.

"I'm not sure Sid had any real friends, just loads of acquaintances. All pubs used to have characters people remembered years after they were dead and gone. That's because people used the same pub for forty or fifty years. So if you come back tonight, someone will tell you a story about Sid. He's not been gone long enough for people to have forgotten him altogether. But things don't stay the same these days, do they? People move far more readily than they did, which is why fewer characters are around. They don't have time to develop. Well, that's my take on it, for what it's worth."

"How long has Adriana worked here?" asked Lydia.

"Hard to remember," said Frank. "She's talking about going home next year. I'll miss her. She's a hard worker, worth two of our local kids. They think the world owes them a living."

"Thanks for the background, Mr Wooding," said Suzie. "We'd better get to the Chronicle before they finish work for the day."

Frank Wooding tidied cloths and beer mats as he watched Lydia and Suzie leave. He wondered whether the Detective Inspector would make a phone call, despite what she told Adriana.

"I hope we can catch Fiona Marsh," said Suzie as they headed for James Street West. "Something must have caused friction between Sid Selman and the editor."

When they arrived outside the Westpoint building, the lights in the offices shone brightly. The rain had started again, and the breeze had a hard edge that wasn't there when they walked from Sydney Buildings to The Raven.

"Perhaps we should have brought the car back to Green Park," said Suzie. "It will be a trek in this weather before we can drive back to London Road."

"Keep positive," said Lydia. "Fiona Marsh might tell us why they couldn't work together any longer and remember where he was moving after he sold his flat."

"Dream on," said Suzie.

They went through the same rigmarole with the Chronicle reception desk to reach the third floor, and Fiona Marsh was equally as flustered as she had appeared earlier.

"We've spoken to the lady who bought Mr Selman's flat," said Suzie. "She said he had a difference of opinion with someone in this building, and that's what caused him to sell up and move on. Could you point us in the direction of that person's office, please? We'd like to get details."

"That won't be possible," said Fiona, recovering her composure. "We've had a change of editor since then. However, I'm sure you appreciate that freelance journalists like Sid Selman bring ideas to the table which need careful consideration before we go into print."

"Your lawyers go through everything with a fine-toothed comb in case you get sued for millions," said Lydia. "We understand. What great scoop did Sid unearth? Was Jane Austen really a man who fooled Bath society for years? Or was it Caroline Herschel who discovered Uranus and not her more famous brother, William?"

"It was nothing like that, I can assure you," said Fiona. "Before you ask, I can't divulge any details; they're confidential."

"We can get a warrant," said Suzie.

"It seems a lot of fuss," said Fiona.

"For what?" asked Lydia.

Fiona Marsh realised these two detectives weren't going to back down.

"Mr Selman wanted us to expose abuse among police officers working in Manvers Street. Our editor looked at the evidence he'd gathered and wasn't convinced it would stand up in court. Then our legal team got involved and discovered Mr Selman had tried something similar in Warminster a couple of years earlier. That complaint hadn't gone the distance, either. The legal team thought Mr Selman was a fantasist who saw corruption and scandal wherever he looked."

"What happened next?" asked Suzie.

"He was called into the editor's office and told we wouldn't pursue his proposed project. He was unhappy with the outcome, had a few harsh words with the editor, and stormed out of the building. We didn't hear from him again. That's all I'm prepared to say without a warrant. I don't think you have enough to support one, anyway."

"Perhaps not," said Suzie. "But we'll be back if our enquiries tomorrow lead us to find Sid Selman, and the evidence he shows us can be substantiated."

"If there's nothing else, I'd like to go home," said Fiona. "We work regular hours here."

Suzie and Lydia returned to the ground floor and stood outside on the pavement.

"I wonder whether any of those buses over there go anywhere near Sydney Buildings?" said Lydia.

They were soon sat on a bus heading for the University of Bath, and ten minutes later, they hopped off close to Lydia's car.

"That avoided a twenty-minute walk in the rain," said Lydia.

"I'd forgotten what a bus journey was like," said Suzie. "I haven't been on a bus since I went into Devizes School on the day I left."

Lydia set off for London Road.

"You can drop me in the car park when we get back, Lydia," said Suzie. "Gus will be wondering where I am. We'll pick this up again in the morning. I want to try the Bath Central Library first, and then we'll badger Denise Blanchard's neighbours if we don't turn up something useful."

"I've no idea what Alex has been doing today," said Lydia. "He promised to ring when he got the chance."

Suzie wondered how Gus had fared. When she left him this morning, he looked like a fish out of water.

Thursday, 8 November 2018

"DID YOU HAVE A GOOD EVENING?" asked Suzie when Lydia arrived in her office bang on nine o'clock.

"Quiet," said Lydia. "Alex rang just after nine. He'd had a full day in north London. Neil had been in touch. He was disappointed to learn that because of an international break, there wouldn't be an opportunity to get assigned to crowd control at a Premier League game. Alex told me the protestors could target bridges over the Thames next Saturday."

"More opportunity for hanging banners in prominent positions, I suppose," said Suzie. "I don't envy the Met trying to anticipate the pressure points. They can't cover them all."

"How was Gus?" asked Lydia. "Had the red mist lifted?"

"Bless him, he'd made a start on the to-do-list I left him," said Suzie. "We went out for dinner last night. I drove, as I wasn't drinking. We would have been like two drowned rats if we'd walked. Our friends usually cycle to the pub, but even they yielded to the constant downpour, and Brett used his car. The landlord put a damper on the evening; he told Brett his grandfather hadn't been in for a couple of days."

"That's Bert Penman, isn't it?" said Lydia. "Gus mentioned what a good friend he is."

"Bert's eighty-five, and Gus knows he can't last forever. Brett has been busy with veterinary work this week, so he hadn't called in, and Clemency, the vicar, is avoiding the allotment until she can buy new wellington boots. A lady called Irene North has lived with Bert for a while, so if something had happened, she would have contacted Brett, I'm sure."

"Perhaps they've both been taken ill," said Lydia. "Have they had their flu jab? Or it could be tummy trouble."

"Brett had an emergency operation on a collie today in Wootton Bassett, so Gus agreed to call in to see Bert and Irene. Then, he'll take it from there."

"I assume the Central Library lives up to its name?" said Lydia.

"I don't know where the original library was," said Suzie, "but now it's housed in The Podium shopping centre, a two-minute walk from Pulteney Bridge. We'll park in the underground car park there. Are you ready?"

"An eager beaver, that's me," said Lydia. She still had her car keys in her hand.

Forty-five minutes later, they had safely parked the Mini and were inside the lift.

Suzie stepped inside the first-floor library. She could make out the sound of a photocopier and a printer in the distance. There were computers in abundance, humming away. They should be able to get away with a whispered conversation if the opportunity arose.

Lydia spotted a young woman carrying several books.

"That's too many for someone to take home for the weekend," she said. "She must work here."

The assistant librarian slowed when she heard Lydia speak.

"Who's in charge here?" asked Suzie, showing the woman her warrant card.

"Police?" she replied. "You want the gentleman in the reference section."

Suzie nodded her gratitude and walked around the corner, where she found a middle-aged man, surrounded by books, sitting at a large table. When the man heard Suzie and Lydia approach, he looked up. Lydia thought he was exactly what she considered a librarian should look like. He wore a beige sleeveless pullover with a lemon-coloured button-down shirt. His tie was brown, as were his trousers.

"Detective Inspector Ferris, Wiltshire Police," said Suzie. "My colleague is Lydia Logan Barre. We want to speak to anyone here who remembers a Mr Sid Selman. We believe he was a frequent visitor to this library a couple of years ago. Who's the best person to speak to?"

"I suppose that would be me, ma'am," the man replied.

He blinked several times behind his glasses. Suzie wondered whether being surrounded by books all day had led the chief librarian to watch hours of British police series on TV. She couldn't remember anyone other than a police officer calling her ma'am.

"You knew Mr Selman?" she asked.

"Oh, yes, ma'am. Sid was here almost as often as me. We should try to keep our voices down, ma'am. They're not as strict as when I was a boy, but they like us to respect others."

"When you say 'they'?" said Suzie. She was confused. "Sorry, the young woman gave us the impression you were in charge. Aren't you the chief librarian?"

"Heavens, no, ma'am. I'm a police officer, a Detective Sergeant from Manvers Street."

Suzie realised the assistant librarian's first thought when she'd produced her warrant card and asked who was in charge had been of the semi-permanent fixture in their reference section. Education was a wonderful thing, but it was wasted on the young.

Suzie and Lydia quietly moved chairs nearer the table to continue the conversation.

"What case are you working on?" asked Suzie. "Is it okay to interrupt you for a while?"

"Oh, I haven't been on an active case for several years, ma'am. My superiors keep me busy researching background for cases they hand to the younger detectives. The less time I spend in the office, the better. That seems to be the way of things. It was easier to hide me away in the old Manvers Street building, but our office space has halved since we moved across the road."

"There was nowhere to hide you," said Lydia.

"Quite," said the Sergeant, blinking again.

"Tell us about Sid Selman," said Suzie.

"Sid started coming here in the early part of 2014. It would have been March while the Literature Festival was in full flow. There were fewer empty seats here back then, I can tell you. We didn't speak to one another, just a nod to acknowledge we'd recognised a fellow avid reader. Later in the year, when the buzz created by the festival had died, I discovered Sid's name and former occupation."

"We know his background, Sergeant," said Suzie. "We're interested in what he was doing while he was here."

"Not my place to interfere, ma'am," he replied. "When we did discuss anything, it tended to concern the future of this place. The Council planned to save money by opening what they called a One Stop Shop for a raft of their services. A slimmed-down library was an option to be included in a building called Lewis House. Sid and I agreed it would be a travesty."

"The library is still here," said Lydia. "The Podium has been open for almost thirty years. So why would anyone want to move this lovely library away from the heart of the city?"

"To save money, miss. History doesn't butter any parsnips, not even in an ancient city like Bath. Residents protested in their thousands to stop the library from being downsized and relocated to Lewis House and then further protested to prevent the relocation of those One Stop Shop services here a few months ago. A terrific example of people power at work."

"How does any of this connect to Sid Selman?" asked Suzie.

"After we discussed the proposed move, Sid wrote an article for the Chronicle. He already had a weekly column which attracted a small but enthusiastic following. When that article appeared, his standing in the city rose. Sid told me it wasn't as heartening as the national reaction to some of the pieces he'd written while working in Fleet Street, but it proved he could still make a difference."

"What went wrong?" asked Suzie.

"Sid asked me whether I felt aggrieved at how I was treated. He wanted me to say I'd suffered abuse, you know, nothing untoward, but age-related abuse. He thought my superiors were misguided. The same went for the editors of the newspapers who turned their backs on any reporter over the age of fifty. I wasn't happy about going down that road, so we stopped talking to one another. He didn't come to the quiz nights any more at Widcombe Social Club."

"Isn't that close to where he lived?" asked Lydia.

"Yes, miss. They only had to walk a little over half a mile. I've gone there for years with my three pals. We've entered a team of four in the quiz for as long as I can remember."

"Had Sid made friends with someone in the flats at Sydney Buildings?" asked Suzie.

"I wouldn't know, ma'am. He brought a partner with him the first time they attended. Two of my friends were on holiday, and I'd asked Sid if he was interested in making up the numbers. We came second that night, an improvement on our usual performance."

"Did he bring someone different the next time he came?" asked Lydia.

"No, miss. He was always with the same lady. Sid told me he wasn't available on a couple of occasions when I didn't have a full team, and then in the summer of 2015, they arrived without prior warning. The organisers weren't happy about a six-person team taking part, so Sid and his wife played on their own. They did surprisingly well."

"Sid was married," said Suzie. "That's news to us. What was his wife's name?"

"Althea, ma'am," said the Detective Sergeant. "A Filipino lady."

Suzie looked at Lydia. Where had they heard about someone from the Far East?

"Sid Selman with a much younger woman. I didn't expect that," said Lydia.

"Oh, Althea wasn't as young as yourself, miss. I would say she was in her mid-forties, perhaps a little older—a very sensible woman, strong on Geography and Science. My pals would agree with me. Sid and Althea were very much in love. You can forget that theirs was a marriage of convenience or that Sid was an older man conned by a young bar girl while on holiday in Manila or Cebu."

"Please tell me you know where they went when they left Sydney Buildings," said Suzie.

"Bristol, ma'am," said the detective. "Sid wanted to pursue his ambition to write for the Evening Post, but as he felt his recent past would count against him, he changed his name. So, he became Sonny Ramos after his late father-in-law for articles he submitted to the Evening Post. Unfortunately, Althea's father died just weeks after the wedding. Sid and Althea were happy to remain single, but her father's liver cancer spurred the couple to satisfy Sonny's wishes that they tie the knot."

"Do you have an address for Sid?" asked Lydia.

"Bradley Stoke, miss," said the detective. "That's all I can tell you, I'm afraid. But the Evening Post will be able to put you in touch, I'm sure."

"You've been a great help, Sergeant," said Suzie. "I hope things improve for you. Having you hidden away in this library seems a terrible waste of an experienced detective."

"What is your name?" asked Lydia.

"Sergeant Dodds, miss. I might not be hidden away here for much longer. I've heard a rumour a young Detective Chief Inspector is moving to Bath after a successful stint with the Met. Someone suggested putting my name forward as her potential partner. I think they thought it humorous. I can't see a partnership between two people with our age difference working, ma'am. Can you?"

"You'd be surprised, " said Suzie, tapping her small bump as she eased herself out of the chair.

Chapter Five

"BRADLEY STOKE IS A RABBIT WARREN," said Lydia as they descended in the lift to the car park.

"Perhaps, but as our friendly sergeant suggested, the Evening Post will have contact details for Sonny Ramos," said Suzie. "Unless he's upset someone there too, by now."

"Where to next, Suzie?" asked Lydia.

"Back to London Road," said Suzie. "Divya will have compiled that missing information for us, and we can ask her to do some digging on Sonny Ramos."

Lydia drove them out of Bath, and forty-five minutes later, with lunchtime fast approaching, they parked outside the main building on London Road. When they reached the top of the stairs, Vera Butler waved a hand.

"Divya Yadav delivered a file for you, Suzie," she said. "I've put in on your desk. Do you want me to ask Kassie to bring her trolley around in a little while? If you stay in the office this afternoon, you don't want to miss lunch."

"That would be great, Vera. Thanks," said Suzie.

Once they were inside her office, Suzie checked the

details of which businesses were operating in Warminster town centre in the eighteen months before the poster campaign started.

"Marjorie's was there, as Bernie Cotton told us," she said. "I've realised there was something else we should have asked Divya to do."

Lydia thought back over what they'd learned in the past two days.

"We know Bernie started visiting the hair salon as soon as they moved into town. She'd had a mobile hairdresser visit them in Longbridge Deverill before that. The girl had trimmed Will's hair too. A Filipino girl worked in the hair salon, doing menial tasks, and left within weeks. Bernie Cotton sold us another dummy. She referred to the staff as girls and explained that they were ten to fifteen years younger than many of their clients."

"Exactly," said Suzie. "Bernie referred to the foreign girl sweeping up and doing various chores as a *young* girl. So we assumed that might mean an eighteen-year-old."

"Someone in their mid-forties *would* be young to a group of ladies in their seventies and eighties," said Lydia. "I wonder how Althea met Sid Selman? Nothing Bernie told us suggested that Will had his haircut at the salon. He must have found a barber shop in town."

"I'd like to know where those campaign posters were positioned," said Suzie. "If Divya could get details of the street furniture in the town centre, that would help."

"We could use Google street view to see whether there was a lamppost directly outside Marjorie's salon," said Lydia.

"Things could have changed," said Suzie. "Was the street layout the same in 2011 as today?"

"To access old street view photos, you must tap the

Street View image you're looking at," said Lydia. "Then tap to see more dates."

"Really? As Gus keeps telling me, one new fact every day is the high road to success," said Suzie. "That sounds simple enough, provided it works. For example, we could see what Warminster town centre looked like at various stages during the dates we're interested in. We'll catch sight of Sid Selman and Althea Ramos if we're lucky."

"Sid won't be holding a paste brush," said Lydia. "We agreed he must have distributed his posters at night or at weekends when everything was quiet, and Althea wasn't working. If he came back during the day to see what reaction his posters were getting, we might capture the moment their eyes met through the window of Marjorie's."

"Ever the romantic, Lydia," said Suzie. "Perhaps I'm cynical, but Sid Selman didn't sound the sort of bloke to lose his heart over a pretty face. Hark at me. Gus is the one who's on a diversity and inclusivity course next week, and here I am making unqualified stereotypical assumptions."

"We have no idea what Althea looked like," said Lydia. "And apart from knowing Sid was over sixty and possibly a borderline alcoholic, we don't know whether he once won a George Clooney look-alike contest. However, Sergeant Dodds told us Althea was a valuable addition to their pub quiz team. So, she was over-qualified for the job she had at Marjorie's."

"I wonder," said Suzie. "We assumed the domestic slavery allegation raised by Sid Selman referred to the young Asian girl in the hair salon before we discovered their true relationship. I asked Divya to check whether she was illegally brought to this country by an organised crime group. There's nothing in this file about her."

Suzie called Divya Yadav in the Hub.

"Hi, Divya, it's Suzie Ferris. Did you find anything on that Filipino woman who worked at the hairdresser's in Warminster?"

Lydia could tell there was plenty to hear.

"Ah, okay, that's interesting," said Suzie finally. "Thanks."

"Your frown suggests the water just got murkier," said Lydia.

"Marjorie's knew her as Althea de Angelo," said Suzie. "She came to the UK from Manila in 2008 with her husband, Ferdinand. They settled in Nottingham, but Althea ran away three years later to escape physical and mental abuse. The salon manager must have given her a job, plus a room above the shop."

"What happened to Ferdinand de Angelo?" asked Lydia.

"No idea. But we should ask Divya to check whether Althea divorced Ferdinand before marrying Sid Selman," said Suzie. "The way Sergeant Dodds described it, they flew to the Philippines to get married, so Althea's father could see his daughter married before he died."

"It's odd how we refer to our friendly sergeant by his surname, isn't it?" said Lydia.

"He was an odd character. Perhaps he doesn't have a first name," said Suzie.

A tap on the door interrupted the conversation.

"Good afternoon, ladies," said Kassie Trotter. "Coffee?"

"Yes, please, Kassie," said Suzie. "We're both black, with one sugar."

"Is that each or between you?" asked Kassie. "Only kidding. What about a bite to eat?"

"I'm famished," said Lydia, studying the items on

Kassie's trolly. "I'll be kind to Suzie and have the healthy option," she said.

Kassie was soon on her way, minus two salad baguettes.

"I didn't realise how hungry I was," Suzie said after finishing their lunch.

"Back to Althea de Angelo," said Lydia. "So, she arrived in Warminster and found a sympathetic employer who went above and beyond to help her. Her husband, Ferdinand, sounds like a piece of work. Perhaps he was looking for her."

"I queried why she was only earning minimum wage," said Suzie. "But she accepted whatever menial job was available. Unfortunately, Althea felt she couldn't fill out applications for middle-management positions or higher."

"If Sid was trying to keep Althea away from Ferdinand by moving to Bath, no wonder he covered his tracks as well as he did," said Lydia. "Nobody mentioned Althea to Denise Blanchard. She thought Sid must have had a cleaner when we suggested he lived in a tip. Again, we assumed his lifestyle matched our image of a drunk with a chip on his shoulder."

"Sid must have kept Althea hidden away in that flat at Sydney Buildings for the first year after leaving Warminster," said Suzie. "Perhaps they only went out together under cover of darkness. If Althea were a battered wife on the run and in love with Sid, she would have done anything to avoid raising suspicion."

"Then they risked the odd social evening with Sergeant Dodds and his cronies," said Lydia, "until they flew abroad to get married."

"Now we know her background; there's no reason to question how Althea travelled home for the wedding. She had a valid passport, albeit in her married name. I haven't met the woman, but I hope she divorced Ferdinand before tying the knot with Sid Selman. I'll get Divya on that straightaway."

Suzie made the call, and for the rest of the afternoon, they analysed the data on the town centre businesses. At five o'clock, they had almost completed their task.

"Back to the grindstone in the morning," said Suzie. "Divya hopes to get what we need by coffee time. If she finds Sid and Althea, we'll drive to Bradley Stoke and have a quiet chat. Before we leave here, I want to drill down through the more relevant street-view images to find Sid and Althea. Either together or alone. I want to take those images with us."

"How many addresses among the businesses we've analysed do you think are related to Sid's poster campaign?" asked Lydia.

"Less than five," sighed Suzie. "Nobody whose name appears over the door, or is registered as the landlord, is known to us. What we've found so far supports what Mark Colbourne and Melanie Spicer thought at the time. Nothing was going on of any genuine concern."

Lydia drove home to Chippenham. She faced another evening alone, waiting for a phone call from Alex. After the day they'd had, she stopped for a takeaway and congratulated herself for putting a new bottle of Chardonnay in the fridge this morning before she left home.

When Suzie reached the bungalow, Gus had prepared their evening meal.

"You've got thirty minutes before it's ready to serve, darling," he said. "Before you dash off to shower and change, I have news on Bert and Irene. I drove to see them mid-morning and found them wrapped in throws, trying to keep warm by the open fire."

"They hadn't had their flu jabs," said Suzie. "Typical Bert, still thinks he's invincible."

"Not on this occasion," said Gus. "They went to the clinic on the same day they received the invitation to get protection, had the jab, and forty-eight hours later went down with the worst cold either of them can remember."

"The luck of the draw, I suppose," said Suzie. "Did they call the doctor?"

"Irene called and received a list of suggestions on how to deal with the aches and pains. They should ring to make an appointment if their condition hasn't improved by Monday."

"Did you call Brett?" asked Suzie.

"He and The Reverend will keep tabs on them over the next three days," said Gus. "Brett thought the worst would be over in another twenty-four hours."

"Did you stay with them long?" asked Suzie.

"No, don't worry. Irene made sure I kept well away. She wasn't that worried about me getting the flu. She was more concerned for you and the baby."

Suzie hugged Gus and went for her shower. When she returned to the kitchen, he was dishing up dinner.

"Enjoy," he said as he sat down opposite her. "Tell me about your rainy day in Bath."

"I met a Detective Sergeant today who didn't think relationships between an older man and a younger woman had much chance of success. I told him he was misguided."

"I didn't realise you were speaking to anyone from Manvers Street," said Gus. "Did your case take a different turn?"

"The DS was in the library, where we hunted for anyone who knew Sid Selman. By the sound of it, he knew Sid better than most and told us Sid and his wife had moved to Bradley Stoke."

"Good luck finding him there unless you have an address and a decent map," said Gus. "Hang on. I don't remember Geoff telling me Sid Selman was ever married."

"Sid married a lady he met in Warminster," said Suzie. "We haven't uncovered all the details yet, but Althea worked at a hair salon in the town centre from 2011. Sid moved to Bath two years later, and Althea went to live with him. They married in the summer of 2015."

"A washed-up hack in his early sixties marries a shop girl," said Gus. "They'll make a movie of that one day. It doesn't match the image Kenneth and Geoff painted."

"I think Sid changed his ways," said Suzie. "He may have earned a reputation for enjoying a drink in London, but from what we heard today, he'd cut back on his drinking. As for the shop girl, Althea is fifteen years younger than Sid and an intelligent woman who escaped an abusive marriage."

"The fact they're making frequent moves doesn't augur well," said Gus. "Did this DS of yours believe Althea was in danger?"

"We don't know yet," said Suzie. "Divya is chasing down the husband's whereabouts and checking a divorce was finalised before the couple flew to the Philippines to get hitched."

"How does any of this connect to your corruption case?" asked Gus.

Suzie grinned.

"Heaven only knows. I keep discovering something I didn't think was likely when I started this job for Geoff Mercer. Lydia even asked whether Kenneth selected the

Clark case for you to investigate because he knew something was behind the complaints that led to the poster campaign."

"I was told upfront not to get involved in the Selman business," said Gus. "My team was miffed. They thought photographic evidence and potential witness statements Selman claimed to have could have been vital in learning who killed Millie Clark. They were wrong, as it turned out. Whatever you discover tomorrow won't impact that murder case one jot."

"Have we still got two slices of the cheesecake?" asked Suzie.

"I see our work conversation over," said Gus. "Fair enough. I believe we do. Would you like a coffee afterwards? We can relax in the lounge and watch Question Time with the sound muted."

"That sounds like a plan," said Suzie. "Politics bore me. Before we go into the lounge, can you show me the to-do list? I want to check your progress."

"You need to write a new one," said Gus. "I must have left it in my back pocket when I washed my trousers today. Then, when I emptied the washing machine, it took ages to collect the bits."

Friday, 9 November 2018

WHEN SUZIE ARRIVED at London Road, she found Lydia was already scanning Google street view images of Warminster town centre.

"You're quick off the mark," she said. "What time did you get here?"

"Only ten minutes ago," said Lydia. "Nothing new from

Alex last night. I was nodding off when he rang. He was in a pub somewhere with a couple of other officers drafted in ahead of next weekend."

"He left it late to call, I suppose," said Suzie. "Typical bloke."

"It wasn't that late," admitted Lydia. "I'd had two glasses of wine with my chicken curry, and the day caught up with me."

"Two glasses of wine," sighed Suzie. "Oh, how I remember those days."

She sat beside Lydia and studied the screen.

"What am I looking at?"

"This is what the town centre looked like in 2011. We're heading towards the corner of Weymouth Street, where the illegal activities were supposedly centred," said Lydia. "The bridal boutique on our right has been there throughout, and the charity shop. Now we're passing the Weatherspoon's pub. Just beyond the jewellers is Costa Coffee. Our hair salon is coming up on our right, next to the bakery."

"Stop," said Suzie. "Look, who's that outside Marjorie's?"

"We won't be able to see their faces," said Lydia as she retraced her steps. "They blank out the features for privacy. Although, I'm pretty certain I recognise that man by his posture and the way he walks. It's Tom Brewer, and the woman he's meeting outside the hair salon is his wife, Cynthia."

"There's too much reflection from the shop window to tell whether anyone inside the salon is watching them," said Suzie. "The other people on the pavement on that side of the street are too young to be Sid Selman. I must admit I never expected to see Tom Brewer."

"Should we be surprised to see someone we know?"

asked Lydia. "Tom was still a DI in town, and they lived near the police station. It wasn't until later they moved out to Heytesbury. Cynthia wasn't as badly affected by dementia as now, but if she showed early signs in 2011, perhaps Tom would take her to the hairdressers and collect her afterwards. Tom didn't go inside; he waited on the pavement a few yards away until he saw Cynthia step outside the door. We can't be certain either of them spoke to Althea."

"Let's switch our attention again to the left-hand-side of the street," said Suzie. "Keep your eyes peeled for Sid Selman."

"You do remember we haven't got a photograph of him," said Lydia. "We should contact that DS at Manvers Street for a description."

"It might be quicker to call the library," said Suzie.

As she went to lift the phone, it rang.

"No worries, Divya. Bring everything you have to my office."

"Divya beat the clock," said Lydia. "It's nowhere near coffee-time."

Two minutes later, there was a knock at the door.

"Here's a summary of where the street furniture was in the Market Place between the dates you specified," said Divya. "There haven't been many adjustments. They had to replace a 1950s lamppost in 2013 after a delivery lorry mounted the kerb and demolished it. Other than that, little has changed. One thing to remember; I indicated which properties were empty for a period after a business closed. Remember to add those to your list of potential poster sites. Nobody takes heed of the 'Bill Posters Will Be Prosecuted' notices these days."

"Good thinking, Divya," said Lydia. "We haven't seen any posters on random shop windows in 2011."

"I've checked the marital status of both Sid Selman *and* Althea de Angelo," said Divya. "Just in case Sid was already married while he was in London. He'd never married. Althea didn't divorce Ferdinand de Angelo but don't panic. He died of a heart attack several months before the wedding, aged fifty-eight. Details of his sudden death were published online and in local Nottingham newspapers. Sid and Althea may have learned of his death that way, but a local firm of solicitors ran one of those ads in the national press where they ask people with a claim to the estate to get in touch. I haven't followed up to find out whether they ever had a response."

"My, you've been busy, Divya," said Lydia.

"Just one more thing to tell us," said Suzie.

"An address for Sid Selman and Althea Ramos?" asked Divya. "How about a three-bedroomed end of terrace in Daisy Close? The details of how to get there are on this card."

"Bless you," said Suzie. "If Kassie is on her way in the next five minutes, we'll grab a coffee before we leave."

"My second cup in the Hub will get cold," said Divya. "I'd better get back. Bye."

"How the other half lives," sighed Suzie. "Thanks for your help, Divya."

"It's why we're there, Suzie. You know that."

Lydia followed Divya out of the office and spotted Kassie Trotter. She asked Kassie if she could spare two minutes after dealing with DS Mercer.

"I'll show Mr Mercer my baps, and after he's decided which one he fancies, I'll pop along. Two coffees was it?" said Kassie, ever the innocent.

"Please, Kassie," said Lydia. "Can I get your phone

number? If I'm here every day next week, we should check we don't turn up looking like tall bookends."

"I've only got one charcoal grey pinstripe suit, miss," said Kassie. "Why don't you risk Mr Truelove's blood pressure and wear your black leather skirt? Live dangerously."

Vera Butler was walking past as Kassie spoke.

"What Gus Freeman doesn't see, he can't criticise Lydia. Go for it. I wish I had your legs."

Lydia returned to the office to find Suzie browsing through the street view images.

"We haven't got time to check for updated images," she said. "Depending on what we learn this morning, we'll take a closer look when we get back from Bradley Stoke."

They left the office just before ten. One hour later, they had reached Bradley Stoke, and after a couple of wrong turns, Lydia drew up outside the house in Daisy Close.

"No car on the drive," said Lydia.

"We have no evidence that either can drive," said Suzie. "Sid walked around Bath, and he and Althea walked to that social club on quiz night."

"The curtain twitched," said Lydia. "Come on. Let's go before they do a runner."

"Relax," said Suzie. "They don't have anything to hide. If anything, Sid Selman should be eager to spill the beans over whatever agitated him in Warminster."

They walked the short distance from the pavement to the front door. Lydia rang the bell, and Suzie had her warrant card ready. A short, plump lady answered the door. Althea Selman was elegantly dressed, with long dark hair. Suzie tried to imagine her thirty years younger and fifty pounds lighter. She would have turned heads, that's for sure.

"Althea?" she asked. "Is it Selman or Ramos?"

"Who are you? What do you want?" asked Althea. She spoke quietly with a heavy accent.

"Wiltshire Police. I'm Detective Inspector Suzie Ferris. My colleague is Ms Logan Barre. We wish to speak with you and your husband. Is he in?"

"Sid's in his office, writing," said Althea. "You had better come in. I'm Mrs Selman, by the way."

Althea showed them into the lounge and invited them to sit. She left them to go upstairs.

They could hear voices from the room above. Two minutes later, Althea walked into the room, followed by Sid Selman.

George Clooney had nothing to worry about. Sid Selman was of medium height with greying tousled hair. Lydia wondered whether his latest article was proving difficult to write. Sid was casually dressed, with a navy blue cardigan over a pale blue polo shirt. Lydia couldn't tell whether the slacks were black or blue. She noticed Sid wore carpet slippers, so he wasn't planning on running away.

"I wondered whether this day would ever come," said Sid. "How did you find us?"

"We asked a police officer," said Suzie.

Sid nodded.

"You carried out a poster campaign in Warminster town centre," said Suzie. "On several occasions, you claimed to have approached the police to provide evidence, but they refused to talk to you. What can you tell us about that?"

"Let me get one thing straight first," said Sid. "Who asked you to look into this business after five years?"

"Our Chief Constable, Kenneth Truelove," said Suzie.

"He worked in Warminster," said Sid. "How can I be sure this will be treated fairly?"

TED TAYLER

"Tell them everything, Sid," said Althea. "These two
ladies weren't involved in what happened. Let's trust them."

Sid left the room and went upstairs to his office. When
he returned, he was carrying a folder and a mobile phone.

"This is the evidence I gathered," he said. "Some of it
was probably rubbish, but I had to stop Althea from getting
hurt."

Sid opened the folder and emptied a load of
photographs onto the coffee table in front of him. Lydia
picked one and showed it to Suzie. They had no idea who
the man was, but Sid told Lydia to turn the photo over.

"DS Chris Lawry," said Lydia. "Where is that building?
Is it in the Market Place?"

"It's in a narrow side street off the Market Place," said
Sid. "I've got half a dozen photos of that detective visiting a
woman for a massage. He went there twice a week for three
weeks."

"Were the premises registered as a beauty studio?" asked
Suzie. "It could have been a genuine series of treatments for
a muscle problem. What else have you got?"

Lydia separated the six shots of Chris Lawry entering,
or leaving, the door to a first-floor flat. Then she picked up
another photo and looked at the back.

"PC Hugh Sharpe," she said.

"I knew Hugh Sharpe," said Suzie. "He must be retired
now. How often does he appear?"

"Once a week," said Sid. "Always at the same time, half-
past six in the evening."

"After he'd finished his shift," said Suzie. "If he'd been
on his feet all day…."

"I told you some of them could have been tenuous,"
said Sid. "If we had solely concentrated on the main man,
we might have been six feet under by now."

"The information we received suggested you had been harassed and intimidated," said Suzie. "Who was responsible for that?"

"Althea was the one who was harassed and intimidated, to begin with," said Sid. "I was threatened with violence by this man later."

Sid pushed a photo across the table towards Suzie.

"This must have been taken late at night," she said. "It's hard to make out who that is. He reminds me of a young Detective Constable that worked out of Polebarn Road in Trowbridge. Before leaving the force, he performed various tasks in the Trowbridge, Westbury, and Warminster areas. He never showed the aptitude to progress any higher than a DC; I can't remember his name."

"Rob Haines," said Sid. "He didn't know I had taken this photo."

"Haines, that was him," said Suzie. "Every team he worked with that included female officers wanted him moved on as soon as possible. A nasty piece of work."

"He drove to Avon Road and forced his way into my home," said Sid. "It was almost midnight on a Saturday, and I'd been keeping watch on Althea's flat during the week. He told me I didn't know who I was dealing with. If I didn't stop the poster campaign and interfering in Althea's life, things would get sticky for both of us."

"Who's on the remaining photos?" asked Lydia.

"If you think there's an innocent explanation for the photos you haven't looked at yet, you should watch this video first."

Sid Selman picked up the mobile phone and searched for the item he wanted.

Suzie and Lydia recognised Marjorie's hair salon.

"Where were you when you filmed this?" asked Suzie.

"In a narrow gap between two shops fifteen yards further along, on the opposite side of the street. You can see the time and date, the eighteenth of August 2012."

A tall shape appeared on the pavement, keeping close to the darkened shop fronts. When they reached the door to the first-floor flat above the hair salon, they stopped and rang the bell. A light appeared in the stairwell, and a short, plump woman answered the door. Suzie watched as the man looked left and right, then pushed his way inside, closing the door behind him. The light went out in the flat upstairs less than five minutes later.

"Is this the only video you filmed?" asked Suzie.

Sid shook his head.

"We thought if we had evidence, it would stop," said Althea.

Lydia sensed she was on the verge of tears. "He was too powerful; we couldn't trust anyone to listen. When Sid told me what that man Haines had said, we decided my only option was to run away again."

"I think we should hear your story now, Althea," said Suzie. "Why did you choose to come to Warminster after leaving your husband, Ferdinand, in Nottingham? You couldn't have known anyone here."

"My father had urged me to marry Ferdinand de Angelo," said Althea. "He was a wealthy man with a thriving business in the city. We were a poor family, and I had four younger sisters. I didn't love Ferdinand, but he treated me well at first. His business suffered setbacks, and suddenly I became the focus of his frustrations. Ferdinand would come home after another fruitless day trying to secure new customers, and the smallest thing would set him off. I covered the bruises with make-up as best I could and wore sunglasses on grey, cloudy days."

"I suppose he said he was sorry and promised never to do it again," said Lydia.

"Not at all," said Althea. "He never apologised once for how he treated me. Things got worse for his business in 2011, and the creditors were circling. One night, Ferdinand went crazy, punching and kicking me, before getting in his car and driving away. He said someone in Sheffield owed him money, which was his last resort. Somehow, I made it outside the house, caught a bus, and reached the hospital. They told me several ribs were fractured, as was my wrist. A nurse asked how it had happened. I told her I'd tripped on a loose runner on the stairs and put out my arm to break my fall. I could tell she didn't believe me. She left me in the cubicle for several minutes. I was about to slip away because I had to get home before Ferdinand returned from Sheffield. I was frightened the nurse had gone to call the police."

"Did you get home in time?" asked Lydia.

"Another lady came into the cubicle to talk to me before I could make it outside," said Althea. "She wasn't wearing a uniform. Her name was Heather, and she said I ought to leave Ferdinand because he would never change his ways. Heather knew of a refuge for battered wives in Nottingham and agreed to take me there, but I said that wouldn't work. Ferdinand knew so many important people in the city; it would only be a matter of time before he found me. So, Heather helped me outside and into her car. She drove me home, and there was no sign of Ferdinand. She helped me pack a suitcase. I gathered my important documents and crammed them into my handbag. Heather drove out of Nottingham; I had no idea where we were going. I slept on the sofa at her house in Beeston. Then we drove to a lorry park close to Junction 23 on the M1 the next morning. That's where I met Judy, a trucker driving south. Judy had been in my shoes several years before, and she'd met Heather at that refuge I mentioned. No questions asked. As soon as Heather told her I needed to get as far away from Nottingham as possible, Judy stowed my suitcase behind the passenger seat and helped me up into the cab. My wrist and ribs were hurting like hell."

"Where was Judy headed?" asked Suzie.

"Wincanton," said Althea.

"Why did Judy drop you off in Warminster on the way to Wincanton?"

"One reason was she wasn't supposed to have passengers," said Althea. "But mainly because Sheila, the owner of Marjorie's, is her older sister, and Judy knew she'd help someone in trouble."

"The salon has been called Marjorie's since it opened decades ago," said Sid.

"We learned yesterday that Sheila put you up in the flat and gave you a job in the salon," said Suzie. "We thought you were being exploited, but Sheila was helping you stay hidden from Ferdinand."

Althea nodded.

"As the weeks passed, I thought I was going to be safe, and then one morning in February 2012, a lady came into the salon to have her hair done. Her husband came to fetch her an hour later, and I saw how he looked at me. It was as if he was undressing me. He spoke quietly with Sheila as I prepared everything for the next customer to sit in the chair. When they had left the shop, I asked Sheila what had been said. She told me not to worry. Her friend's husband was a senior police officer."

Chapter Six

SUZIE DREW the remaining photographs together and flicked through them one by one.

"What happened next, Althea?" she asked.

"The doorbell rang late on a Saturday night. I had always gone to bed early since I left Nottingham. I wasn't brave enough to go out in town alone. Sheila or one of the girls in the salon would come with me when I went shopping in the daytime. I kept myself to myself. None of the customers was aware of my background. It wasn't a great existence, but I was no longer getting punched and kicked for no reason."

"You found this man on your doorstep?" asked Suzie showing Althea one of the photos. "The same man in the video on Sid's mobile phone?"

"Yes," said Althea. "He was drunk and told me he'd fancied me from the moment he set eyes on me. I told him I wasn't interested in him, but he pushed me into the hallway and shut the door. He said he had checked the name Sheila gave him and knew I was still married to Ferdinand de

Angelo, a businessman from Nottingham. He threatened to call Ferdinand and tell him where to find me if I wasn't nice to him. I protested, but he dragged me upstairs, took me into the bedroom and forced himself on me. When he'd finished, he told me he'd be back. One word to Sheila or anybody else, and he'd make that call. I thought I'd gone from one nightmare to another."

Suzie flicked through the photos again.

"These photos were taken at different times," she said. "The lighting's different, and the shop window displays next door varies. So what dates are covered by those videos, Mr Selman?"

"The first was in September 2012," said Sid. "The last one in March the following year."

"How did you get involved?" asked Suzie.

"I had started collecting evidence on Chris Lawry and Hugh Sharpe at the beginning of the year. Articles of mine were being published in the local newspapers, but they were lightweight pieces that didn't stretch me. I could knock off a thousand words in three hours to satisfy their editor. I needed something to get my teeth into, something worthy of my talent. I chanced upon PC Sharpe hobbling up the stairs to a flat off Market place one evening. He walked like a man of eighty, and I visualised a different reason for his being there. It started as a laugh. Then, Chris Lawry offered a second opportunity for me to follow someone discretely and take photographs, All the while, I was praying something big would turn up to make my story capable of grabbing the headlines, not hidden away on page fifty-three next to the crossword and the horoscope."

"So, you stalked Warminster police officers hoping to find someone guilty of wrongdoing," said Suzie.

"I'm not proud of how it started," said Sid. "I had been

to a pub in town and was walking through the Market Place, hoping to get a taxi back to Avon Road. I spotted the light above a doorway across the road. A man crept out, turning off the light as he stepped outside. Then he closed the door and hurried away, glancing over his shoulder now and then. I thought it suspicious. I couldn't believe it was someone leaving home, not at midnight. So he must have lived somewhere else. Who lived in the flat, I wondered? I noticed a light had come on upstairs, but it went out again a few minutes later. Walking further down the street to the taxi rank, I let my imagination run wild. Was he a husband playing away from home? Or could there be a brothel in operation at that address? I'd heard nothing to substantiate that line of thinking since I'd lived in the town. But I decided to add the address to my list of places to monitor. So, when I next spent the evening in town on a Saturday night, I filmed that first video. Then, I strolled past the door on Monday morning and realised it was connected with the salon."

"I had just finished sweeping the shop floor," said Althea. "Sheila asked me to wash down the tiles in the salon entrance and the wood panelling underneath the plate-glass windows. We'd had snow that lasted just twenty-four hours, and passing traffic had sprayed the shop front with grey slush. So I walked through the door with my bucket and mop, and there he was. Sid looked straight at me, and my heart skipped a beat."

Lydia glanced at Suzie, but she was giving nothing away.

"When did you start seeing one another?" asked Suzie.

"It was difficult," said Althea. "I never knew when I would get another late-night visit, and there was always the chance Ferdinand would find me without any outside help.

Judy hadn't called in to see her sister in months, and I wasn't sure if I could trust Sheila if she had known the couple for years. I was desperate. The only person I thought might help me was Sid, but I didn't even know his name at that stage."

"I got the idea for the poster campaign," said Sid. "I thought if I exaggerated the severity of what I'd seen happening, it might deter Althea's tormentor from harassing her. He wouldn't want people focusing on the comings and goings in the town centre. I felt the safest time to put the posters in the most prominent positions was on Sunday nights, and on one of those occasions, we got the chance to speak for the first time."

"I was drawing the curtains in the bedroom before having another early night," said Althea. "I spotted Sid furtively moving from one side of the road to another, grabbed a dressing gown, and went downstairs. I called out and asked what he was up to."

"I told Althea what I'd witnessed that Saturday night," said Sid. "She was embarrassed to admit the police officer had been to her flat uninvited several times. I was livid. He'd abused his position as a senior police officer and raped Althea without fear of repercussions."

"Sid wanted to take the evidence he'd gathered to the police," said Althea. "We both realised it wouldn't be enough on its own. I was prepared to suffer for a little longer if the man went to prison. But then the other officer visited Sid at home and threatened to hurt us. It felt then like it wasn't just the man at the top who was rotten; everyone working at the station was prepared to take his word against ours. The threat of Ferdinand finding me was always at the back of my mind too, and I began to believe there was no escape. Sid's kindness was the only thing that kept me going. He didn't judge me for what I was prepared to do to help him gather more evidence."

"I continued to keep watch on the flat, despite the threats of violence," said Sid. "You can see the times and dates on the back of the photographs, and I'll forward the videos to you whenever you wish. The poster campaign drew more attention later that year when a girl was murdered. I shamelessly exploited that case to strengthen my claims that Wiltshire Police knew who had killed the girl but ignored witnesses who linked the killing to the criminal activities in the town centre. I'm not proud of that, but we needed to use every trick in the book. I knew the truth would come out if the matter were properly investigated. My actions might earn me a rap over the knuckles, but it was a small price to pay for putting a sexual predator behind bars."

"Why were there no more videos after March?" asked Lydia.

"The visits became far less frequent," said Althea. "For which I was thankful. I knew why that might have been in the salon one day. We hadn't seen his wife for a few weeks. Sheila told me she wasn't well."

"She was diagnosed with senile dementia around that time," said Lydia. "Her husband was fast approaching retirement. So they planned to move to the country and take well-earned holidays."

"My heart bleeds," said Sid. "Haines called on me a second time while that murder investigation was in full swing. I'm not sure what he would have done if he'd found me home."

"How did you discover he'd been in Avon Road?" asked Suzie.

"A nosy neighbour, who never missed anything day or

night," said Sid. "She popped over the road to tell me what she'd seen when I got home the next morning."

Lydia saw Althea staring at her lap. She looked embarrassed.

"What did she see?" asked Suzie.

"She thought I'd committed a crime," said Sid. "Why else would a police officer be standing on my doorstep at ten-thirty at night, with a baton raised, ready to strike whoever opened the door? When nobody answered, he kicked the door several times and drove away."

"It's fair to say your relationship with Althea had progressed somewhat," said Lydia. "You spent the night at her flat, didn't you?"

"We both wanted to be able to live our lives as we pleased," said Althea. "As I'd not been bothered for several weeks, we agreed it was time to put a stop to things. Sid was ready to answer the door if he'd turned up."

"I realised the visit from Haines confirmed the police knew I was still seeing Althea," said Sid. "We had to be careful, so I looked for somewhere we could move to which would allow me to keep tabs on events in Warminster and still find work. The basement flat in Sydney Buildings was the perfect spot."

"How did you learn of Ferdinand's death?" asked Lydia.

"I gathered hundreds of contacts around the country while I worked in Fleet Street. I spoke to someone in Nottingham as soon as I heard Althea's story. He kept me appraised of Ferdinand's bankruptcy, and in due course, he called to say he'd dropped dead on the street outside a bedsit near the University where he lived."

"You realised you could go outside the flat in the evenings," said Lydia. "There was no need to hide. That's why you agreed to go to the quiz nights at Widcombe Social Club."

"I realised you knew about that when you said you asked a police officer," said Sid.

"I'll have those videos now, Mr Selman," said Suzie. "We can transfer them to my phone. Is there anything else you gathered that wasn't in this folder?"

"No, that's the lot. I'll give you the name and address of my neighbour from Avon Road," said Sid. "I'd appreciate it if you don't drop me in it. She did us a great favour by looking out of her bedroom window that night."

"Don't worry," said Suzie. "She'll be able to tell her neighbours she helped put two dangerous men behind bars. Right, I think that's all we need for now. Many thanks for your help. I wish you every happiness for the future."

"Thank you," said Althea. "I hope everything goes well and you have a healthy, happy baby."

Sid and Althea followed Suzie and Lydia to the front door.

"Will you continue to submit stories as Sonny Ramos to the Bristol Evening Post, Mr Selman?" asked Lydia.

"I shouldn't rock the boat," said Sid. "Althea writes at least half of the articles, and since she discovered her inner voice, the column has drawn more attention."

"We're in a much more prominent position these days," giggled Althea. "On page seven, nowhere near the crossword and horoscope."

"As for quiz nights, we've found three pubs nearby that we regularly attend," said Sid. "I must call the sergeant and tell him there's one place that allows six people per team. It would be nice to meet up again."

It was almost one o'clock when Suzie and Lydia arrived at London Road.

"I'll see whether Geoff Mercer is in his office," said Suzie. "He needs to be brought up to speed. I don't envy him telling the Chief Constable what we've found."

"What can I do while you're gone?" asked Lydia.

"Set up an interview with DS Chris Lawry," said Suzie. "Polebarn Road will have his contact details, and he can come to my office asap. As for Hugh Sharpe, HR at Polebarn Road will know where he's spending his retirement. I don't know where Rob Haines went when he quit the force. Try Divya. Maybe she can find him through social media. He always considered himself irresistible to women. So it's nailed on that he'll be active on Facebook and Instagram, posting loads of selfies."

"That should keep me busy," said Lydia. "I'll tell Divya not to bother following up on that 'to whom it may concern' advert from the Nottingham solicitors when I speak to her. I don't think Althea would ever have bothered getting in touch, even if Ferdinand had still been a wealthy man. She wanted nothing to do with him."

"Two men abused Althea," said Suzie. "Yet she's still found love with Sid Selman. It's the sort of story Vicky Bennison would love to hear about."

"You'd better get to DS Mercer's office," said Lydia. "He could be off to a riveting budget meeting this afternoon. So I'll start on this list. You can fill me in about Vicky Bennison later."

Suzie tapped on Geoff Mercer's door and went inside.

Lydia went to Suzie's office and called Divya. Once the ball was rolling, she phoned Polebarn Road in Trowbridge. Chris Lawry was interviewing a suspect in Westbury but would drive to Devizes as soon as he was finished.

Hugh Sharpe and his wife hadn't moved far after he retired. Lydia was given an address in Chapmanslade. She checked the map on her phone to check its location and discovered it was a small village four miles from Warminster, Westbury, and Frome. Lydia thought a place on the border with Somerset in the middle of three towns was a decent place to live if you enjoyed a change of scenery for your weekly shop.

Lydia wondered whether to call Hugh Sharpe to arrange an appointment for Monday. Sid Selman admitted he'd exaggerated matters to get a reaction. Maybe Suzie could get what she wanted with a quick phone call.

Divya called back before Lydia had reached a decision. She'd found Rob Haines easily. Suzie was right; he was prolific on social media. Alive and still causing trouble, living in Portsmouth. Haines had been a bouncer at a night-club for the past nine months.

"I'll read you the piece from the newspaper report, Lydia," said Divya.

"Officers were called to the nightclub at three in the morning. A member of a door staff team viciously assaulted a man outside the club and dragged him to the floor. Pictures and videos of the scene circulated on social media, seemingly showing the security employee punching and kicking a man before forcing him to the ground. It happened after the young man was ejected from the club. An external security company employed the man involved. All CCTV regarding the incident, including mobile phone footage, had been passed to the police for investigation."

"Has the case got to court yet?" asked Lydia.

"Haines was remanded on bail," said Divya.

"You couldn't make it up, could you?" said Lydia. "Still, if he's adhering to his bail conditions, we can interview him."

"I'll email you his address," said Divya. "He has to

continue to live there, can't contact the man he's accused of assaulting, and his passport has been withheld. So yes, I'd say there's every chance you'll be able to speak to him."

"He might not like what he's going to hear," said Suzie.

Divya ended the call, and Lydia returned to thoughts of Hugh Sharpe. Perhaps she could call him? Suzie had to ask whether he'd visited a massage parlour, which could be awkward if his wife was hovering in the background.

Suzie breezed into her office and dropped Sid Selman's folder on her desk.

"Right," she said. "We're off. Geoff Mercer will make the arrest, and I'll be there for support. Perhaps you can look after the wife."

"Chris Lawry will be here in the next hour," said Lydia. "We won't get back in time."

"I'll tell Reception as we leave. Lawry will be kept under wraps until we need him. Anything from Hugh Sharpe?"

"I thought a phone call would be best to avoid unnecessary embarrassment."

"Perhaps," said Lydia. "How about Divya? Has she found Rob Haines?"

"I have an address in Portsmouth," said Lydia. "He's on bail for aggravated assault."

"Why am I not surprised?" said Lydia. "We'll deal with them when we get back. Geoff's waiting downstairs."

Lydia paused by the front door while Suzie briefed the young sergeant on Reception, and soon they were in Geoff's car heading for the A36 and the Cley Hill roundabout. Lydia checked her watch. They would reach Primrose Cottage by two o'clock.

"Leave the talking to me," said Geoff. "I've contacted social services, and someone's on her way. We don't want a protracted visit. Instead, I'll tell him what we know, read him his rights, and assure him his wife will be well looked after. A quick in and out, agreed?"

"Yes, Sir," said Suzie and Lydia.

Geoff led the way from the car. Tom Brewer opened the door before they could knock.

"It must be serious if they've levered your backside out of the chair, Mercer," he said.

"Don't try to kid us that you don't know what this is about, Tom," said Geoff. "Tom Brewer, you are under arrest, and I must caution you that you do not have to say anything. But it may harm your defence if you do not mention when questioned something which you later rely on in court. Anything you do say may be given in evidence."

"Cynthia's not well," said Tom. "I can't leave her. Can't I come to London Road next week and clear it up, whatever this nonsense is?"

"It's too late for that," said Geoff. "We have sufficient evidence supplied by Sid Selman and statements from Sid and his wife Althea to make our charges stick. Rob Haines will be charged with making threats to kill on your behalf."

Lydia spotted a small saloon car parked behind Geoff, and soon a middle-aged lady bustled up the pathway to the house. She wore a light-blue uniform under a quilted jacket.

"Maria Bryant," she said. "Social Services."

"Cynthia's in the lounge," said Tom. "I'll get my coat. Can I at least say goodbye?"

"DI Ferris and Ms Logan Barre will go with you," said Geoff. He returned to his car to wait. He'd had difficult days during his lengthy police career, but today marked a new low.

Two minutes later, Tom and Suzie Ferris got into the back while Lydia sat beside Geoff.

The conversation was at a premium on the return journey. Tom Brewer was handed over to the duty sergeant in Reception, and Geoff ensured everything was by the book. There would be tonnes of media attention once this arrest leaked out. They couldn't afford a slip-up.

Suzie and Lydia had gone upstairs to her office. As he turned away from the desk, Geoff spotted an anxious looking individual sitting in the corner of the entrance hall.

"I can't put a name to the face," he said. "Who are you here to see?"

"DI Ferris, Sir. I'm DS Lawry, based in Trowbridge."

"Follow me, DS Lawry," said Geoff. "I'll show you to her office. How are you getting on at Polebarn Road?"

"Fine, until this afternoon, Sir," said Chris Lawry. "I can't imagine what this is about."

"You worked in Warminster for a while, I believe?" said Geoff.

"Two years, Sir. Mr Brewer was my guvnor. I couldn't believe my eyes when you brought him in just now."

"Don't ask, DS Lawry," sighed Geoff. "I'll know where to come if you mention a word of what you witnessed downstairs. Do you understand?"

Chris Lawry nodded his head.

Geoff left Chris Lawry outside Suzie's door and continued walking to Kenneth Truelove's office. Time to update the boss.

Chris Lawry knocked, heard a voice, and entered.

"Come in, DS Lawry," said Suzie. "We have questions about your time in Warminster."

Chris Lawry sat down, and Lydia slid Sid Selman's photographs across the desktop.

"Do you recognise this part of Warminster?" asked Suzie. Chris Lawry nodded.

"What was the purpose of your visit to the first-floor flat?" asked Suzie.

"I ricked my back, moving furniture at my mother-in-law's house. I was in agony for several days, and then one of the lads suggested I visit Emma. He said she'd have me fixed up in no time."

"Emma?" asked Lydia.

"Emma Bonds, miss. She's a qualified masseuse. All above board, honest."

"We can check," said Suzie.

"Who gave you Emma's name?" asked Lydia.

"One of the older uniformed lads, Hugh Sharpe," said Chris. "After forty years pounding the pavements, poor old Hugh's feet were in a right state."

"Which is why he was a regular customer after a long day shift," said Suzie. "I think we can dispense with that phone call, Lydia."

"Is that it?" asked Chris Lawry.

"When did you last have your eyes checked, DS Lawry?" asked Suzie.

"Three or four years ago, ma'am," he replied.

"I'd make an appointment if I were you," said Suzie. "A semi-retired reporter in his sixties was able to follow you and take these photos without you spotting him."

A sheepish-looking Chris Lawry left the room. As soon as the door closed behind him, Lydia stifled a laugh.

"Hugh Sharpe was just as bad," said Suzie. "Perhaps we don't expect members of the public to follow us and record what we're doing routinely, but those two should have been more aware of their surroundings."

"What do we do next?" asked Lydia.

"I'm awaiting instructions from DS Mercer," said Suzie. "The Chief Constable might want someone else to lead the interview with Tom Brewer, perhaps ACC Colbourne. Then, Geoff would attend, leaving us at a loose end."

"Could you interview Rob Haines?" asked Lydia.

"I'd like to, but we need something from Tom Brewer first," said Suzie.

Lydia thought for a moment, then clicked her fingers.

"Got it," she said. "What did Tom Brewer have on Rob Haines?"

"Haines was always a piece of work," said Suzie. "My guess is Tom persuaded him to put the frighteners on Sid and Althea in return for not turning him in."

"Geoff Mercer might prefer to leave Rob Haines for a few days until he's got Tom Brewer to get everything off his chest. We should spend the rest of the afternoon getting our paperwork in order, and unless we hear otherwise, we'll head home and pick things up again on Monday."

"I don't expect to see Alex this weekend," said Lydia. "It will give me a chance to call my mother to discuss our plans for Christmas. I'll call Chidozie and Rosa, too, to see how things are going in Dubai."

"I don't expect to be busy this weekend," sighed Suzie. "Gus will be checking that Bert Penman's health is improving and hoping a fire breaks out in the conference room to avoid his training course next week. Then, I'll put my feet up once we've done the weekly shop."

They didn't hear from Geoff Mercer, and they went downstairs at five o'clock.

Vera Butler and Kassie Trotter were just ahead of them.

"It's the A-Team," said Vera. "Did you two enjoy working together?"

"It wasn't like starting from scratch," said Suzie. "We've bumped into one another socially since Lydia started working with Gus. So yes, I think we've done okay."

"More of the same next week," said Kassie. "Lydia needs something to occupy her while Mr Freeman goes back to school."

"You two are a laugh a minute," said Suzie.

Vera and Kassie went their separate ways. Vera walked to her house a few hundred yards from the London Road HQ, and Kassie turned left to walk to the rugby club, where Noah, her boyfriend, would be waiting after a vigorous training session.

"Today's events beg the question," said Lydia as they stopped by Suzie's Golf. "Is there enough left to do on this special project for an extra pair of hands all week?"

"Don't fret, Lydia," said Suzie. "Geoff Mercer will think of something."

Lydia walked to her Mini and set off for Chippenham. Suzie was already on her way to Urchfont. Neither woman saw Kenneth Truelove watching them from his office window.

Monday, 12 November 2018

"TIME TO GO, DARLING," said Suzie. "I'll drive us to London Road. There's no point taking both cars this week."

"Don't remind me. I know I'm not going anywhere," said Gus.

Suzie consoled herself with the thought they'd had a quiet but enjoyable weekend. Brett had dropped by the bungalow at lunchtime on Saturday to say Bert was feeling much better. Irene wasn't recovering as quickly as his grandfather, but he was hopeful they could forget about the hassle of making appointments to see a doctor today. The

Reverend had called later that afternoon to check they were still on for a meal at the Fox and Hounds. The weather continued to dampen everyone's spirits, but somehow they coped, and this morning a new week dawned, and the sun made a welcome reappearance.

Suzie left the driveway and entered the lane more sedately than usual. There was no point making Gus any grumpier than he was already. She arrived in the car park at five to nine, parked the Golf, and they climbed the steps to the front door together.

"You need to sign in, and don't forget to pick up your lanyard," she said.

"Yes, miss," said Gus. "I knew it was a mistake to let Tess persuade me to throw out my school short trousers."

"I'll see you tonight, darling," said Suzie. "Do you need me to remind you where the conference room is?"

Gus scowled. He fetched his lanyard from Reception. The swipe card it carried would allow him to enter the Hub building and reach the second-floor suite of offices. As he crossed the car park, he spotted Lydia hurrying towards the front door.

"Good luck, guv," she called. "I didn't have my alarm clock beside me this morning. I spoke to Alex last night. He sends his best wishes."

Gus raised a hand in response, then entered the Hub. He looked for a friendly face but saw nobody he recognised. Divya Yadav must be running late too. When he reached the second floor, he exited the lift and looked for the conference room door. Inside, just one woman was waiting for him.

"Freeman. Gus Freeman," he said.

"I've been expecting you, Mr Freeman. Come in," replied the woman. "I'm Lisa Truman."

As he walked to the only desk and chair in the room, Gus cursed Monty Norman but couldn't avoid humming a familiar theme tune.

WHEN LYDIA ARRIVED in Suzie's office, she found it empty. Then, Vera Butler appeared in the doorway. Who else? Nobody reached the first floor without Vera spotting an intruder.

"Geoff Mercer called Suzie into his office as soon as she got here," said Vera.

"Thank you, Vera," said Lydia.

"Gus will be with Lisa Truman now," said Vera, stepping into the office. "No matter how much she tries to brainwash him, he'll come through unscathed. We all needed to change our ways, value diversity, and be committed to promoting good community relations and equal opportunities among our employees. I can see sense in that philosophy and do everything I can to support it. But some things don't change; there will never be a man in Kassie's role, for instance. Criminals will laugh at us and continue to thrive until we come down on them hard."

"I'm sure you're right, Vera," said Lydia.

"Cases like the one you've been working on don't do us any favours," said Vera. "If we can't keep our house in order, how can we preach to others that they should obey the law?"

"When I met Tom Brewer and saw him with Cynthia, I thought he was a caring, loving husband. It just goes to show that nothing is ever as it seems."

Vera shook her head and left the office.

Suzie soon returned from Geoff's office. She stood by the door with her car keys in her hand. "Right, Lydia.

We're off to Portsmouth to interview Rob Haines. He'll be at the police station in Gosport. I'll drive on this occasion."

Lydia grabbed her bag and dashed after Suzie. They were soon heading out of Devizes towards Salisbury.

"What's the latest with Tom Brewer?" she asked.

"Mark Colbourne headed up the initial interview with Tom Brewer on Saturday morning," said Suzie. "Geoff didn't go into detail. However, Tom couldn't deny the evidence from the photos and videos. His solicitor asked for a break after a couple of hours to allow Tom to check on Cynthia. Mark Colbourne agreed but insisted they resumed after a sixty-minute interval."

"Did Tom reveal anything about his relationship with Rob Haines?" asked Lydia.

"Mark had a job to stop him talking when they resumed the interview," said Suzie. "His solicitor must have told him he didn't have a prayer."

Suzie got them to Gosport Police Station in an impressive hour and forty-five minutes. They went through the usual rigmarole in Reception and finally entered an interview room at eleven o'clock. Rob Haines was already inside, with a duty solicitor sitting beside him. Suzie made the introductions and explained why they wanted to speak to him. Rob Haines sat in silence until she'd finished.

"If I tell you what I know, will it help me?" he asked.

"I can't promise anything," said Suzie. "Aggravated assault is a serious offence, and it was committed in Hampshire, not Wiltshire. Let's say it won't do you any harm to fill in the gaps of what we already know."

"Tom Brewer has already dropped me in it then," shrugged Haines.

"You lived in Westbury while stationed in Warminster," said Suzie. "Tom Brewer became suspicious about the amount of money you appeared to have whenever you met at a social occasion. He wondered whether you were moonlighting. Wiltshire Police monitor matters to ensure our people are playing by the rules. Tom Brewer was convinced you were involved in something sleazy, which your superiors wouldn't have sanctioned."

"He was a crafty devil," said Haines. "It was my fault. I boasted to colleagues about my expensive holidays with a girlfriend in Mauritius and Turkey. Tom asked me for her name, and when he dug into her background, he learned Nancy had a history of involvement in prostitution. Tom called me into the office one day and said he'd arranged for a covert camera to be fixed overlooking the flat Nancy owned in the middle of Westbury. I was warned to keep quiet if I wanted to save my career. That camera filmed scores of men visiting what purported to be a private address. Tom ensured I was working when the flat was raided, and Nancy and her younger cousin were arrested."

"Were you living with Nancy?" asked Suzie.

"No, I rented a flat in the same block," said Haines. "Nancy and Dee Dee pleaded guilty at Swindon Crown Court and received suspended sentences."

"Although your choice of girlfriend was questionable, I'm struggling to see how Tom Brewer had such a hold over you," said Lydia. "You hadn't committed any offence."

"Where do you think my money came from?" he said. "Nancy took the lion's share, and her cousin took the rest of what they earned. I benefitted from enjoying Nancy's company and her money when she wasn't working. So I started another profitable side-line for my benefit. Unfortunately, Tom Brewer installed another camera on my side of the block of flats that I knew nothing about. I used my unmarked police car to follow punters as they left the flat. I pulled them over, flashed my warrant card, and suggested they hand over cash to avoid me dropping in to see their wives or girlfriends. That scam earned me maybe two hundred quid a week. Tom saw me on that second camera using my unmarked car off-duty and followed me, catching me in the act. He said I could be charged with corruption, misconduct in public office, and heaven knows what."

"Tom Brewer told you he was prepared to forget what he saw provided you did him a favour," said Suzie. "Is that right?"

"On the button," said Haines. "I moved to Warminster after Nancy and I had split up. One night, Tom called me and gave me the address on Avon Road of a bloke called Selman. Tom wanted me to scare Selman, get him to stop stirring up trouble. It meant nothing to me. I did what he asked, and a couple of months later, Tom wanted the bloke hurt badly. I wasn't happy about going that far, but Tom swore the slate would be clean if I did. When I got there, the bloke wasn't home. Tom still had me on the hook. I quit the force, found a job as far away from Warminster as possible, and hoped never to hear from him again."

"Did you know why he wanted Sid Selman out of the way?" asked Lydia.

"Not a clue," said Haines.

Suzie got a signed statement from Haines before they left, and they were on the return journey to Devizes before twelve.

"What sentence is he facing?" asked Lydia.

"Five years," said Suzie. "As for what Haines admitted he did on Tom Brewer's behalf, that might add an extra six months inside. His duty solicitor will try to do a deal based on his cooperation. The CPS might agree to the sentences being served concurrently. That's not my problem. I'm happy we can hand Geoff Mercer the final piece of the jigsaw."

"They say you get more like a person the longer you live with them," said Lydia. "That could have been Gus speaking."

"Heavens, I shall have to watch myself," said Suzie.

They drove back across Salisbury Plain to Devizes in silence.

As Suzie parked the Golf at London Road, she spotted movement in a window on the first floor. Kenneth Truelove was watching them.

"Will you have a quiet word with ACC Colbourne, Suzie?" asked Lydia as they climbed the stairs to the mezzanine.

"Geoff will bring him up to speed once I've reported on our Gosport trip," said Suzie. "Why? What did you have in mind?

Lydia stopped by Geoff Mercer's door as Suzie raised a hand to knock.

"Tell him even in red herring season; a live one can always slip through the net."

Chapter Seven

THE LATE-NIGHT TAKEAWAY

Monday, 19 November 2018

"RISE AND SHINE," said Gus. "I don't want to be late on my first day back."

"Cheeky," said Suzie, opening one eye. "It's hardly seven-thirty."

Gus padded towards the bathroom. The shower was like him, showing its age, and it needed a minute or two to warm up. The long wet spell of weather from last week was a distant memory, and frosty mornings were now the order of the day.

Suzie joined Gus in the kitchen just before eight.

"Breakfast is served, ma'am," said Gus.

"What on earth are you having?" said Suzie as she started on her bowl of oats, blueberries, and raspberries.

"Porridge," said Gus. "I remember the advert, central heating for kids. I don't see why it shouldn't work for grown-ups too."

"So you're back to work today with a full complement

of Crime Review Team personnel," said Suzie. "That wasn't so difficult, was it? I told you it was only temporary."

"I hope I don't have to suffer too many war stories from last weekend's protests," said Gus. "I'd prefer a quick catch-up and a call from Vera to say Kenneth has brought the meeting forward to ten o'clock. After that, I want to get up and running on the new case."

"Our Chief Constable is a busy man," said Suzie. "The PCC called in for a surprise visit on Thursday afternoon. On Friday morning, Vera hastily rearranged Kenneth's timetable for this week. I took a peek before I left at five o'clock, and your meeting was unaffected. Sorry, sweetheart, you'll be having lunch with Geoff and the boss."

"Curses, foiled again," said Gus.

At twenty-past-eight, they left the bungalow and walked to the cars.

"Didn't you forget something?" asked Suzie.

Gus patted his jacket pockets.

"Don't think so. Car keys, mobile phone, pocket money."

"Lisa Truman gave you a certificate on Friday, didn't she?" said Suzie. "Surely, you'll want to display it on the office wall?"

"What? A piece of paper saying I completed the course on diversity and inclusivity. That's as bad as having a school report where the highlight was congratulations from the Head on having a perfect attendance record. A rough translation of which was - at least he turned up."

"You're incorrigible, Gus Freeman," said Suzie. "Usual time tonight?"

"All things being equal," said Gus.

Suzie led the way through the gateway and into the lane, and Gus flashed his lights as she turned off towards

London Road. He wondered how long it would be before some killjoy decided flashing should become illegal. Gus cruised down Caen Hill at a shade over the speed limit and only slowed as he neared the town centre. He had no choice because of a parked delivery van, but what's life without a bit of risk, he thought.

As he entered the Church Street car park, he spotted Grace getting out of Blessing's Nissan Micra. He parked beside them and got out.

"Morning, guv," said Blessing. "I've missed you."

"Likewise, I'm sure," said Gus. "Good to see you two enjoying the benefits of sharing a car. Wiltshire has spent enough money on signage encouraging motorists to find someone to fill the empty seats in their vehicles."

"It's not always convenient, Gus," said Grace.

"True," said Gus. "What's the plan for next week?"

Blessing giggled.

"I'm not sure Grace's Smart car will cope."

"It'll be cosy, that's for sure," said Grace. "It's only fair that we share the driving."

As they waited for the lift doors to open, Neil Davis parked beside the Focus. Gus spotted Alex Hardy's car entering the car park. The band was back together.

Two minutes later, the team was upstairs in the office. As Gus hung his jacket on the back of his chair, the conversation was already in full swing.

"Eighty-five people were arrested as thousands of demonstrators occupied five bridges in Central London," said Alex.

"Where were you, Alex?" asked Blessing.

"Southwark," said Alex. "The protestors began massing on the main bridges from ten o'clock on Saturday morning. By eleven, all the crossings had been blocked."

"I saw footage of people locking themselves together," said Grace. "Most of the crowd just linked arms and sang songs. I watched the CCTV camera feeds in a surveillance suite inside the Curtis Green building on the Victoria Embankment."

"Get you," said Lydia. "On the Commissioner's doorstep. Did you make sure they got your name for future reference?"

"I was a small cog in a huge wheel," said Grace. "I hope I didn't let Wiltshire down."

"The media reckon it was one of the biggest acts of peaceful civil disobedience in the UK for decades," said Neil. "I was stationed in Parliament Square."

"Was it exciting where you were, Alex?" asked Blessing.

"For a couple of hours," said Alex. "Then the crowds abandoned Southwark and moved to Blackfriars. It was a short distance to Westminster from there. That was their ultimate aim."

"Waterloo and Lambeth were the other bridges they occupied," said Grace. "All five bridges soon reopened, and most arrests were for obstruction under the Highways Act."

"I missed all the fun," said Blessing. "They sent me to Paddington Station, where I spent eight hours watching people moving from the platforms to the Underground."

"Were you watching CCTV screens too, Blessing?" asked Lydia.

"No, I spent the week doing the Tube equivalent of the Knowledge that black cab drivers have to pass," said Blessing. "More experienced London Transport Police officers were strengthening security within the system. I was supposed to help any travellers who weren't sure how to reach their onward destination."

Gus was the only person in the office not to laugh. Blessing's poor sense of direction was legendary. What was it Kenneth had said? Horses for courses. Someone blundered there.

"I got flustered," said Blessing. "It seemed like everyone who passed me needed my help."

"You did your best, Blessing, I'm sure," said Gus. "Now your stint helping the Met is over, we can get back to what we're here for."

"What were you able to do while we were away, guv?" asked Neil.

Gus realised Alex was the only team member to know what he and Lydia had been doing.

"Lydia can fill you in briefly on her special assignment," said Gus.

"Get you," said Grace.

"Touché," said Lydia. "I worked at London Road with Suzie, sorry, DI Ferris, on the alleged corruption complaint we were told to ignore. Sid Selman had laid a trail of red herrings that led us to Tom Brewer and an ex-DC called Rob Haines. No organised crime groups were operating in Warminster town centre, and they had no illegal immigrants. In some ways, it was much worse, but you'll hear all about it when the press gets wind of it."

"Gosh, lucky duck," said Blessing. "Were you alone in the office, guv?"

"I spent the week at London Road, too, Blessing," said Gus. "To undergo a training session specifically designed for a woolly mammoth."

"Intriguing," said Grace. "Did Lydia tell you what it was about yesterday, Alex?"

"Nothing we haven't all been through," said Alex. "Look on the bright side. With the PCC tightening the purse strings, would they spend money on training someone if they planned to dispense with their services shortly?"

Gus hadn't thought of that. It gave him a glimmer of hope the axe wasn't about to fall.

"You can't rely on that," said Neil. "Every football club chairman has given his manager the dreaded vote of confidence, only to sack him within forty-eight hours."

"That's football, Neil," said Blessing. "It's not real life."

"I'll say it again, Blessing," said Gus. "I've missed you. Let's see if we can fire up the Gaggia after the extended break. You and I will do the hot drinks run this morning."

Gus and Blessing headed to the restroom. As soon as the door closed, Neil and Grace turned to Lydia.

"My lips are sealed," she replied. "As Alex said, it was no big deal."

Gus soon returned and delivered coffees to Alex and Lydia. He nodded his thanks for having his back.

Blessing handed Neil his coffee and placed Grace's potion on her desk.

"I wonder where we'll be going next?" said Blessing as she sat down.

"I'm not leaving the office to find out for another ninety minutes, Blessing," said Gus. "If any of you feel the urge to discuss last week's events, please try not to disturb me. I want to flick through my course notes one last time before I bump heads with the Chief Constable."

As eleven-thirty approached, Gus donned his jacket and walked to the lift. The chatter about the Extinction Rebellion protests hadn't lasted long. Alex and Neil were now comparing the relative merits of several pubs in the capital. Grace told Lydia and Grace about the excellent meals served in the canteen in the building the Met moved to in 2016, still referred to as New Scotland Yard.

Gus parked the Focus in the visitor's car park at London Road with two minutes to spare. He signed in, trotted upstairs to the admin area, and took stock of his surroundings. A voice boomed out from behind him.

"Vera has a dental appointment, Mr Freeman," said Kassie Trotter.

"Don't creep up on me like that, Kassie," said Gus. "Silent but deadly, that new trolley of yours."

"Mr Truelove said he missed the four-minute warning," laughed Kassie.

"I haven't seen you since I was last in his office," said Gus. "How did the visit with Noah go?"

"Very well, thank you, Mr Freeman. Betty enjoyed my Battenberg, and I've secured a weekly order. She's given her husband a list of her favourite cakes, and last Monday, he chose Lamingtons. So when I pop in later, you'll hear what he thinks is best for next Sunday afternoon's tea."

"I've heard enough about cakes," said Gus. "What did Kenneth and Betty make of Noah?"

"Betty said he's a big boy," said Kassie.

Gus spotted Geoff Mercer leaving his office, ready to walk across the mezzanine for the meeting with Kenneth. Gus decided he should join him before Kassie said anything further.

"Morning, Gus," said Geoff. "Did your team make it back in one piece?"

"All present and correct," said Gus. "Suzie filled me in at the weekend on the good work Lydia helped her achieve last week. What a shock."

"I didn't see it coming," agreed Geoff. "Least said when we get in here, d'you agree?"

Gus nodded.

The Chief Constable was seated at his desk when they entered.

"Welcome back, Freeman," he said. "Good work on the Clark case. I've read everything from cover to cover now. A clean deck and all that."

He opened his top drawer and removed a thin folder.

"This case has troubled us for almost a decade," said Kenneth. "You're off to Swindon again. Matthew Archer, thirty-three years old, was beaten to death on Friday the sixth in February 2009 as he delivered a takeaway. Universally known as Matt, Archer worked as a delivery driver for the Jade Garden restaurant in Haydon Wick for eighteen months."

"Thirty-three?" said Gus. "That's a job more suited to teenagers on scooters, like the ones who respond to my urgent phone call for pizza. Was Archer single? Had he just come out of prison and had taken any job he could get?"

"Archer was married with a daughter, Jasmine, aged seven," said Kenneth. "His wife's name was Janet, thirty-one. They had moved to Swindon from Luton, Bedford-shire, eight years previously. Archer had a clean record and was employed at the local leisure centre during the day. Janet had returned to work after the birth of their daughter, but the recession hit the firm she worked for, and Janet got made redundant. Matt Archer took the evening job at the Jade Garden to bolster their finances. The couple struggled to keep up with their mortgage payments, and although they weren't in trouble on that score when he died, unre-solved matters caused the investigating team headaches."

"Who was running the investigation, Sir," asked Geoff Mercer.

"DI Dave Arrowsmith was the man in charge," said Kenneth. "His second-in-command was DS Natasha Chandler. Both officers are still at Gablecross and have moved up in rank to DCI and DI. Have you worked with either of them, Mercer?"

"I've had dealings with DCI Arrowsmith, Sir," said Geoff. "Unless I'm mistaken, Natasha Chandler is on maternity leave."

"That shouldn't prevent her from sparing thirty minutes to speak to Freeman or DI Packenham. I'd be disappointed if one of our DIs couldn't multi-task."

"What were these unresolved matters, Sir?" asked Gus.

"The Archer family relied on their Honda Jazz to get Matt to the leisure centre and for the numerous short trips on behalf of the Jade Garden. Janet would often drive Matt to work in the morning, drop Jasmine at school, and return in the afternoon to collect her. It's a sign of the times, Freeman. Parents are reluctant to allow their children to walk to school unescorted. My mother took me to school on the first day, pushing me out of the back door the following morning and asking if I remembered the way."

"I assume these unresolved matters were connected to the Honda Jazz, Sir," said Gus.

Kenneth wasn't prone to ramble. Gus realised it was a clear sign Tom Brewer's fall from grace had affected him deeply.

"Dave Arrowsmith believed someone had a grudge against Matt Archer or his wife. The Jazz had been vandalised on several occasions. On their driveway, in the leisure centre car park, and while inside the local Lidl supermarket doing the weekly shopping."

"Minor damage?" asked Geoff.

"The damage was escalating," said Kenneth. "The first instance was a dented bumper, then a cracked headlight glass.

Matt Archer never bothered to report these incidents. He thought they could have been caused by a coming together of his car and another vehicle in a car park. The snapped wing mirror occurred while the car was parked outside the house on New Year's Eve, and all three slept inside. The sudden noise woke Janet Archer, but when she looked out of the bedroom window, she saw nobody, and it wasn't until the following morning that the extent of the damage was apparent."

"No doubt Matt Archer put that down to drunks hanging around late at night," said Geoff. "Not an uncommon occurrence in Swindon or anywhere else at that time of year."

"A month before he died, someone scraped a coin the length of the car. Although they could ill-afford the expense, Archer booked the car for a respray. Things quietened for a while, and then in February, the Jade Garden received an order for a takeaway to be delivered to a farmhouse near Bremhill Bridge."

"What time was the order placed?" asked Gus.

"Twenty-five past nine," said Kenneth.

"Was Matt Archer in the restaurant at the time?" asked Geoff.

"Archer was delivering to three addresses off Westfield Way," said Kenneth. "Lily Liang, the owner's wife, expected him back within ten minutes. The order from the farmhouse wasn't at the top of Mrs Liang's list. Whoever rang it in stipulated that they wanted to eat at half-past ten. It made no odds to Michael Liang in the kitchen. Lily stopped taking delivery orders at ten o'clock, and with the help of their children, Adam, and Danielle, the family and their staff dealt with walk-in customers who wanted a takeaway or to eat at a table."

"I assume they had a cut-off point for those customers?" asked Gus.

"They shut the doors just before eleven," said Kenneth. "Michael had learned to set the clocks forward five minutes, which frustrated many drinkers who always took full advantage of the ten-minute drinking-up time in the local bars. But it saved him and his family from coping with an unruly mob after the pubs closed during the week. The restaurant was in darkness when any hungry souls were milling around in the early hours at the weekends. Other food outlets were available within walking distance of places that stayed open until two in the morning or later. Michael Liang was fifty-nine, one year older than his wife. They'd worked extra-long hours when they first opened the Jade Garden to get the business established. Michael believed he'd earned the right to a quieter spell before he retired."

"I'm concerned this folder is painfully thin," said Gus. "Was an order from the farmhouse a regular occurrence? Did Lily Liang know the person who called?"

"Arrowsmith and Chandler had worked together for a couple of years and always conducted a thorough investigation," said Kenneth. "They failed to progress in the first seventy-two hours in this instance and appealed for information. I'll explain why in a moment, but they wanted to hear if someone had seen anything suspicious between nine-fifteen and nine-thirty on the night in question. A chap called Saul Brinkworth called in to say he'd seen a man making a call from a public phone box near Moredon Post Office. That's about four hundred yards from the Jade Garden."

"The only odd thing about that is the man was extremely fortunate to find one in working order," said Geoff Mercer.

"The caller had left the engine running in his Mazda 3," said Kenneth. "Brinkworth sensed the man was trying to hide the fact he was using the phone. He didn't want to draw attention to himself and turned his body away from anyone passing by to keep his face hidden. Brinkworth carried on walking into town to his local pub and forgot about the incident until he heard the appeal from the police."

"What sort of description was this eyewitness able to give?" asked Gus. "Was he alone?"

"The man was white, medium height, late twenties to early thirties," said Kenneth. "Brinkworth thought he looked like he worked out. He had dark hair, a full-length dark coat, and a scarf that would have been covering half his face if he'd turned towards him. Brinkworth told police the car's tinted windows made it impossible to see if there was a passenger, but he did hear the Mazda driving away as he continued to walk down Moredon Road. The car travelled in the opposite direction on Purton Road."

"That would take him out towards Bremhill Bridge," said Geoff. "Perhaps someone from the farmhouse was placing their order as they were on their way home?"

"Lily Liang told the detectives that when she received the call, she asked the caller for directions. The farmhouse was at the limit of the radius they set for deliveries. Lily Liang couldn't recall getting a delivery from the farm all the years they had been at the Jade Garden."

"Who was the owner?" asked Gus.

"John Payne," said Kenneth. "He's in his late seventies now, but at the time, he was still involved in the day-to-day running of the farm. His son, John Junior, is in charge these days. Matt Archer returned from Westfield Way, and Lily handed him the next batch of meals to go out. He set off for Saffron Close, Boscombe Road, and Helmsdale. When Matt returned, Lily explained about his last delivery of the night and handed him a slip of paper with the directions. Adam, the eldest boy, twenty-nine, delivered the remaining orders on his way home. Matt Archer left the Jade Garden at ten minutes past ten."

"Every delivery we've heard about so far was within a five-minute drive of the restaurant," said Gus. "How far away was the Payne farm?"

"A ten-minute drive," said Kenneth. "Archer followed the Purton Road to a place called Common Platt, turned right to join the B4553 through Bremhill Bridge, and the instructions told him to turn left just before reaching Packhorse Lane. Blades Farm was half a mile from the road. It was a strange journey to him, but Archer must have reached the entrance to the lane leading to the farmhouse by twenty-five past ten. He couldn't go further, as the gates were closed and padlocked. Archer didn't have the phone number of the farm, so he called the Jade Garden to speak to Lily Liang. She had to hunt for the number in the directory and ring the farmhouse landline on Matt's behalf. John Payne's wife, Rosemary, answered and told Lily that her husband, and their three sons, were already in bed. Nobody had ordered a Chinese takeaway from Blades Farm that evening. Lily then spoke to Matt Archer, told him it was a hoax call, apologised, and said he should take the meal home and enjoy it. Lily hated good food going to waste. Matt thanked her and said he would see her at the usual time the following evening."

"So, Archer was in the middle of nowhere in his Honda Jazz with a takeaway on the passenger seat," said Geoff. "Why didn't he drive home and have a free supper with his wife? What happened?"

"John Payne and his sons were up early the next morning," Kenneth said. "The younger boys were in the milking parlour. John and his eldest boy set off for another of their fields on Packhorse Lane to start work. When they reached the farm entrance, John Junior got out of the Land Rover to unlock the gates. He shouted to his father, saying there was a Honda Jazz blocking the way down the narrow lane, and they wouldn't be able to get past. John Payne approached the Jazz and found the doors unlocked, the headlights still on, and a Jade Garden carrier bag on the passenger seat."

"Someone lured Matt Archer to the remote location and dragged him from his car," said Gus. "Where did they take him? Was it the man Saul Brinkworth saw making the phone call an hour earlier?"

"That was something DI Arrowsmith and his team needed to find out," said Kenneth. "Nobody from the farm had phoned the police at this stage. All John Payne had was an abandoned car, so he and his son split up. The father walked back along the lane towards Common Platt. He knew that was the direction the Honda Jazz must have travelled with the so-called delivery. His son walked past the abandoned car and searched the B4553 leading to Packhorse Lane. He called his father two minutes later to tell him he'd found a body. Matt Archer was lying face down on the grass verge underneath the hedgerow. When his father joined John Junior, they called the police without touching anything."

"Why did John Payne assume they were looking for a dead body?" asked Gus.

"Rosemary Payne had told her husband about the conversation with the Chinese restaurant owner, which got her out of bed," said Kenneth. "He realised the car's presence, plus the cold takeaway suggested something had happened to the driver."

"Did Dave Arrowsmith attend the murder scene straight away?" asked Gus.

"Uniformed officers arrived first," said Kenneth. "They cordoned off the area close to the Honda Jazz and closed the lane to through traffic."

"What time was this?" asked Gus.

"It was still only a quarter to eight," said Kenneth.

"I wonder why Janet Archer wasn't climbing the walls," said Gus.

"It was a Saturday morning, don't forget," said Geoff. "Farmers don't get a lie-in, but many people do, especially when there's no school. Janet Archer wasn't aware Matt hadn't returned home."

"Who notified the wife?" asked Gus.

"That came later," said Kenneth. "First, uniforms secured the area and awaited the arrival of the police surgeon. They had to wait until they received official confirmation they were dealing with an unexplained death."

"Stuart Fitzwalter would have been the police surgeon responding to that call in 2009," said Gus. "The chap Eve Northwood stood in for on occasion."

"Correct," said Kenneth. "Arrowsmith and Chandler were summoned by Gablecross as soon as John Payne called 999. They drove to Blades Farm and arrived at five to eight. The forensic team were ten minutes behind them in a van. Stuart Fitzwalter inspected the body and determined that Matt Archer had been beaten around the head with a blunt instrument. He died of severe head injuries. The time of death would be determined later. John Payne could tell the police surgeon that Matt Archer was still alive at half-past ten because he'd called the Jade Garden then. The restaurant owner got his wife, Rosemary, out of bed five minutes later with a story that someone had ordered a Chinese meal to be delivered to Blades Farm at precisely ten-thirty. The restaurant owner couldn't understand why they'd locked the gates. Before she ended the call with his wife, Rosemary, the Chinese lady had put her on hold while she told her delivery driver he had had a wasted journey and could go home."

"Lily Liang had spoken to Matt in person, not by text," said Geoff. "So, the attack happened straight after she passed the message."

"If it hadn't, the farmer and his son wouldn't have discovered the Honda Jazz blocking the lane," said Gus. "Because Matt Archer would have been well on his way back to Haydon Wick. The car was still where he'd parked it when he found the gates locked."

"Isn't it possible the car was moved," said Kenneth, "then returned to where it was found?"

"Maybe," said Gus, "but why did the killer, or killers, block the lane? It drew attention to the car. It could have stayed there for days if they'd parked it closer to the body by the hedge. The obvious assumption would be the car had been abandoned, perhaps by joyriders, and thankfully they hadn't set it alight."

"At the autopsy, Stuart Fitzwalter judged time of death as occurring between ten-thirty and eleven-thirty," said Kenneth. "A fingertip search was carried out extending from the farm entrance to fifty yards beyond where the body was discovered, but police never found a trace of any murder weapon."

"What was the possible motive?" asked Gus.

"Someone could have been behind the damage to his

car," said Geoff Mercer. "It might not have been a series of random attacks."

"Arrowsmith and Chandler hunted high and low for anyone who held a grudge against Matt Archer, or his wife, without luck," said Kenneth. "At that time of night, there were unlikely to be eyewitnesses to a Mazda 3 spotted in the vicinity of Blades Farm. So, whether Saul Brinkworth's car was connected to the phantom takeaway order was never determined."

"No wonder the file is so thin," said Gus. "They didn't know much for certain, did they?"

"Just one thing," said Kenneth. "The Jade Garden carrier bag containers held portions of chicken curry, rice, and two spring rolls."

"We've got several lines of enquiry to pursue," said Gus.

"I thought you'd tell us you didn't know where to start, Gus," said Geoff.

"We have to start somewhere," said Gus. "We'll dig into what was happening in Luton before the family moved to Swindon. Then there's the leisure centre where Matt Archer was employed."

"I've always thought it suspicious for someone to *want* to become a member of one of those places," said Geoff.

"It's obvious you've never been tempted, Mercer," said the Chief Constable.

"Exercise can be useful and enjoyable, Sir," said Gus. "So they tell me. From what I've heard, Matt Archer was in a happy marriage, but I don't know his role at the leisure centre. Was he a trainer who was hands-on with women of all ages throughout the day? Perhaps a jealous husband wanted to do him harm? Maybe a lonely wife wanted more than Matt Archer was prepared to supply. Feral teenagers might not have caused minor damage to the car. There are a lot of possibilities. For instance, I want my team to talk with all four members of the Liang family from the Jade Garden."

"I can't see how they could be involved," said Kenneth.

"Adam Liang made deliveries on his way home that Friday night," said Gus. "Perhaps it was normal for him to share the load with Matt Archer. It's possible Adam was responsible for the delivery process before Matt Archer arrived on the scene."

"Fair comment," said Kenneth. "It was very much a family business."

"When the mystery caller placed the order, he may have expected Adam Liang to make the delivery," said Geoff. "If they had been away from Swindon for eighteen months, they wouldn't know the Jade Garden had taken on an extra driver."

"We must stick to our tried and trusted methods," Kenneth said. "The attack on Matt Archer was brutal, and Arrowsmith and Chandler didn't uncover any long-running feud between Archer and any of the people we've mentioned so far. "

"Quiet, unassuming people can become killers," said Gus, "given the right motivation, but at first glance, this murder seems to be the work of an experienced criminal. We'll involve the whizz-kids in the Hub on this one. The investigating team may have overlooked someone with a penchant for violence who had suddenly resurfaced in Swindon."

"Recently released from prison, perhaps," said Geoff.

"Matt Archer was *never* in trouble with the law," said Kenneth. "Not just since he moved to Swindon. Any idea that this vendetta started with his life in Luton seems unlikely, which brings us back to Adam Liang. Was he the real target?"

"If the attack was personal, then there was no reason for Archer to die," said Gus. "Once he'd reached Blades Farm, whoever was lying in wait would soon see they had the wrong man."

"Archer called Lily Liang," said Kenneth. "Rosemary Payne told her there must have been a mistake. Archer would have driven home, unaware of any danger."

"If the killer carried on regardless of who was making the delivery, that suggests it was a contract hit," said Geoff. "We're talking about Haydon Wick, not Chicago in the Twenties. It sounds like someone was paid to carry out the attack and followed orders, unaware the delivery driver they found at Blades Farm wasn't the intended victim."

"It's a muddle, alright," said Gus. "DCI Arrowsmith will be high on my list of interviewees. There must be more he can add to the scant detail within that murder file. We can visit DI Chandler and her new-born child. Let's hope the two lead detectives can offer more than one eyewitness."

"After nine years, the trail will be as cold as that chicken curry," said Geoff Mercer. "Where's Kassie? I'm getting peckish."

"I told Kassie to change her trolley route today," said Kenneth. "There's another matter I need to discuss with Freeman."

Chapter Eight

THE CHIEF CONSTABLE stood and walked to the window.

"While you hid away in the Hub last week, Freeman, I kept my eye on DI Ferris and Ms Logan Barre."

"Suzie didn't discuss the details of DS Mercer's special project with me, Sir," said Gus. "I wouldn't have pressed her for information, but she kept everything under wraps."

"I wasn't being critical of how DI Ferris handled things or suggesting she spoke out of turn," said Kenneth. "Indeed, both women performed extremely well in tricky circumstances. Betty and I prayed for Cynthia at the weekend; she didn't deserve any of this. As for Tom Brewer, well, you think you know someone. But, no, I need to tell you that DI Ferris had completed the investigation by Monday, apart from tying the ribbon on the paperwork."

"I wasn't aware of that, Sir," said Gus. "What were they up to for the rest of the week?"

"I want Ms Logan Barre to have an insight into those opportunities that exist for someone with her capabilities. You met Vicky Bennison, didn't you?"

"On the Gerry Hogan case, yes, Sir," said Gus. "Suzie was in touch with Vicky several times after we wrapped up that mystery."

DS Vicky Bennison had been badly injured during an anti-austerity protest march in London three years ago. The physical wounds healed, but the mental scars never left her. After leaving the police, disillusioned, she'd gone to work for a victim support charity in Abingdon. It was clear Vicky spent many hours rebuilding self-confidence and trust in others with the victims of a crime she met through the charity, despite the fact her personal battles continued.

Gus always believed Vicky's bravery and tenacity were a significant loss to the police and convinced Suzie to meet with her and explore ways to work together. Only two months ago, Vicky had been attacked by the husband of one of the women Vicky, and the charity was helping. As a result, she suffered broken ribs, a damaged spleen, and a fractured skull. Suzie had visited Vicky in the hospital and helped her through her first few days at home.

Although Suzie had hoped to persuade Vicky to rejoin Wiltshire Police, that hope had faded.

"DS Mercer and I have kept tabs on the victim support charities in the county," said Kenneth. "When we learned Vicky would never return to work with us in that capacity, we agreed we should ensure the work DI Ferris started should not be wasted. We owe it to DS Bennison to support those charities in any way we can. Ms Logan Barre has now seen first-hand what Vicky's former colleagues face. Whether that's where her future lies, I can't say. It's her decision."

"I've always known Lydia was on a faster track than some of her colleagues," said Gus.

"We wanted to keep you in the loop, Freeman," said Kenneth. "It's only fair. You had no say in the personnel you were given when you returned to the fold. Mercer and I hand-picked them, and perhaps, if we weren't friends, we could move someone like Ms Logan Barre at a moment's notice. The time will come when she leaves you for good. That time isn't now. However, I want you to accept that whenever Mercer has the opportunity to give her an insight into a potential career move, Ms Logan Barre won't be available to you."

"I understand, Sir," said Gus. "We've coped with being short-handed since DS Sherman jumped ship. I don't suppose there's any chance of getting a replacement for him?"

"Not while the current PCC is holding the purse strings, Freeman," said the Chief Constable.

"I'll try to restrict Lydia's taster sessions to one week at a time, Gus," said Geoff. "DS Davis will be entitled to take time off next month when Melody has the baby. I'll lose a Detective Inspector from London Road when Suzie starts maternity leave. We must manage these situations as best we can."

Gus studied the thin folder on his lap and wondered how many more of these he could bring to a successful conclusion.

"Chin up, Freeman," said Kenneth. "Things are never as bad as they seem."

A loud knock at the door told them the buxom baker was outside with their lunch.

"Come," said Kenneth.

Kassie wheeled her trolley into the room and whipped away the cloth covering her goodies.

"Just what the doctor ordered," she said. "Your baps

and wraps, followed by two Viennese whirls. One's never enough, as they're only a mouthful."

"I've got this week's order, Kassie," said Kenneth. "Betty fancies some Cherry Bakewell."

"I'll get half-a-dozen ready for Friday, Mr Truelove," said Kassie.

As Geoff demolished his sausage bap, Kassie served the three coffees.

"Did you enjoy my Lamingtons on Sunday, Mr Truelove?" asked Kassie.

"I did," he replied. "Betty started singing the theme tune to 'Neighbours' when she'd eaten her first one. The significance was lost on me, but she had fond memories of the name mentioned on one of her favourite soaps."

"Perhaps Betty couldn't remember the 'Shortland Street' theme," said Gus.

That comment drew a blank from Geoff Mercer and the Chief Constable.

"You're so knowledgeable, Mr Freeman," said Kassie. "The Lamington has been an Australian favourite for decades, but strong evidence has emerged recently that the recipe originated in New Zealand."

"I don't care where it comes from, Kassie," said Kenneth. "It's the taste that counts."

Kassie seemed an inch or two taller as she wheeled her trolley through the door.

"We'll let you get back to the office as soon as you've finished that wrap and your coffee, Freeman," said Kenneth. "I'm sorry there's not more to go on."

"We've worked with less, Sir," said Gus.

Geoff Mercer was starting his second bap and looked in no rush to leave.

"Mercer's staying for the next meeting, Freeman," said

Kenneth. "The PCC has us jumping through hoops this week. Nothing for you to worry about."

Gus placed his empty cup and plate on the tray on Kenneth's desk and headed for the door.

Nothing to worry about, he thought. That's easy for him to say. Three teams of two were easy to organise, and he could give everyone their chance to benefit from his experience. Of course, when they had to manage without Lydia, it meant some poor devil was left alone in the office.

As he drove the Focus down Caen Hill towards the Old Police Station office, he remembered Kenneth's other words. Things were never as bad as they seemed.

It was only a fortnight before Neil would get a phone call from Melody's mother telling him to drop everything. If Lydia got the call from Geoff Mercer simultaneously, they would be back to an even number. Somehow, he had to view that as a bonus.

Gus parked the Focus next to Blessing's Nissan Micra for the second time that day. With Neil and Lydia missing, they would be reduced to two teams of two. He pressed the button to call the lift.

"Welcome back, guv," said Neil.

"Thank you, Neil," said Gus. "I wish I had more to bring you."

He placed the slim folder on Grace's desk. "An unsolved murder from Swindon this time, Grace. Why don't you start the ball rolling?"

Grace followed the pattern of previous investigations. She extracted the crime scene photos and secured them to a whiteboard. Gus waited until the final picture was in place, and then he walked across and stood beside her.

"Matthew Archer was a thirty-three-year-old employee at a leisure centre in Haydon Wick, Swindon. Everyone knew him as Matt, married to Janet, thirty-one. The couple had moved to Swindon from Luton in 2001, and their daughter, Jasmine, was born the following year."

"How awful," said Blessing.

"Jasmine's okay for a girl's name, isn't it?" asked Neil.

"No, I meant, why would anyone want to kill him?" said Blessing.

"I can't see evidence that the original investigation ever determined that, Blessing," said Gus. "We must do better. Can you and Neil get the street maps for Haydon Wick on the wall, please? Dig out our map of the greater Swindon area while you're at it. So we can see where the major events took place."

Gus pointed to the picture of Matt's blood-soaked body in the ditch beside the B4553.

"A brutal attack crushed Matt's skull as he tried desperately to save his life," said Gus. "Stuart Fitzwalter, the police surgeon, believed there was just one assailant. However, he couldn't identify the weapon used, and nothing was found in the surrounding area despite a fingertip search."

"When was Matt Archer murdered, guv?" asked Alex.

"Friday the sixth in February 2009, as he tried to deliver a takeaway," said Gus. "Archer had worked as a delivery driver in the evenings for eighteen months."

"Where did the attack take place, guv?" asked Neil. "Surely, someone would have seen something in Haydon Wick on a Friday night? Which restaurant did he work for?"

"The Jade Garden," said Gus.

"That's on the main road," said Neil. "I've been there for a meal, and they served top nosh. It was a few years ago now, though, when Melody and I were dating."

"A busy part of town," said Alex. "Was Archer waylaid

in a side street and taken to the location we can see in the photos? The attack *was* there, wasn't it?"

"Lily Liang at the Jade Garden received a telephone order at twenty-five past nine," said Gus. "It was to be delivered to a farmhouse near Bremhill Bridge at precisely ten-thirty. Mrs Liang had never had an order from that farm before, and it was almost out of range for addresses where she and her husband, Michael, guaranteed to make deliveries."

"Did Mrs Liang ask for a telephone number, Gus?" asked Grace.

"I don't see any evidence of that in the murder file, guv," said Alex.

"What are you driving at, Grace?" asked Gus.

"Takeaways, pubs, and restaurants like to have a land-line to check whether the caller is genuine. They'd like to match the phone number to an address, especially when dealing with cash on delivery."

"The Jade Garden had a steady stream of customers that night," said Gus. "Some were seated in the restaurant, while others called in to collect a phoned order. They also had random walk-ins who popped in on their way home, and meanwhile, Matt Archer was ferrying deliveries to addresses within a two-mile radius. The farmhouse order was some way down their list of priorities, especially as Matt Archer had to make it his last trip."

"When did they stop taking delivery orders, guv?" asked Alex.

"Ten o'clock," said Gus. "The doors shut at eleven. I'm not sure when they stopped taking the call and collect orders; perhaps that was also ten. It would be a good fit to reduce the numbers in the building to those eating in the restaurant."

"It's more difficult to start a fight when you're sat down," said Neil.

"When did Matt Archer leave the Jade Garden?" asked Lydia.

"Lily Liang had noted the directions to Blades Farm from the person who called her," said Gus. "She handed the slip of paper to Archer before he left the restaurant at ten minutes past ten."

"How long did it take him to reach the farm, guv?" asked Alex.

"At least ten minutes," said Gus. "Archer would have followed the Purton Road to Common Platt and took a minor road through Bremhill Bridge. It's the only logical route, and whoever rang Lily Liang gave specific directions, so Archer didn't get lost. The entrance to Blades Farm was on the left, fifty yards before he reached the next junction. Archer would have seen the signpost in his headlights just beyond the farm entrance. The farmhouse was half a mile from the entrance up a dirt track."

"What's a common plait, guv?" asked Blessing.

"Not a hairstyle, Blessing," said Neil. "Common Platt was a hamlet. There was an old-style greyhound racing track on common land when my Dad was a teenager. Flapping, they called the sport back then. The group of dwellings on the common's edge made it just about worthy of a place name. Recently it's been the focus of new builds, and the gap between it and Purton has been all but eliminated. You'll be able to follow the route Archer took on the map now that I've finally got the map on the wall. Sorry, it took so long, guv."

"Every little helps, Neil," said Gus. "We could spend several hours in that neck of the woods trying to work out what happened next. OK, so, at twenty-five past ten, Matt

Archer turned into the farm entrance and swung the Jazz around to point back the way he came, along the B4553."

Gus pointed to the crime scene photo showing the position of the Honda Jazz when the police arrived the following morning.

"Archer thought he'd get out, drop off the takeaway, and be on his way home to a warm bed more quickly," said Alex. "That made sense if the farmhouse was nearby, guv, but you said it was half a mile from the gateway."

"Archer found the gates closed and padlocked," said Gus. "There was no hungry farmer to greet him with the right amount of money, and Archer didn't have the phone number of the farm. So he called Lily Liang and asked what he should do. She put Archer on hold while she called Blades Farm. Rosemary Payne, the farmer's wife, had had to stop reading to get out of bed to answer the phone. Her husband, John, and their three sons were already asleep. She confirmed none of them had ordered a takeaway that evening. Lily returned to Archer and told him the call must have been someone's idea of a joke. As far as Mrs Liang was concerned, Matt Archer was then driving home with a free supper and would be back at work at six o'clock the following evening. She continued to help serve customers in the restaurant, and it was after midnight before she drove home with her husband, Michael."

"The attacker must have been lying in wait," said Grace. "Time of death had to be within minutes of that final conversation between Mrs Liang and Matt Archer."

"If nobody at the farm called in the order, who did?" asked Lydia.

"Stuart Fitzwalter stated Archer died between ten-thirty and eleven-thirty," said Gus. "I agree with Grace. The killer had to strike quickly to prevent Archer from driving away."

"If I'd been Archer," said Neil. "I would have jumped out of the car, thinking that the gate would be unlocked as the delivery was expected. Once he realised he couldn't push it open because it was padlocked, he called Mrs Liang. We all know how unreliable mobile phone service can be in the countryside. It would have been worse in 2009, so Matt Archer stayed out of the car, standing by the gate, waiting for instructions from Mrs Liang. If you check the fourth crime scene photo, he only had to grab the carrier bag from the passenger seat when someone arrived to collect it. The padlocked end of the gate was closest to the passenger door."

"That makes sense, guv," said Alex. "Farmers are tight on security due to the rash of large equipment thefts in recent years. Matt Archer probably expected someone on a quad bike to roar down the track from the farmhouse to unlock the gate and settle the bill for a family meal. Especially as it was supposed to be for a ten-thirty supper."

"Archer wasn't aware his trip was a waste of time until he heard from Lily Liang," said Blessing.

"I can't promise we have was the answer to Lydia's question," said Gus, "but after searching for a weapon, and a motive, for seventy-two hours without luck, the police appealed for eyewitnesses to a telephone call at twenty-five past nine on the previous Friday night."

"Sounded like a long-shot, guv," said Neil. "If I was in a crowded pub in Haydon Wick that night, I could have seen a dozen people on their mobiles, chatting to someone. How would I know they were ringing the Jade Garden above all the noise?"

"The caller could have withheld their number while phoning from a private address," said Grace. "Nobody would have witnessed them then. Who was running this investigation, anyway?"

"DI Dave Arrowsmith and DS Natasha Chandler," said Gus. "They'd worked together at Gablecross for a couple of years and were considered a good team. They wanted to hear if someone had seen anything suspicious between nine-fifteen and nine-thirty. Only one person responded with information that appeared to fit the timeframe and the known circumstances. A local resident called Saul Brinkworth saw a man making a call from a public phone box near Moredon Post Office."

"That's just up the road from the Jade Garden," said Neil.

"Four hundred yards, according to the murder file," said Alex.

"Brinkworth told police the man in the phone box drove a Mazda 3," said Gus. "He'd left his engine running while he made the call. Saul Brinkworth was on his way into town for a night out, but something about how the man acted caught his attention. He was furtive and moved position whenever someone walked past. The description given to Arrowsmith and Chandler was of a white man in his late twenties or early thirties. The guy was of medium height, with dark hair, and looked like he could handle himself. Although he was driving rather than on foot, he wore a full-length dark overcoat, and the lower half of his face was covered by a scarf. Brinkworth couldn't see if anyone else was in the car, and the Mazda left soon after he had stopped looking across the road. He heard it roar off in the direction of Purton Road."

Grace was studying the map on the wall beside her desk.

"That was the most direct route to Bremhill Bridge," she said. "The Mazda could have followed the same route as Archer to reach Blades Farm. I can see why Arrowsmith and Chandler linked that sighting to the subsequent murder."

"A tenuous link," said Lydia. "I'm concerned it could be a red herring. Suzie and I encountered several recently."

"You've lost me, Lydia," said Grace. "We don't know much about what you and DI Ferris worked on while we were in London."

"That ex-Fleet Street reporter, Sid Selman, took two police officers with genuine ailments and used photographs to create the illusion of a thriving vice den operating in the centre of Warminster. DI Clare Edwards looked into the matter in 2013 and found nothing. Since then, ACCs Mark Colbourne and Melanie Sloper have done a follow-up check with the same result. There was nothing to find in the place where they were looking. The real crime went undetected for years because they were chasing the red herring."

"What evidence do you have that the man in the phone box wasn't speaking to Lily Liang?" asked Gus.

"None, guv," said Lydia. "But there isn't any evidence to prove he was, either. The police heard from Saul Brinkworth, who said he was passing the phone box near the Jade Garden between the times they specified in the appeal. Then he told them the Mazda was going in the right direction to reach a turning that would eventually lead to Blades Farm. It's sketchy, guv, don't you think?"

"Early days," said Gus with a shrug. "Was Saul Brinkworth known to the police? Could he have deliberately misled the investigation? Perhaps *he* made the call from the phone box as a prank, and everything else was a figment of his imagination. All we have to go on so far is what's in the original murder file. Let's step though the aftermath of the murder, and then we'll decide who we wish to interview and in which order."

"Who found the body, Gus?" asked Grace.

"John Payne and his eldest son, John Junior," said Gus. "They set off early next morning to drive to a field on Packhorse Lane. When they reached the farm entrance, John Junior went to unlock the gates and found the Honda Jazz blocking the exit. The two younger lads were milking cows in a building near the farmhouse and hadn't ventured towards the lane that morning. Rosemary Payne was stripping beds and picking clothes off the boys' bedroom floor. John Payne Senior checked the Honda by the farm entrance and found the doors unlocked, with the headlights on. Another photo behind me shows the Jade Garden carrier bag on the passenger seat."

"Did John Payne call the police straight away, guv?" asked Blessing.

"There was no evidence of foul play, Blessing," said Gus. "A quiet, country lane sees its fair share of abandoned vehicles. John Payne had heard the content of the late-night telephone conversation from his wife, so he knew the delivery driver had stood on that spot at ten-thirty last night. So why were his car and the food still there? Why leave the lights on and the doors unlocked if he'd run out of petrol? It didn't make sense, so he told his son to carry on down the lane towards the Packhorse Lane junction while he walked back the way the Jazz had come. John Junior found Matt Archer lying face down on the grass verge underneath the hedgerow. That's where the violent attack occurred, as we can see from the pooled blood on the ground and the spatter indicated on the hedge in the photos."

"Archer was pushed or dragged away from the gateway to be bludgeoned to death," said Alex.

"Once John Payne had walked to where his son was, they called the police," said Gus.

"Who was first on the scene?" asked Neil.

"Uniformed officers from Gablecross arrived first at a quarter to eight," said Gus. "They cordoned off the area close to the Jazz and closed the B4553 to through traffic. Then, with the crime scene secured, they waited for the police surgeon. They needed official confirmation they were dealing with a confirmed death before driving to Haydon Wick to notify Janet Archer. DI Arrowsmith and DS Chandler reached Blades Farm at five to eight. The forensic team were still ten minutes away. When Stuart Fitzwalter arrived just ahead of them, he inspected the body and told the detectives that Matt Archer had died of severe head injuries."

"Who notified Janet Archer?" asked Grace.

"Two uniformed officers," said Gus. "One of whom was PCSO Beverley Coulson. Janet and her daughter, Jasmine, were still in bed. Janet had no idea Matt hadn't come home. It wasn't unheard of for Matt to fall asleep on the sofa after a fourteen-hour day. Friday nights were busy at the Jade Garden, and a full shift at the leisure centre before that took its toll."

"Why was Matt Archer working these extra hours, guv?" asked Lydia. "Did the couple have money troubles?"

"The murder file says Janet Archer returned to work after Jasmine was born," said Alex. "Plenty of firms were hit by the recession, and she was made redundant. It was a struggle to keep up with mortgage payments, but there were no red flags on their financials when Matt was killed."

"So, we're not looking for an over-zealous loan shark chasing his extortionate payments," said Neil.

"It doesn't appear so," said Alex. "But the file has a few

paragraphs on another matter that DI Arrowsmith thought important."

"Dave Arrowsmith believed someone had a grudge against Matt Archer or his wife," said Gus. "The Jazz had been vandalised on four different occasions. Matt and Janet were reliant on the Honda Jazz. He used it to get to work at the leisure centre and on the trips that he made in the evenings delivering takeaways. Janet sometimes drove Matt to work if the weather was bad. Then she took Jasmine to school and now and then visited one of Swindon's outlet centres."

"The person who made the hoax call could have been behind the damage to the family car," said Blessing. "Those attacks might have been random, I suppose, but taken together with what happened at Blades Farm, it sounds more than a grudge."

"That's a line of enquiry we'll follow, Blessing," said Grace. "The true motive for the vicious attack on Matt Archer has never been established. I see that as a priority."

Gus was deep in thought, and the others waited for him to continue leading them through the initial investigation's main events.

"You've started me thinking about red herrings, Lydia," he said. "The Chief Constable asked me earlier whether it was possible the Honda Jazz had been moved and then returned to the place where John Payne and his son found it."

"If the killer didn't want the body found for a day or two, they could have found a quieter spot for the car," said Lydia. "Maybe Matt Archer was killed to send a message? I have no idea who to and why, but leaving the car where it was sure to be found early on Saturday morning meant the message, if there was one, was spreading across various media outlets by lunchtime."

"We're on the same wavelength," said Gus. "The object of the attack was to get rid of Matt Archer, and let someone connected to him know they should, what, stop what they were doing? It's frustrating not being able to see a clear motive for the murder. Matt Archer's record was clean, and he was a stand-up guy, as far as we can tell. There's nothing in the murder file to suggest the motive might have come from his work at the leisure centre, or the Jade Garden, where his employers were more than happy with his work. If the grudge started back in Luton in the 1990s, retribution was a long time coming. We'll have to dig back into his past to discover whether he crossed swords with someone it was best to avoid."

"One thing I've thought of, guv," said Blessing. "Whether the killer was the driver of the Mazda 3 or not, they still needed to drive from Haydon Wick to Blades Farm. Did nobody see a vehicle on the main roads before they turned off onto the side roads and lanes?"

"Fat chance of anyone remembering seeing a Honda, or a Mazda after nine years, Blessing," said Neil. "If the murder file didn't include a sheaf of CCTV images from the centre of Haydon Wick from Friday night, either they didn't check or found nothing."

"Once a car took the side roads at that time of night, they could travel miles without seeing another vehicle," said Grace.

"It's possible someone from Common Platt was out walking the dog," said Lydia.

"If they did, they didn't come forward with the information," said Neil.

"Maybe, nobody asked them," said Alex. "I can't see an

address outside Haydon Wick for anyone Arrowsmith and Chandler interviewed other than the names we've heard."

"Are there any names you would like to add to the list?" asked Gus. "Who do we have so far?"

"The detectives, the PCSO who visited Mrs Archer, the Payne family, and the husband and wife who ran the Jade Garden," said Blessing. "Oh, and Janet Archer."

"We'd need to identify colleagues from the leisure centre, guv," said Neil.

"What about people who use the place?" asked Alex. "The Jazz was vandalised outside the leisure centre, wasn't it?"

"It was," said Gus. "I'd like to talk with all four members of the Liang family from the Jade Garden too. Because she had to send Matt Archer away for his final delivery at ten past ten, Lily Liang asked Adam Liang to deliver the remaining orders on his way home."

"Was that normal, guv?" asked Neil. "Anyway, does it matter?"

"Adam may have been responsible for the delivery process before Matt Archer arrived," said Blessing.

"My thoughts exactly, Blessing," said Gus. "Adam was twenty-nine at the time. His father was thirty years older. It wouldn't surprise me to learn that Adam is now in charge of the Jade Garden, and Michael and Lily have retired. It's not uncommon for Chinese restaurants to be independent operations, and many are family businesses."

"At this stage, we don't have many concrete facts, do we?" said Grace. "I want to tackle it from a different angle. We have a victim who died from blunt-force trauma. Divya Yadav would tell us that statistically, the victim likely knew their killer. Therefore, someone wanted Matt Archer dead. He may have had a clean record, but it wouldn't be the first time a criminal went undetected for decades. Yes, Archer had worked at the Jade Garden for a few hours per night for eighteen months, but he'd worked full-time at the leisure centre for eight years. That's where we should concentrate our attention if we want to establish a motive."

"What job was Archer doing before he moved to Swindon?" asked Lydia. "Perhaps the motive originated at a leisure centre in Luton?"

"Add those names to the list by all means," said Gus, "when you've identified them all."

Gus tried to determine how many people might have come into close contact with Matt Archer at a leisure centre. They could be talking hundreds, even thousands if they had to delve into the last century. What contact was there when delivering a takeaway? It was minimal if the Domino pizza guys and gals who dropped by the bungalow were anything to go by.

Chapter Nine

"YOU DON'T SEEM KEEN, GUS," said Grace.

"There were four separate acts of vandalism carried out on Matt Archer's Honda Jazz," said Gus. "Two incidents happened when the car was parked outside the family home. A wing mirror was broken on New Year's Eve, and a coin scraped along the side of the car a week later. Not exactly a precursor to an attack with a blunt instrument designed to bring Matt's life to an end. If we check with Gablecross, they'll know the names of likely lads on that Haydon Wick estate regularly in trouble nine years ago. As for the other minor incidents, they can easily be explained by normal wear-and-tear when your car spends extended periods in a busy car park. Matt Archer's Jazz was parked outside the leisure centre for up to forty hours a week, and if we checked CCTV from a supermarket car park today, I'd bet we'd see the odd bump and broken tail light."

"When you put it like that, it does seem a leap to go from a coin scrape to a vicious assault," said Alex. "Does that mean you think the answer lies at the Jade Garden, guv?"

"The Jazz was never targeted while Matt Archer was making deliveries," said Gus. "Matt and Janet didn't receive calls at home, luring them to a remote spot on a fool's errand. No, the phone call was to the Jade Garden."

"I get what you're driving at now, guv," said Blessing. "It could have been the Liang family the caller had an issue with. Matt Archer was the unlucky victim."

"Grace mentioned Divya Yadav earlier and pointed out that most attacks are personal. The original investigation never found evidence to support that, but would it have been carried out with such clinical precision if it was personal? Archer's murder feels like the work of an experienced criminal. There was a high degree of planning involved. The killer arranged for a food delivery to arrive at Blades Farm by ten-thirty. We know the call was made at nine twenty-five. Therefore they had at least fifty minutes to get to the farm, park their car somewhere discreet, and find a good place to hide."

"They could have lived in Common Platt for all we know, guv," said Neil. "Walking to the farm entrance from there wouldn't take long. So the Mazda 3 could be a red herring."

"What could have sparked a vendetta between someone and the Liang family, Gus?" asked Grace.

"A disgruntled customer?" suggested Neil.

"We've all had a dodgy takeaway meal, Neil," said Alex. "It's never prompted us to bash one of the staff to death. We write it off to experience and visit a different establishment."

"Let's take a break," said Gus. "Everyone has a good understanding of the basics now. Can you split setting up interviews with the main protagonists between you, Alex and Grace? Then, Neil and Blessing, I'd like you to visit the Haydon Wick leisure centre in the morning to find out what Matt Archer's job entailed. Nine years is a long time, and staff turnover is notoriously high in that sector. You might struggle to find staff who remember him."

"The same goes for customers, Gus," said Neil. "If I were ever tempted to join a gym, my membership wouldn't last longer than a year."

"There will be people who regularly go swimming if there's a pool," said Lydia. "People of all ages."

"Don't forget the man Saul Brinkworth saw in the phone box, guv," said Alex. "He reckoned the bloke looked as if he worked out. That could be the nexus we're seeking."

"Jamie told me he's seen the effects of anabolic steroid use on young soldiers trying to get a rapid improvement in their body shape," said Blessing. "The drugs make them more aggressive and temperamental."

"Roid rage," said Neil. "That's an angle we can pursue tomorrow, guv."

"By all means, Neil," said Gus. "Whoever killed Matt Archer wasn't a mild-mannered accountant. Keep in mind Grace's desire to go wide in the hunt for staff and customers who had a grudge against Archer. The leisure centre should have records of past employees and members. If anything you hear raises suspicions, then ask for addresses. You might meet resistance, but remind them we're investigating a murder."

"Got it, guv," said Neil and Blessing.

"Do you have something I can do, guv?" asked Lydia.

"You can do a deep-dive into social media, Lydia," said Gus. "Did the Jade Garden have a good reputation online?

Were there any occasions when the police were called there because of a late-night disturbance? You know what we're looking for. Try to find comments about the leisure centre, too. Any facility that attracts hundreds of people from across a town as big as Swindon will have suffered flash-points over the years. Was there anything of note between 2001 and 2009? Use your imagination. After the experience you gained working with DI Ferris, your sleuthing abilities should have improved."

"That should keep me busy tomorrow," said Lydia.

"That's the general idea, Lydia," said Gus.

The team made their way to the lift in pairs at five o'clock. Grace and Blessing had already left Church Street in the sturdy Nissan Micra when Alex and Lydia stepped into the car park. Alex was edging into traffic when Gus and Neil exited the lift.

"Have you ever been tempted to join a gym, Neil?" asked Gus.

"Melody has suggested I needed to lose weight once or twice since we got married, guv," said Neil. "Why? Do you think I'd struggle to get through a physical?"

"Don't ask me," said Gus. "I've never been inside a gym except while on duty. My allotment keeps my waistline as trim as any bloke my age warrants. We might need to tread carefully after our other half gives birth. They might think it a great idea for us to join them at the gym when they're getting their figures back."

"The best way out of that is to suggest they go together while we stay home looking after the baby, guv," said Neil. "Childcare is so expensive, isn't it?"

"Good thinking, Neil," said Gus. "See you when you get back from Haydon Wick."

Gus followed Neil's car to the traffic lights by

Wadworth's Brewery. Neil turned left to head home to Melody, and Gus drove straight ahead through the market place and past the Bear pub. He should be home by twenty to six. Suzie would have arrived at the bungalow already, and with luck, she had started to cook a meal. Gus wasn't in the mood for a takeaway for some reason.

Tuesday, 20 November 2018

"GOOD HUNTING TODAY, SWEETHEART," said Suzie as she stood beside her Golf.

"I gave everyone else a list of tasks, and that leaves me spinning my wheels this morning," said Gus. "Until I receive an interview schedule or positive feedback from Neil and Blessing from Haydon Wick, I can only get my files set up in readiness."

"Don't forget Divya Yadav," said Suzie as she prepared to leave.

"How could I forget the Hub," said Gus. He shivered at the memory of his brief spell on the second floor.

Suzie sprayed the side of the bungalow with gravel and disappeared into the lane. Gus wondered how the rambling roses survived such wanton disregard for their delicate nature. He had to remind himself that Christmas was only a month away because more new buds were about to open among Tess's favourites. The world was a'changing.

The two small cars parked in the bays reserved for the Crime Review Team meant he was last to arrive. Grace had brought her Smart car today, and Lydia's red Mini gave their side of the car park a colourful look. Gus slotted his dark grey Focus between them.

Two minutes later, he was removing his jacket and sitting at his desk.

"I've set up a meeting with Adam Liang at the Jade Garden, Gus," said Grace. "If we wish to speak with his parents, we'll have to use Zoom. They're retired and living in the south of France."

"I thought as much," said Gus. "The retired part, anyway, although I wouldn't have thought of France as being their first choice. What about the daughter, Danielle? Is she still involved in the family business?"

"Yes, guv," said Alex. "Adam told me she would be available tomorrow. Danielle's visiting suppliers in London today."

"Who's interviewing Adam Liang, Gus?" asked Grace.

"We'll do that, I think," said Gus. "I'll drive."

"Why am I not surprised," said Grace.

"If you leave now, you should reach the Jade Garden by ten o'clock, guv," said Alex. "Adam will be in his office above the restaurant. They don't open at lunchtime these days."

"Come on then, Grace," said Gus. "Get your coat. We're off."

They were soon in the Focus, heading towards Calne and waiting for the heater to kick in to reduce the chill of the cold start to the day.

"Neil tells me it's quicker to get to Haydon Wick via Wootton Bassett," said Gus.

"Local knowledge," said Grace. "I'll catch up, given time."

"How are you settling in at Worton Farm?" asked Gus.

"I'm happier now than I was for the first few days," said Grace. "I wasn't sleeping well and knew the others in the office thought I was a bit of a grouch."

"It takes time to get used to new surroundings," said Gus. "Did you feel you benefited from your time in London?"

"Of course," said Grace. "It's always good to see how other forces operate."

"We're supposed to be singing from the same hymn sheet, Grace," said Gus.

"The Met always seem to be on a different verse to the rest of us," said Grace. "You would have had a fit if you saw how officers mixing with the protesters behaved. It was difficult to tell whether they were policing the march or participating in it. I'm glad it was mostly trouble-free; the boots on the ground were far from being able to react to an incident."

"You can knock them into shape when you get the top job, Grace," said Gus.

Alex hadn't been far out with his estimate, and Gus parked outside the Jade Garden just before ten. Grace was first to the door and pressed the bell. Gus tried to recognise the tune played by the chimes but failed. Before he could ask Grace, the door opened.

"Wiltshire Police, I presume?" said Adam Liang. He looked every inch the successful businessman, with a light-grey three-piece suit, a pink shirt and tie, and shiny, black leather shoes. His father, Michael, had run the Jade Garden from the kitchen. Adam must have employed a chef since his father retired, and he was not helping out with late-night deliveries as he had done nine years earlier; that was certain.

Grace and Gus followed Adam upstairs.

"My sister Danielle's office, is on the left. We have a staff restroom on the right. My office is straight ahead."

Gus looked around the large room with two floor-to-ceiling windows overlooking the street. Danielle had come off second-best in the office stakes, regardless of how well her room was decorated.

"Please be seated. How may I help you?" asked Adam.

Gus and Grace sat in the two chairs that had been placed opposite Adam's large desk. Gus could see the space on the outside wall they usually occupied. The restaurant owner sat in a black leather chair that was too big for him. No matter how successful he'd become, Adam Liang would always be a shade over five feet tall.

"My name is Freeman," said Gus. "A consultant with a Crime Review Team investigating unsolved murders."

"I'm DI Packenham," said Grace. "Mr Freeman and I are colleagues. We're reviewing Matthew Archer's murder from February 2009."

"Not an easy matter to forget," said Adam. "My family was interviewed at the time. There was very little we could offer to help the detectives achieve a positive outcome."

"How did your father react when he received an application from Matt Archer for the delivery driver's job?" asked Gus.

"I don't follow you," said Adam.

"You were a family business," said Gus. "In my experience, very few jobs in restaurants and takeaways are available to outsiders. It's easy to understand why that was the case. The language barrier would be a real problem when the pressure mounts. Communication needs to be spot-on. So, everyone from the chef to the kitchen and waiting staff would be Chinese, Thai, Turkish, Indian, Greek, or Italian, depending on the food served. Undoubtedly, in these modern times, some people would take issue with that. I can imagine you and Danielle worked here in some capacity from an early age."

"I was eight when my father started me working in the kitchen," said Adam. "Danielle took on my position preparing vegetables when she reached the same age. My father insisted we never go near the takeaway counter or where customers might catch sight of us working."

"There's nothing wrong with acquiring a strong work ethic," said Gus. "So, what age were you when you started making deliveries?"

"We didn't always have a delivery service," said Adam. "Licensing hours changed in 2005, and more bars and clubs stayed open later. My father was forced to change the way we operated. I was twenty-one and had a car, so I was chosen to make the deliveries. Danielle was just old enough to want driving lessons. My father elected to share the duties with me to save money. Once Danielle had passed her test, at the fifth attempt, we shared the deliveries between us. It wasn't too bad then because not many customers could use their mobile phones to view the menus online and ring us with their selection. Most incoming calls were for customers wanting to collect their meals from the waiting area by the front door. My father sectioned off the restaurant area during 2006 to accommodate the extra footfall."

"Two years later, Matt Archer took over the delivery duties," said Grace. "What did you and Danielle think about that?"

"We were comfortable with the decision," said Adam. "My parents had to do what they thought was best for the business. Danielle and I took the weight off our mother's shoulders. She was tired. For years our mother had been responsible for everything outside the kitchen. After the changes, she coped with the phone orders, and we ensured the restaurant's clients received the highest standard of food and service. We had to be flexible, so my father would shout instructions from the kitchen when delivery orders piled up. Finally, on the night you're talking about, he told my mother as there weren't many customers in the restaurant, she should switch me to deliveries to help reduce the backlog."

"Was that a common occurrence?" asked Gus.

"Only at the busiest times. Weekends mostly," said Adam.

"So, *you* could have made the Blades Farm delivery," said Grace.

"But nobody could be certain which driver would pick up which order," said Gus.

"Sorry, I don't follow you," said Adam.

"The detectives who investigated the murder nine years ago thought someone had a grudge against Matt Archer," said Grace. "Mr Freeman is pointing out that the person who attacked Matt Archer called your mother to place an order. They then lay in wait outside Blades Farm until the delivery arrived at ten-thirty, as agreed, and attacked the driver. On another night, it could have been you delivering that meal, or even Danielle, if your father deemed it necessary to reduce cover in the restaurant."

"I suppose so," said Adam. "But what does it mean?"

"It's too soon in our investigation to determine that Mr Liang," said Gus. "When did your parents retire?"

Adam Liang laid back in his chair. Gus prepared to listen to a well-rehearsed potted history of the Jade Garden.

"They retired in 2015," said Adam. "My parents said goodbye to Haydon Wick after thirty years of being in business. It was heartbreaking and emotional because, like many other British-born Chinese families, the business had been their whole life. My parents emigrated from Hong Kong in the Eighties to start a family and search for a better quality of life. As both were uneducated, their only option was to work in low-skilled jobs or run a fish and chip shop or restaurant. There was little competition in Haydon Wick in 1985, and by working long hours and putting up with the abuse many families in similar circumstances had to suffer, they thrived."

"They wanted to provide the best life for you and Danielle, so you didn't have to go through the same hardships as they did," said Gus.

"Exactly," said Adam. "We owe them everything."

"What do you remember of that Friday night nine years ago?" asked Gus.

Adam leaned forward and looked at the ceiling.

"I left home, about forty minutes after my parents, to drive here in my car. Danielle always took longer to get ready and drove into town, arriving five minutes before we opened. Our parents were already in the kitchen with our other staff. It was normal for them to arrive at four o'clock, two hours before we opened. We have multiple people working on each dish and use high-quality equipment to cook food quickly. We often have pre-made ingredients we can heat up or assemble. The operation needs to be slick and understood by everyone if we wish to maximise the number of customers we can satisfy."

"We appreciate the basics, Mr Liang," said Grace. "Let's fast-forward to when your father realised deliveries were falling behind."

"I was monitoring the serving staff in the restaurant. We had two new youngsters who needed a prompt now and then to serve customers from the right side. Both were under eighteen, so if a customer on their table wanted a fresh drink, I was ready to jump in. Danielle was doing table checks, ensuring her customers were happy with their meals.

I heard my father shout from the kitchen. As soon as there was a lull in the restaurant, I asked Danielle to cover the bar and went to speak to my mother."

"What time was this?" asked Gus.

"I can't be accurate," said Adam Liang. "A few minutes after ten o'clock."

"Where was Matt Archer?" asked Grace.

"On his way back from his latest trip. Matt walked through the door seconds after I joined my mother from the restaurant."

"What did your mother do then?" asked Grace.

"She explained that a delivery to Blades Farm had to be made for ten-thirty. The customer had given her directions that she'd written down. Also on the counter were several deliveries for addresses closer to the restaurant. I grabbed those and headed for the door. I heard my mother telling Matt he could make the Blades Farm trip his last for the night. There weren't many opportunities for an early night for either of us. I realised my father was panicking, as usual."

"What do you mean?" asked Grace.

"We had inexperienced staff in the kitchen too. As I grabbed the deliveries, I realised that several meals for collection had been put in the wrong place. There weren't any more deliveries that night. We had only taken a handful of calls after half-past nine."

"Matt Archer left at ten past ten to drive to Blades Farm while you delivered to addresses that were on your way home," said Gus.

"Correct," said Adam. "We heard about the murder the following day. Two uniformed police officers came to the restaurant at five o'clock to notify my parents. They phoned me at home, and Danielle and I drove here before six. We had a family conference and decided to keep the takeaway service running. My mother phoned customers who were due to arrive at the restaurant. She apologised for the inconvenience, and while Danielle stayed to help my mother, I dealt with the deliveries. It was a strange evening. People were asking if what they had heard was true. Many were upset because they knew Matt, either from here or from the leisure centre. He was a popular guy."

"How did you two get on?" asked Gus.

"We didn't mix socially," said Adam. "Like my parents, my life centred on the Jade Garden; it still does. Matt was married with a young daughter. Our lives didn't cross outside this building."

"I was interested in the dynamic within this building," said Gus. "Matt was thirty-three, and although your parents were the people who gave him the delivery job, you were the eldest son of the owners. Did he resent having to take orders from someone four years younger?"

"It was rare for anyone other than my mother to deal with Matt," said Adam. "I can't remember if I was ever asked to supervise him."

"You were a single man at the time of the murder," said Grace. "Has that situation changed?"

"Times have changed in many areas of life, DI Packenham," said Adam. "My parents believe traditions are important. My father searched for a wife from a suitable family in the UK as soon as I left school. He's actively searching now in Arles, where my parents live. Only last month he called me with details of a potential candidate. I see no rings on your fingers, yet you are perhaps my sister's age. Neither of you is married. I'm in no rush to marry, but I haven't ruled it out. The girl my father wants me to meet when I next visit could become Mrs Liang one day."

"Why did your parents choose to retire to the south of France?" asked Gus.

"I can't believe you asked that, Gus," said Grace.

Adam Liang laughed for the first time since they'd arrived.

"Arles is a beautiful city on the edge of the Camargue," he said. "My mother loves to paint, and if it inspired Van Gogh, then why not live near Arles? The main reasons were the doctors believed it was vital for my mother's health that she lived somewhere warmer, and we have family in Saint-Remy-de-Provence."

"We don't have many questions left, for now, Mr Liang," said Gus. "You mentioned a high turnover of staff, some of whom were under eighteen. Were there any staff members Matt Archer was close to or perhaps had an argument with?"

"Not that I can recall, Mr Freeman," said Adam. "There was no cause for Matt to enter the kitchen or the restaurant. Instead, he would park outside, and my mother would tell him where to deliver and in what order. He'd return for another trip, and if there were a lull, he'd sit in the restroom along the corridor, reading a book. The other staff members would only pop up here for a comfort break. They wouldn't have time to sit and chat."

"Did you and Danielle use the same facilities?" asked Grace.

"Of course," said Adam, "as did my parents. They're separate from the part of the restroom where the staff have their lockers and where Matt would have rested. The customer toilets are downstairs, with access from the restaurant."

"Can you recall any fights or disturbances in the take-away area when Matt picked up a delivery?" Gus asked.

"What about a complaint from a customer about a delivery Matt had made?"

"I would be lying if we didn't have incidents as you describe," Adam said. "My father's view was the customer was always right in anything related to the food he served. So, he gave an automatic refund if anyone was unhappy. He had the sense to close earlier than some fast-food outlets to minimise the number of drunks we suffered. Our instructions were to call the police immediately if anything happened. You can check how many times that was, but again, I don't remember Matt being involved, and he certainly was never the cause of any disturbance."

"Danielle is away on business, is that right?" asked Gus.

"Yes, she's in London visiting suppliers," said Adam. "If you return in the morning at the same time, I'll ensure she's in her office. Was there anything else?"

"Not at this time, Mr Liang," said Gus. "If we think of something, no doubt we'll find you here tomorrow morning."

"Whatever you need, you only have to ask," said Adam. He followed Gus and Grace to the top of the stairs.

"Did Matt and his wife ever eat in the restaurant?" asked Grace as they reached the front door.

"They were customers of ours before Matt answered the advert for a delivery driver. They celebrated birthdays and their anniversary here. We saw less of them after their daughter was born, of course. Why do you ask?"

"Matt was always with his wife?" asked Grace.

"Always," said Adam.

"Thank you, Mr Liang," said Grace. "We'll see you tomorrow."

Adam Liang closed the door and returned to his office.

Gus pulled away from the Jade Garden and set off towards Wootton Bassett.

"What made you decide a Columbo moment was needed?" asked Gus.

"Clutching at straws," said Grace. "Matt Archer never put a foot out of place, did he? He was on good terms with the owners and had no problem with Adam, Danielle, or the other staff. Nobody complained about his behaviour on the premises or when he delivered their orders. The man was a saint. I hoped to learn he was closer to Danielle than Adam Liang liked or he was seeing a married woman from the leisure centre. Whatever prompted someone to murder him doesn't appear connected to the Jade Garden."

"Early days yet, Grace," said Gus. "Things are not always as they seem."

Chapter Ten

"DOES Jamie spend much time in the gym, Blessing?" asked Neil as they neared Swindon. "Your guy's as fit as a butcher's dog."

"A military policeman needs to stay fit," said Blessing. "That goes for an officer like Jamie and the troops in trouble with the law he deals with. So, I'm not complaining."

Neil laughed.

"Who do we have to ask for this morning?" he asked.

"Brendan Kelson is the manager's name," said Blessing. "Do you know where we're going?"

"Thames Avenue," said Neil. "I know Swindon pretty well. The leisure centre shares its building with the bowls club and sits next door to a supermarket. We can't miss it. There are plenty of parking spaces, too, so we won't have to walk far."

"Just as well," said Blessing. "I hated the rain we had every day earlier in the month, but at least it was warmer."

Neil soon parked outside the giant modern building that

housed various sporting facilities. He was looking forward to learning what Matt Archer had done here.

Neil and Blessing walked to the main entrance and asked for Mr Kelson.

The young girl behind the counter picked up the phone.

"Brendan, the police are here," she whispered.

Blessing checked out the red, white, and blue décor. "It's patriotic, isn't it, Neil?"

Neil shrugged.

"Once you've seen one leisure centre, you've seen them all. Or so they tell me."

Two minutes later, a tall, thin man in his forties hurried towards them, apologised for keeping them waiting, and asked them to follow him. His office was just around the corner.

Neil made the introductions and reminded the manager why they were there.

"I'm not sure how much I can help," said Brendan. "I've only been here since we took over. You said you're interested in someone who worked here years ago?"

"Matthew Archer," said Neil. "He was employed here between 2001 and 2009."

"You're probably aware the Council used to be the guardian of facilities such as ours, DS Davis. Over the years, they've been unable to keep pace with the rapid changes in their ratepayers' leisure requirements. Hence, they've closed old buildings altogether and put places such as this out to tender. A company such as ours can deliver what the public demands."

"We're not that interested in what you can deliver," said Neil. "We want to find out who murdered Matt Archer and why. So the only thing I need you to tell me is, what did he do here? If you can't do that, and the Council possesses those details, then we'll ask them."

"Perhaps there's a member of staff who remembers Mr Archer. If so, we'd like to talk to them," said Blessing.

"Edward Hyde is the building's longest-serving employee," said Brendon. "He's in charge of maintenance. Our company kept him on because his knowledge was invaluable. Edward is possibly the only person on our books here back then."

"Where do we find Mr Hyde?" asked Neil.

"If you return to the front desk, Maisie will call him for you. He could be anywhere."

Blessing steered Neil out of the office before Neil said a word.

Maisie was eager to please and put out a tannoy call for Mr Hyde to report to Reception.

"You were a bit short with Mr Kelson, Neil," said Blessing when they moved away from the counter to wait for Edward Hyde.

"They could have saved us a lot of time by telling us the place was under new management yesterday afternoon," said Neil. "Let's hope Mr Hyde has a good memory."

When a grey-haired man in green overalls came in the main entrance, Blessing knew they would soon find out. Maisie pointed towards her as soon as Edward Hyde reached the counter.

"What appears to be the problem," he said. "Which piece of equipment were you using?"

"Wiltshire Police," said Blessing. "I'm Detective Constable Umeh, and this is Detective Sergeant Davis. We want to talk to you about Matthew Archer, not your treadmills."

"I remember Matt," said Mr Hyde. "An awful thing to

happen that was, and you never discovered who killed him, did you?"

"That's right, Mr Hyde," said Neil. "It's our job to put that right."

"Call me Eddie," said the maintenance man. "Let's go to my office. It's quieter there. It's a five-minute walk. Is that okay?"

Blessing buttoned up her coat and stuffed her hands in her pockets. Why did she leave her gloves in Neil's car?

"Some people would call this a workman's hut," said Eddie when they reached the large wooden building. "But it's been home to me for twenty-five years. Matt worked here when the centre was last re-furbished, back in 2006. Which is it to be, tea or coffee? I've got biscuits if you're hungry."

Blessing looked around the large shed and saw that Eddie Hyde had squeezed in a few home comforts among the industrial racking that held everything he might ever need to keep the building from falling apart.

"Coffee, please," she said. "White for both of us, and one sugar for DS Davis."

Eddie put the kettle on and fetched a milk carton from a fridge under a nearby workbench. Neil's eyes lit up when Eddie removed a fresh packet of Hobnobs from a desk drawer.

They were soon settled with their coffee and biscuits, Blessing and Neil leaning against the sturdy wooden bench while Eddie sat on the only chair available.

"Matt moved to Swindon from Luton, if I remember rightly," said Eddie. "He was a fitness instructor. Some refer to them as personal trainers, but in a place like this, you get all sorts. There's little chance for a one-on-one session, so the instructors mostly work with groups. If you checked

Matt's job description, it would say he engaged clients in exercise routines and weight loss programmes and helped them to reach their individual goals."

"Was he popular with the clients?" asked Neil.

"You heard me say that fitness instructors were there to help people lose weight," said Eddie. "What do you think? For some people, keeping their weight under control is a constant battle. A battle they're keen to face up to, and Matt would help in every way he could, but he wasn't a fan of the other sort."

"People who join in January and have lost interest by Easter," said Neil.

"We have plenty of those," said Eddie. "A few renew their membership the following year and try again. No, Matt knew being a hard taskmaster with those determined to succeed was the best way forward, and they appreciated it. You wouldn't hear a bad word from anyone who lost the excess weight and kept it off. He didn't like wasting his time on those who gave up, despite the likelihood they would keel over and die within five years if they didn't take drastic action. A couple in that category might tell you they thought Matt was a bully."

"He wanted what was best for them," said Blessing.

"That's the way I saw it," said Eddie.

"What about the bosses who were here then?" asked Neil.

"Matt was never censured or told to take a softer approach," said Eddie. "Not as far as I knew. I'm here, there, and everywhere, so it's not likely I missed it."

"Can you remember anyone on the staff who argued with Matt?" asked Blessing. "Not about his single-minded attitude to helping people achieve their personal goals, but perhaps on a personal matter?"

"Something personal?" asked Eddie. "What do you mean?"

"Was Matt close to a particular staff member?" asked Neil. "Maybe a female who worked here in some capacity?"

"No, you're barking up the wrong tree there, Sergeant," said Eddie. "Matt and Janet were devoted to one another. She would drop him off outside in the car park some days. You only had to see them together; they were as happy as pigs in, you know what."

"You said Matt and the other fitness instructors rarely worked alone with a client," said Blessing. "Could someone have paid him to make a home visit?"

"That would have been against the rules," said Eddie. "I wouldn't have known about that if it did happen. Matt wouldn't have told anyone here, would he? But any opportunity for a personal session was off the cards once he took on the delivery job at the Chinese restaurant."

"Did Matt ever tell you why they moved here from Luton?" asked Neil. "I imagine there were plenty of vacancies for fitness instructors across Bedfordshire."

"He'd recently got his accreditation at the gym he worked at in Luton," said Eddie. "Haydon Wick was a promotion for him. Matt saw it as a win-win; they both earned more money, and house prices were lower here than in Luton. So he didn't leave the place under a cloud if that's what you're driving at."

"We're looking for a thread to follow that doesn't lead to a dead end," said Neil puffing out his cheeks. "If Matt Archer was the hard-working, loyal, likeable bloke everyone says he was, why did someone bash him over the head and kill him?"

"I asked myself that question for ages nine years ago, young man," said Eddie. He collected their three empty mugs and returned the Hobnobs to the desk drawer. "I'll wash these mugs and get back to work. I don't believe the thread you're looking for will be found on these premises."

Neil and Blessing were inclined to agree.

"Time to return to the office," said Neil. "Thanks for the hospitality and the background information on Matt, Mr Hyde. Our boss will need to come up with another cunning plan."

Eddie followed them out of the shed and said goodbye before walking toward the bowling green. Blessing and Neil trudged to the car park, and soon they were on Thames Avenue heading for Devizes and onward to the Old Police Station office.

GUS AND GRACE returned to the office at half-past eleven. Alex and Lydia could tell from their faces they were no further forward than when they left.

"Have you heard from Neil and Blessing yet?" asked Gus.

"Nothing so far, guv," said Alex. "I've scheduled an interview with DCI Arrowsmith at Gablecross for lunchtime tomorrow. He can only spare us an hour. I thought it would help if you drove straight there after seeing Danielle Liang."

"That sounds fine, Alex," said Gus. "Any luck getting hold of DI Chandler?"

"Natasha could speak to someone later this afternoon, guv," said Lydia. "Perhaps Alex and I could cover that one for you?"

"Fine," said Gus. "Drive to her place, interview her, and then make your way home to Chippenham."

"I take it things didn't become any brighter this morning, guv," said Alex.

Gus gave Alex and Lydia the gist of what Adam Liang had told them. Then he and Grace started updating their digital files. As the clock on the wall ticked around to noon, the lift descended to the ground floor.

"The wanderers return," said Gus as Neil and Blessing entered the office.

"I hope you had better luck than us, guv," said Neil. "If Eddie Hyde, the maintenance man, was telling the truth, Matt Archer was universally loved, except for a couple of clients who took offence at him criticising them for not taking their weight loss programme seriously."

"You pointed out it was a big step from snapping a wing mirror to braining someone, guv," said Blessing. "We found another way of putting it. Nobody kills someone because they tell them they're overweight. Edward Hyde was adamant Matt and his wife were devoted to one another. No way he was playing away. As for the switch from Luton to Swindon, Matt was promoted to a fully accredited fitness instructor. Neil wondered whether Matt had seen a female client in the evenings before his delivery job. When we speak to Janet Archer, we can explore that angle. Ask if Matt had a regular appointment in the evenings."

"Matt could have told his wife he played five-a-side football, guv," said Neil. "That would have explained why he came home hot and sweaty."

"TMI, Neil," said Grace. "Based on everything else we've heard, it sounds unlikely."

"There has to be something that prompted the attack at Blades Farm," said Gus. "What progress did you make on social media, Lydia?"

"I found what I expected to find, guv," she replied. "The Jade Garden has had a 4.4-star rating since the review site started in 2007. That related to both the takeaway side of the business and the restaurant. If they had a disgruntled customer, they didn't go into print. I didn't see any mileage in going back further because Matt Archer wasn't working there."

"Fair enough," said Gus. "What about any trouble?"

"I've checked the Swindon Advertiser from 2005 to 2010, and in 2006 the police were called to separate a group of rival football fans brawling outside the Jade Gardens. The incident between Swindon Town and Bristol Rovers supporters had started inside the takeaway section. Other than that, a late-night customer in 2007 called the police to complain he'd been short-changed. He swore blind he'd handed Mrs Liang a twenty-pound note and only received change from a tenner. The uniforms who attended the Jade Gardens thought the man was too drunk to know what he'd handed Mrs Liang. She thought he was trying to avoid telling his wife how much he'd spent on booze on his night out."

"That's it?" asked Grace. "I don't spend much time in town late at night, but I thought fast-food outlets were a trouble magnet."

"Not the Jade Gardens," said Lydia. "Although, the police probably don't get called out to deal with minor incidents. A shop owner might suffer five minutes of bother, and everyone goes home. The police wouldn't arrive in time to make a difference. If someone's smashed a door or a window, the owners board it up and phone the insurance company in the morning."

"I suppose the leisure centre has a stellar reputation, too," said Gus.

"A similar rating, guv," said Lydia. "No reports of any fights breaking out in the large sports hall."

"A company with leisure centres across the country picked

up the franchise a couple of years back, guv," said Neil. "That's why we had to speak to Eddie Hyde, the maintenance man. The manager reckoned nobody else was still around when Matt Archer worked there. It's a younger person's game."

"Well, get your files together, and tell DI Chandler you're on your way. Where does she live, anyway?"

"Shrivenham, guv," said Alex. "I shouldn't get lost after the years I spent riding my motorbike in that locality."

"Will it be a problem going back, Alex?" asked Blessing.

"Alex has driven past the spot where he crashed, Blessing," said Lydia. "He'd taken all manner of detours to avoid it in the past. It was important for him to overcome the fear if he wanted to move on."

Alex rang Natasha Chandler and told her they would be with her at three o'clock.

The office fell quiet as everyone worked on the Freeman Files. Gus and Grace were first to finish. She came and sat beside his desk.

"I'm concerned, Gus," she said. "By tomorrow afternoon, we'll have spoken to two of the main people from the Jade Gardens, contacted the leisure centre, and seen both detectives from the original investigation. Where on earth do we go next?"

"Neil and Blessing can arrange to visit Janet Archer," said Gus. "We could ask Danielle Liang to set up a video-call to her parents when we're with her tomorrow morning. Perhaps we could drop back to the Jade Gardens after we've spoken to Dave Arrowsmith."

"There aren't many avenues we haven't explored," said Grace.

"True," said Gus. "There's still time for someone to mention a name we haven't heard before. I'm not going to give up after just three days. Tomorrow afternoon we'll assess what we've learned and, if necessary, devise another plan. The motive must be there, somewhere."

Alex and Lydia left for Shrivenham at two o'clock.

"Bring us good news in the morning," said Grace.

Neil phoned Janet Archer and caught her just as she left the house to pick up Jasmine from school. She agreed to talk to them at ten in the morning.

"Same time as this morning, Blessing," said Neil after he ended the call. "I'll pick you up at Worton Farm."

"Thank you, Neil," said Blessing. "Another five minutes in bed, terrific."

Five o'clock seemed to be a long time coming. Gus knew Grace was right; they were making zero progress and running out of options.

As he followed Grace's Smart car out of the Church Street car park, Gus realised he could have offered to pick her up from the farm in the morning. Then he remembered Alex and Lydia could have information from Natasha Chandler that would come in handy when they spoke to Danielle Liang. If they were staying in Swindon for most of the day, they wouldn't hear about it until this time tomorrow.

Best to stick to what they had agreed, thought Gus. Otherwise, Grace might insist on collecting him from the bungalow the next time they had to make an early start. Blessing would soon learn how a sardine felt in its final resting place. There was no way Gus wanted to share the experience.

When Gus turned through the gateway, Suzie was already home and had parked her Golf under the roses. But then, he remembered it was his turn to cook tonight. Gus wished he'd had time to consider what meal he should prepare.

"Hello, darling," said Suzie. "How was your day?"

"Stalemate," said Gus. "We've found nothing that explains why our victim was killed. Everyone agreed he was a lovely chap, had no enemies, and never deserved what happened to him. How was London Road today?"

"Geoff Mercer has handed me another assignment," said Suzie. "Perhaps we could chat about our different problems and opportunities over a drink? I doubt you're in the mood to conjure up a tasty meal after such a frustrating day. I'll order a pizza while you pour yourself a glass of wine."

"What about you, sweetheart?" asked Gus. "I feel guilty."

"Don't be silly; I'll have my usual soft drink. April will be here before we know it."

Gus did as he was told, opened a bottle of Malbec, and wondered whether they would have identified Matt Archer's killer by April.

Wednesday, 21 November 2018

"A NEW DAY, A FRESH START," said Suzie. She kissed Gus before climbing out of bed. "You can make breakfast this morning since you skipped making dinner."

Gus listened for the shower to start before heading for the kitchen. He first checked the central heating wasn't having a lie-in because the place felt chillier than it had at the weekend. Perhaps he was feeling the cold more because of his age. Suzie didn't appear to be complaining, based on the singing he could hear from the bathroom.

The coffee was ready when Suzie joined him, and there were no complaints about the hot, buttered toast and scrambled eggs.

"Have you given up on the porridge?" she asked as she poured her coffee.

"Not at all, " said Gus. "I'll look for a different product at the weekend. Yesterday's sachet didn't taste as good as whatever variety I enjoyed as a kid."

"Dad tells me nothing ever does," said Suzie. "It must be your tastebuds' equivalent of rose-coloured spectacles."

"I'm sure you're right," said Gus. "I'm off for my shower. Any news from Brett or Clemency?"

"Nothing new," said Suzie. "All systems go for a meal at the Lamb tonight."

Gus disappeared to the bathroom, and they were hurrying to their cars at twenty-five past eight. It was too cold to stand around chatting. Suzie led the way into the lane in her Golf, and soon Gus followed a delivery lorry towards Caen Hill while Suzie drove through town to London Road.

Gus overtook the filthy lorry as they descended into the valley. He wondered where the wholesaler was heading. They must have made an early start from Hounslow; too early to run a hose over the exterior. He'd seen the 'Also available in white' comment scrawled in the grime on a rear door before, but it must have taken some skill to write 'If you can read this, call 999' upside down.

The Mini and Smart car bookends were where they were yesterday morning, so Gus eased the Focus into the middle bay. Neil and Blessing could take his spot when they returned from Shrivenham. As he waited for the lift, he wondered whether Janet Archer had started work again if she was available this morning.

"Morning, guv," said Lydia when Gus emerged through the lift doors.

"I bet you were grateful the gritters were out last night, Gus," said Grace. "The car park downstairs wasn't as tricky as the track from the Ferris's farm to the main road. I thought I would end up in the field at one point."

"I didn't notice, Grace," said Gus. "Too many random thoughts cluttering my mind. I'll remember to concentrate when I drive us to Haydon Wick."

"Are you ready for our debrief, guv?" asked Alex.

"I'm all ears, Alex," said Gus. "Keep it short. We must leave in fifteen minutes to reach the Jade Garden by ten."

"We won't tell you about Natasha's beautiful baby then, guv," said Lydia.

"Has DI Chandler decided whether she's returning to work?" asked Gus.

"Yes, guv," said Alex. "Gablecross will see her again in two months. I'd already told her which case we were interested in, so we got straight into it—the details on who arrived at the murder scene at Blades Farm and when were accurate. DI Chandler and her boss arrived at five to eight. The police surgeon confirmed they were dealing with a murder. Matt Archer had been struck repeatedly about the head with a blunt instrument. Later that morning, they visited Janet Archer. That was a couple of hours after uniformed officers notified her of her husband's death. When they arrived, they found PCSO Beverley Coulson had stayed with Mrs Archer and her daughter. Gablecross had told the PCSO before she left the station that as they were short-handed, she should fulfil the role of Family Liaison Officer."

"Had she done anything like that before?" asked Grace.

"No, ma'am," said Alex. "Dave Arrowsmith spoke with

Mrs Archer while Natasha spoke with the PCSO in the hall-way. Nothing had been said to the uniforms to raise any suspicions that Janet Archer had anything to do with her husband's death. Beverley Coulson said Janet was devas-tated by the news. She couldn't accept her husband wasn't going to walk through the front door at any minute. Natasha ensured Beverley knew the right things to say and do until a more qualified person could attend."

"What happened in the next seventy-two hours?" asked Gus.

"They were awaiting forensics and the autopsy, guv," said Lydia. "The search for a weapon had come up empty, and the killer hadn't left behind any obvious evidence. So Arrowsmith and Chandler interviewed the Liang family and their staff early Saturday evening without finding any worthwhile leads. Janet Archer had told them earlier about the vandalism to the Honda Jazz, and they thought there must have been a concerted campaign by an individual with a grudge against Matt or the family."

"Natasha told us they couldn't speak to anyone at the leisure centre until Monday, guv," said Alex. "But when they did, the manager told them he was more than happy with Matt Archer's performance. Matt was a good team player and got on with colleagues and clients. There was nothing to suggest the vandalism was connected to his work at the centre. As for why someone killed him, nobody at the leisure centre had an explanation. It was a mystery."

"So, three days after the murder, Dave Arrowsmith decided to appeal for a witness to the phone call to the Jade Garden," said Gus.

"Natasha said that was his idea, guv," said Alex. "She thought he was clutching at straws, but Saul Brinkworth got in touch. They checked to see if Brinkworth was a frequent flyer who always rang in whenever the police made an appeal. He wasn't, and Natasha told us she believed his statement was genuine. Whether the man Brinkworth saw in the phone box was speaking to Lily Liang was another matter."

"We need to make tracks, Gus," said Grace.

"I'm not hearing anything to suggest Natasha gave you a hot lead for us to follow," said Gus as he grabbed his coat.

"It was interesting to hear her account of everything we've read in the murder file, guv," said Alex. "When you've heard what DCI Arrowsmith has to say, perhaps the accounts won't match. Their recollections of events may vary,"

"An apt turn of phrase, Alex," said Gus. "While we're in Swindon, could you find out how many Mazda 3's were on the roads in Wiltshire in February 2009? I don't recall seeing anything in the files to suggest Gablecross made a serious attempt to locate the driver."

"Always assuming the driver hadn't driven to Haydon Wick from somewhere outside the county, guv," said Lydia.

"Start with Wiltshire, and then expand the search," said Gus. "You'll have plenty of time after you've updated the Freeman files."

Grace and Gus were soon in the lift heading for the Jade Garden.

"Déjà vu, all over again," said Gus as they entered Calne.

"I blame Neil Davis," said Gus. "You would never have made a humorous comment while working at London Road."

"A girl can change," said Grace.

Chapter Eleven

GUS DREW up outside the Jade Garden and parked in the same spot as yesterday.

Grace rang the bell, and although the chimes sounded different from yesterday's, Gus realised why he recognised it.

"Annoying, isn't it?" said Grace.

"Christmas is a month away, and they've got two dozen Christmas songs on a loop."

Adam Liang appeared at the top of the stairs and came down to let them in.

"My sister was taking an important business call," he explained. "Danielle will be free now. Follow me, please."

Gus and Grace followed Adam upstairs. He knocked on the door, opened it, and then ushered in the two detectives.

"Your guests are here, Danielle," he said, disappearing into his office and closing the door.

Danielle Liang was petite, with long dark hair parted in the middle to accentuate her attractive face. Although only a few months separated them, Gus noticed Danielle wore far more make-up than Suzie. Just like her brother, she dressed to impress. The elegant trouser suit and crisp, white blouse fitted where they touched. Gus wondered why Michael Liang struggled to find a suitable husband for his daughter. Perhaps he didn't consider it essential.

"Welcome," said Danielle. "Please be seated."

"Your brother will have explained why we're here, Ms Liang," said Grace. "No doubt he told you what we discussed yesterday after you returned from your meetings in London."

"Adam filled me in just now," said Danielle. "I stayed in London overnight and drove back to Swindon this morning."

"A tiring trip," said Gus. "I trust your visit was successful?"

"The outcome will be mutually beneficial to both our businesses," said Danielle. "What do you wish to ask me?"

"How well did you know Matthew Archer?" asked Gus.

"I met him and his wife when they first visited our restaurant," said Danielle. "I was seventeen and had just moved from working in the kitchens to being face-to-face with the public. They were very polite and forgave my many minor mistakes."

"Several years later, Matt came to work here," said Gus.

"Adam and I were teamed together for the first time in the restaurant. I'd seen my parents trying to compose an advert for a delivery driver and knew their English would let them down. So I offered to help. Matt and Janet came in for a meal that night, and I was working on the advert at the desk when Matt came to settle the bill. I showed him the letter and asked what he thought. He said he'd be interested."

"Why did your parents need to compose an advert?" asked Gus.

"When they arrived from Hong Kong, they searched for other Chinese families living in Swindon to source waiting and kitchen staff," said Danielle. "Things have changed, and people were starting to point fingers."

"You're not legally required to advertise a job, but it's a good idea to do so," said Grace. "Advertising a job means you're less likely to break the law by discriminating, even if you didn't intend to."

"Quite," said Danielle.

"Did your father give Matt the job to deflect any accusation of discrimination?" asked Gus.

"You would need to ask my father," said Danielle. "I think he made his choice because he liked Matt and Janet and trusted them."

"Can you tell us what you remember of the night Matt was killed," asked Gus.

"I arrived for work just before we opened," said Danielle. "I was running late, as usual. Adam was climbing the walls to get everything ready for the first customers. Once we were underway, things ran smoothly. We can see through the window that separates the restaurant from the takeaway section, but there was no sign of trouble. Just people entering and leaving with their Jade Garden carrier bags. I spotted Matt once, at about half-past eight. He was leaving with a batch of deliveries. I watched his Honda Jazz drive away towards Moredon. After that, we were too busy in the restaurant to see, or hear, anything else."

"What happened at around ten o'clock?" asked Grace.

"My father was getting agitated," said Danielle. "We were used to it. He'd be fine for hours, even days, and then he'd explode. He worked so hard in the kitchen, and once in a while, the number of takeaways would accumulate, and he'd start yelling about our reputation. Twenty-five years and you idiots risk ruining it in minutes. That was his usual rant. Nobody in the restaurant would have understood him unless they spoke Cantonese."

"He blew up at ten o'clock," said Gus. "That was when Adam had to leave you to run the restaurant alone."

"I wasn't alone, I had a full complement of staff, and the restaurant side was slowing down. It was a logical decision."

"After the last of your customers left, did you speak to your mother?" asked Gus.

"Yes. Just after eleven," said Danielle. "Adam hadn't returned to the restaurant, and after I said goodnight to my staff, I joined my mother to see if she needed a hand."

"What did she tell you?" asked Grace.

"She said Adam had gone home. Because they wanted to clear the backlog, Matt had taken an order to the other side of Bremhill Bridge, and as Adam had delivered to all of the addresses in the past, he agreed to handle the remaining local ones."

"What happened next?" asked Gus.

"We cleared the stragglers desperate for food and tidied the takeaway section. My father was almost ready to leave. I asked my mother how we came to have an order from so far away, and she shrugged and said we weren't in a position to turn away custom. The recession had hit many local businesses. I drove home, arriving perhaps two minutes ahead of my parents. Adam was already indoors, watching TV with a cold beer. We had no idea what had happened a few miles away. On Saturday afternoon, two uniformed police officers came to the restaurant at five o'clock to notify my parents. My mother phoned us at home, and Adam and I came for a family conference. My father wanted to keep the takeaway service running but close the restaurant. My mother phoned customers who had booked a meal, and I helped her with the takeaways while Adam delivered. We got through it, somehow, but it didn't feel right. Matt was one of us. We should have closed altogether out of respect. We were quieter than usual during the following week, too. I think people stayed away because they didn't know what to say. Do you know what I mean? I remember spending ten minutes chatting with my mother one evening, hoping someone would come through the door or phone for a takeaway."

"When was this, and what did you chat about?" asked Gus.

"Maybe Thursday evening, which is often the quietest night of the week. The detectives working on the case had been backwards and forwards daily, asking questions. Then, that afternoon, they told my mother someone had seen a man in a phone box. It was the same time she logged the call she believed had come from Blades Farm. I asked her what he sounded like. Did he sound threatening? She told me not to be silly, how could she tell whether the man was a killer, just from his voice? He ordered chicken curry, rice, and spring rolls; hardly an order that would stand out from a million others she'd received over the years."

"He was specific about what time the delivery should be made," said Gus. "Ten-thirty, on the dot. Plus, he needed to give her accurate directions for an unfamiliar address. That suggests a longer conversation than some."

"I thought he must have been a local," said Danielle. "But my mother said the man spoke with an accent."

Gus and Grace shared a glance. The murder file never mentioned anything about how the man spoke. All they had was a description of the caller from Saul Brinkworth.

"Did your mother tell the detectives what sort of accent the caller had?" asked Grace.

"I don't think so," said Danielle. "I doubt she could put a name to a regional dialect. She just knew he talked differently to the vast majority of our customers. I suppose he could have been a foreigner who had lived in Swindon long enough to know his way around."

"If we wanted to speak to your parents later today, could you set up a video call?" asked Gus. "We might get our colleagues to provide examples for your mother to listen to."

"If you think it could be important, of course," said Danielle. "I'm happy to call them. What time will you be back?"

"We could return by two o'clock," said Grace. "The tricky part is whether we can put something together between now and then."

"Did you have any further questions?" asked Danielle.

"We understand your parents retired three years ago," said Gus. "Did your mother's health play a big part in that decision?"

"Both my parents had worked long hours for three decades building the business from scratch," said Danielle. "My mother was tired, and my father reluctantly agreed to hand over the reins to Adam and me. He would have kept going until he dropped dead in the kitchen. They are both in their seventies now, but their age and health weren't the only reasons for retiring when they did. The change in people's eating habits, competition, inflation, not being able to keep up with the times, all those things meant our business was in decline. Many other families have been in a similar position. Restaurant numbers fell by three percent in the UK last year, meaning twenty businesses closed each week. To me, these numbers weren't surprising. In addition, we've had to deal with harmful, stereotypical headlines in the media and accusations of serious health warnings associated with Chinese food."

"Did the local press carry these headlines?" asked Grace. "Were you given the right to reply?"

"The local press doesn't carry the same weight or breadth offered by online social media," said Danielle. "We've been here for thirty years, but the abuse can be worse now than when my parents first arrived."

"I can appreciate your parents were puzzled by that reaction after everything they'd contributed to the community," said Gus. "No wonder they thought it time to give up. It didn't deter you and Adam from picking up from where they left off, though?"

"Not at all," said Danielle. "We were savvy enough to appreciate the need for a radical change. The odds are stacked against independent family-run businesses. My parents were very traditional and didn't understand how fast the world was changing. Chinese people of their generation have naturally been cautious and superstitious. Adam convinced me a drop in the number of outlets didn't mean demand was dropping. Chinese food was still the nation's favourite takeaway, but times had changed, and so had people's appetites. The rise of food ordering apps meant smaller, independent businesses like ours were in danger of being left behind if we were stuck in the past."

"So, since 2015, you've adapted to be able to compete with the likes of Deliveroo and Just Eat," said Grace.

"That's right. We had to because our parents didn't understand online ordering systems, websites, and social media. They didn't want any part of it," said Danielle. "When they opened the Jade Garden, Chinese food was new and exotic to Swindon people. As soon as we took control, we had to introduce something new to stay relevant and face the challenge of more competition than ever before."

"You told us the business was in decline," said Gus. "When did you become aware of that?"

"My father kept a tight grip on everything related to the business," said Danielle. "I don't think my mother was aware of how dangerous our position had become. Adam and I were told to remember our place. He promised to leave the Jade Garden in a healthy financial position when he retired. It wasn't something we needed to worry about. He reminded us at the start of 2014 that we'd weathered the effects of the recession in 2009. He said he'd done what was necessary then and would do so again."

"He didn't go into detail, I suppose?" asked Gus.

"Never," said Danielle. "Adam and I knew better than to question his decisions or to argue with him. But, if his mind was made up, there was no dissuading him. He was convinced he knew what was best for the Jade Garden and the family."

"I think we're beginning to understand how important the business was to your parents," said Grace.

"You made it sound like your father considered the restaurant first and his family second," said Gus.

"Perhaps that was harsh," said Danielle. "It was more that the family's life was totally committed to the business. Adam and I had no career options outside this building. We were destined to take over whenever they stepped aside."

"If Adam marries and has children, will he automatically expect them to continue your father's legacy?" asked Grace. "Or perhaps your children would follow in your footsteps?"

"I think it would be naïve to expect the Jade Garden to be around that long," said Danielle.

Gus hoped Grace wouldn't continue this line of questioning. It wasn't leading to the key to Matt Archer's murder. He wondered whether something else Danielle had mentioned was where they should be looking.

"Business seems good at present," said Grace. "Your comment about your trip to London suggested things remain positive."

"I've had to remodel our offering over the last two years," said Danielle. "Our menu was considered old-fashioned and out of touch with what today's younger consumers were looking for in a dining experience. There's been a significant shift towards healthy eating, and more people are embracing a plant-based lifestyle. That was alien to my father's philosophy. He wasn't keen to entertain vegetarian, let alone vegan dishes on our menu. I've researched the new style of Indian restaurants for inspiration in the past twelve months. Chinese takeaway has to be much more than chicken curry or sweet and sour pork balls. Regional Chinese food like Sichuan, Xi'an and Hunan cuisine is on our menu today, not just Cantonese food. Our customers have far more choice and variety since our parents retired. My father would have been too wary of discovering whether diversification could be a good thing. He relied on a handful of wholesalers who came from the same part of Hong Kong as he did. It stifled change."

"I think we've covered everything we need for now," said Gus. "We have an appointment at Gablecross Police Station next. Once we've finished, we'll call and let you know when we'll return. It might be a little later than two o'clock, depending on what our colleagues can provide. Will you have problems getting things ready for us to speak to your parents?"

"I'll call them as soon as you leave," said Danielle. "I have enough time to get my mother to put down her paint-brush and my father to stop watching the racing for ten minutes. I'll see you out."

Gus and Grace followed Danielle Liang downstairs. She held the door open for them.

"Do you want Adam to be present later?" she asked.

"If it's convenient," said Gus.

"I realise this video call could be important," said Danielle, "but our kitchen staff will arrive at four, ready to start preparations for this evening. Adam will want to relay the good news I brought back from my meetings yesterday."

"That's fine," said Gus. "It's your parents we wish to speak to."

Danielle closed the door behind them and went upstairs to her office.

"What did you make of that, Grace?" asked Gus as they headed for Gablecross.

"Danielle had a moment, just like Adam, where she regaled us with what a great job the family had done in difficult circumstances at the Jade Garden," said Grace. "I'm always afraid I'll concentrate on those stories and miss a throwaway comment which would bring our case to a rapid conclusion."

"Funny," said Gus. "I was thinking the same thing. I haven't pinned it down yet, but Danielle pointed us in the right direction, I'm sure of it."

"You don't think she was involved?" asked Grace.

"Heavens, no," said Gus. "Neither of the children was involved in Matt Archer's murder. Phone Alex and set the ball rolling on those regional accents. Perhaps Lydia can chat with Divya Yadav for help."

Grace phoned the Old Police Station office and passed on Gus's request. Alex hadn't heard from Neil and Blessing yet. They were on their way back from Janet Archer's house.

Fifteen minutes later, Gus started the search for a vacant space in the visitor's car park at Gablecross. He'd struggled with this problem before, and noon was peak time.

"DCI Arrowsmith will still be in his office, Gus," said Grace. "Don't panic. I'm sure he won't mind a short delay."

"We haven't got through Reception yet," growled Gus.

Despite Gus's concerns, they soon stood outside the Detective Chief Inspector's office. The door was already open, and Dave Arrowsmith stood up to greet them.

"Gus Freeman," he said. "You haven't damaged your reputation since you returned to work; it's still epic. So who do we have here?"

"DI Grace Packenham, Sir," said Grace.

"How do you do it, Gus?" said Dave Arrowsmith. "Another superstar from London Road on your team."

"Another one?" asked Gus.

"Lydia Logan Barre," said the DCI. "I'm hearing great things about that young lady too."

Gus wondered whether Lydia would still be in the office when they returned. Could the week get any worse?

"How can I help you?" asked Dave Arrowsmith. "DS Hardy mentioned the Archer murder back in 2009. Good to hear Alex is doing well. I remember the day he had his accident. Few officers who attended the scene thought he'd ever walk again."

"Alex is a valuable member of the Crime Review Team, Sir," said Grace. "Gus has done a superb job in the short time he's been with us. However, the Matt Archer case has proved difficult. If only we could pin down a motive. What can you tell us about how you approached the case?"

"Have you spoken to Natasha Chandler?" asked Dave Arrowsmith.

"Our colleagues were with her yesterday afternoon," said Gus.

"I still wonder if we missed something simple," said the DCI. "One thing Natasha and I were known for was conducting a thorough, systematic investigation. We'd worked together on several tricky cases in the past, so it wasn't our first rodeo. You know where the murder took place. Late at night, Matt Archer was in the middle of nowhere, with the closest building half a mile away. His boss had just told him the takeaway order was someone's idea of a joke. She told him to go home, but he didn't get the chance to get back in the car. Whoever had made that call was hiding behind a bush, lying in wait. They hit him over the head, dragged him along the lane, finished the job, and dumped his body in a ditch."

"Forensics and the autopsy didn't yield any significant clues," said Gus. "So you appealed for a witness."

"Natasha thought we should have kept searching for a weapon and interviewed more people who came into contact with the victim. We would have spent weeks chasing down customers who ordered a takeaway that Archer delivered or finding overweight members at the leisure centre who took exception to his weight reduction targets. But, no, my hunch was that the person who called the restaurant with the bogus order was connected to the murder. I still believe that to this day. I suppose you're going to tell me I'm wrong."

"You were probably on the button," said Gus. "The

problem you had was you couldn't prove whether the only witness to answer your appeal was watching the right bloke. Saul Brinkworth just saw a man in a phone box at a time that tallied with what Lily Liang had recorded. When did you start to doubt it was the right phone call?"

"After I'd checked the Mazda," said Dave Arrowsmith. "There were fifty thousand of the little devils sold in Europe the previous year, and the model had been around since the turn of the century. We couldn't guarantee the driver was from Swindon, and even if he was, there were hundreds of owners to chase down and eliminate. If he came from further afield, the number grew like crazy. We would still be interviewing drivers today."

"I don't recall anything in the murder file about trying to trace the caller through the Mazda, Sir," said Grace.

"Odd scraps of files can get lost in the evidence store," said the DCI. "We moved our records to another facility a few years ago because we ran out of space. I'd be surprised if any historical cold case still includes everything from the investigation in its boxes. If we had found CCTV evidence from Archer's final journey to show him being followed by a Mazda 3, we would have kept going, I can assure you. However, it felt like a dead end, so I switched focus."

"I don't recall Natasha Chandler telling us where you looked next, Sir," said Grace. "However, it would be useful if you could take us through your visit to Janet Archer's house and your visit on Monday to speak to the leisure centre manager."

Dave Arrowsmith took a minute to find the relevant notebook in one of his filing cabinets. His account of both meetings matched that of Natasha Chandler.

Gus decided to change their approach.

"Did you ever ask Lily Liang what the caller said?" he asked.

Arrowsmith was out of his chair again, hunting for a notebook that would jog his memory.

"Mrs Liang told me she recorded the time, the order details, the address, and how to get there. She was eager to point out that the man had been particular about when the meal was to be delivered."

"What did he sound like?" asked Gus.

"What do you mean?" asked Arrowsmith. "What difference would it have made?

"If you had known the caller didn't sound like John Payne or one of his sons, it should have raised a red flag. Why would someone order a delivery to Blades Farm at ten-thirty when they didn't live there?"

"I thought of that," said Arrowsmith. "Not at the time, but later, when I was working on the case alone. Mrs Liang kept reminding us they had never had calls from the farm, and it was barely inside the radius to which they delivered. If you wanted Matt Archer to be in a specific place at a certain time to kill him, you wouldn't send him close to your home, would you? So I thought the killer was someone from Swindon who moved Archer as far from town as possible. Either that or someone who lived a distance away had brought him to an isolated spot closer to where they operated without giving any clues to their identity. Archer was a chess piece on a board they moved to suit their plan. Whoever was behind it put a lot of thought into it and left us scratching our heads."

"Did you share any of this with anyone?" asked Gus.

"Not really," said Arrowsmith. "I'd been under pressure to close the case, as usual. However, my ACC was keen to move Natasha to another case with a greater chance of a result. So what did *she* say?"

"You both give a similar account of how the case went," said Gus. "We're returning to the Jade Garden later to speak to Michael and Lily Laing. They're living in Arles, in the south of France, now they've retired. We'd like to see whether Mrs Liang can pinpoint the accent of the man who left the takeaway order."

"How will that help?" asked Arrowsmith. "The caller could have lived in Haydon Wick or near Purton for years."

"It will reduce the number of doors we need to knock on," said Gus.

"There was another thought that crossed my mind at the time," said Arrowsmith. "What if the man making the phone call wasn't the killer, but they were working together?"

"You mean, Saul Brinkworth witnessed a man making the takeaway order, but that was his part in the process done with," said Gus.

"He did have a colleague," said Grace.

"Why not?" asked Arrowsmith. "Brinkworth couldn't see whether anyone else was in the Mazda. A colleague makes as much sense as any other scenario we considered. But, unfortunately, we couldn't get a fix on the motive. Who benefitted from the murder? Nobody, as far as we could tell."

"Did you two ever work together after that case?" asked Gus.

"Not on a murder case, Gus," said Arrowsmith. "No big surprise. Wiltshire isn't the murder capital of the UK."

"You've both moved up the ladder since then," said Gus.

"I miss being at the sharp end," said the DCI. "When you're attending meeting after meeting, it can be a bind."

He looked at his watch.

"Almost time for your next meeting, Sir?" asked Grace.

"Yes, I shall have to love you and leave you. Have you got everything you need from me?"

"I don't think there's anything you can add that will help," said Gus.

"I hope you find the killer, Gus," said the DCI. "But I haven't got any suggestions where you might like to look."

Gus and Grace made their way back through the rabbit warren to the visitor's car park.

"I've heard a rumour that some senior officers get promoted to a level where they can't do any harm, Gus," said Grace.

"It's not a rumour, Grace," said Gus. "It's a necessity."

Chapter Twelve

GUS PAUSED in the Gablecross visitor's car park before driving back to Haydon Wick.

"Call the office, Grace, please," he said. "Check what progress they've made. How will they get the information to us, anyway?"

"The appliance of science, Gus," said Grace. "Leave it to me."

While Grace made the call, Gus went through everything they'd learned today. It was tough trying to separate the real fish from the red herrings.

"Between them, Divya, Lydia, and Alex have compiled a selection of forty regional accents," said Grace after she ended the call. "Then they added another forty male voices using a foreign accent where the core population is white."

"Do you think Lily Liang will last the course?" asked Gus. "It will take ages to listen to that many voices over and over. We've only got until the kitchen staff arrive for work."

"Do we believe Dave Arrowsmith was right?" asked Grace. "Could two people have been involved?"

"It's possible," said Gus.

"Why would two people want to kill Matt Archer?" asked Grace. "Nobody had a grudge against him. If more than one person was involved, does that mean it wasn't personal?"

"That's it, Grace," said Gus slapping the steering wheel. "Danielle Liang did give us the identity of the missing piece of the jigsaw. I thought she had but couldn't separate the wheat from the chaff."

"What now?" asked Grace. "Are you going to let me in on the secret?"

Gus described a possible scenario to Grace as they drove from Gablecross to the Jade Garden. As they left the A419 to join Thamesdown Drive, she was convinced Gus was on the right track. Her phone buzzed.

"The team have sent us everything we need for Lily Liang," she said. "Did you want to speak to Michael Liang first?"

"If Danielle was right about the way he kept his cards very close to his chest, I don't believe we'll learn anything. We must first put a few more pieces into place to show all four family members we're close to the truth."

Gus had to park further along the street when they reached the Jade Garden. The Mercedes with the 2018 plate was probably Adam Liang's executive wheels. The festive chimes brought Danielle Liang to the front door.

"Welcome back," she said. "I hope your meeting went well."

She led them upstairs and showed them into Adam's office.

"We've spoken to our parents, who will answer your questions as best they can," said Danielle. "However, their English has never been great, so they might switch to

Cantonese to clarify a point. Adam will be able to assist you."

Grace could see Michael and Lily Liang on the large screen high on the office wall. They sat side-by-side, looking relaxed.

Gus was unhappy about the need for a translator. Perhaps they should have asked Divya Yadav to locate one and send them here.

"Who do you wish to speak with first, Mr Freeman?" asked Adam. "I'll introduce you, and you can take it from there. Then, as Danielle said, I'll step in if needed."

"We'll start with your father, please," said Gus.

Adam spoke rapidly with his father, who sat quietly beside his wife.

"He's ready, Mr Freeman," said Adam.

"Good afternoon, Mr Liang," said Gus. "Can you tell me which wholesalers you used when you set up your business? Were they local, or did you use a well-established firm already supplying Chinese restaurants in several cities and large towns?"

Grace noticed a slight tension in Michael Liang's demeanour. He rubbed his hands together before replying.

"Nobody local," he said. "I had contact in London. We knew him in Hong Kong."

That tied in with what Danielle had told them.

"Did you have a good relationship with that company?" asked Gus.

"Good," said Michael. "Then, not good. Prices of everything had risen, you understand?"

"So you shopped around for a better deal," said Gus. "That must have been hard for you if the owner was an old friend."

"Business is business, Mr Freeman," said Michael.

"Did you need to keep moving from wholesaler to wholesaler after that to keep your business profitable?" asked Gus.

Michael Liang shook his head.

"We still use the same people today," said Danielle.

"When did you make that change, Mr Liang?" asked Gus.

"Long time ago," said Michael. "I can't remember."

Michael Liang spoke to Adam in Cantonese.

"My father can't understand how this is relevant, Mr Freeman," said Adam. "Danielle told us you wanted my mother to see if she recognised how the man spoke on the phone."

Michael Liang looked ready to move away from his wife's side.

"Tell your father we'll return to that question if we need to," said Gus. "Let's see what your mother can remember."

Grace had prepared the soundtrack the team had provided. Lily Liang was leaning forward in her seat.

"Is your mother hard of hearing, Danielle?" she whispered.

"A little, but she should be wearing her hearing aid."

Danielle spoke to her mother, and Lily Liang fussed with the device behind her right ear. Her husband looked more agitated than before.

"Try it now," said Danielle.

"Do any of these men sound like the man who ordered the takeaway, Mrs Liang?" asked Grace.

Everyone in the office, and the elderly couple in Arles, sat silently as the various regional accents filled the room. Gus watched the parents on the screen while Grace kept an eye on the children. They'd agreed on that approach as they had travelled along Thamesdown Drive.

Lily Liang and her daughter reacted at the same time.

"He sounded like that," said Lily. "I'm sure."

She was more animated than at any time since they arrived in the office.

"I did good, yes?" she asked, beaming from ear to ear.

"Very good, Mrs Liang," said Grace. However, Gus noticed Michael Liang didn't share his wife's excitement.

"The man had a Cockney accent, so what?" said Adam Liang. "My mother is sixty-seven. After nine years, how can she be relied on to pick the right voice?"

"Not all Londoners are Cockneys, Mr Liang," said Grace. "We classify that accent as Estuary English or Received Pronunciation. Unfortunately, we've got other people to interview now, but we'll be back soon."

"Thank your parents for their cooperation," said Gus. "It's been most insightful."

Grace gathered her things and followed Gus out of the office. Michael Liang was talking to his son. It would have been good to know what they were saying, but nothing they had heard this afternoon weakened Gus's version of what had happened nine years ago.

Danielle was two steps behind them on the stairs. She didn't seem as confident and assured as she had this morning.

"Do you think you will find Matt Archer's killer now, Mr Freeman?" she asked.

"We're a step closer, Ms Liang," said Gus.

When they reached the Focus, Grace looked back towards the Jade Garden. Danielle Liang was still staring at them through the open doorway.

"That put the cat amongst the pigeons, didn't it?" she said as she sat beside Gus.

"What did you spot?" asked Gus. "I was concentrating

on the parents. Lily almost jumped out of her seat, and Michael looked like the favourite he'd backed had pulled up lame."

"Adam kept his cool, but Danielle reacted a split second after her mother," said Grace.

"We know Danielle didn't hear the man on the telephone nine years ago," said Gus, "and the voice she heard on the recording could have been anyone. So, why do you think it produced such a response?"

"I'm not sure, but no doubt you can tell me," said Grace.

"The marks had faded a little this afternoon," said Gus.

Grace waited for Gus to carry on, but as the silence lengthened, she realised she would have to wait.

They arrived in the Church Street car park at a few minutes to four. Gus parked beside Neil's car, and he and Grace waited for the lift.

"I can't wait to hear what Neil and Blessing can offer," he said. "Tomorrow morning, we'll have that debrief we spoke about, and, with a following wind, we'll see the finishing line."

When they arrived in the office, Blessing was returning from the restroom with three coffees.

"Almost perfect timing," said Gus. "Could you do the honours, Blessing? Unfortunately, we weren't offered refreshments by DCI Arrowsmith or the Jade Garden."

"On my way, guv," said Blessing.

"I sense a positive vibe, guv," said Lydia. "Did Lily Liang identify her mystery caller?"

"She narrowed it down to a Londoner in his late twenties, early thirties back in 2009," said Grace. "Gus has a theory but won't reveal all the cards he's holding."

"Nothing new there, ma'am," said Neil. "Perhaps we can help?"

"What did you learn from your conversation with Janet Archer, Neil?" asked Gus.

Blessing was returning from the restroom with a black coffee and Grace's drink.

"She's never remarried, guv," she said. "Jasmine is sixteen now and a handful, like most teenagers. They moved from their old address to a two-bedroomed bungalow a fifteen-minute drive away, near South Marston. Jasmine was at school today, and Janet works from home a couple of days a week."

"I thought she must have needed to go back to work after Matt's death," said Gus.

"Janet told us she had various jobs in the first five years, guv," said Neil. "She couldn't settle to anything."

"She told us she ate at the Jade Garden with Jasmine from time to time, guv," said Blessing. "I thought that would be tough for both of them, but Janet said she and Matt had always enjoyed their meals there."

"What has Janet been doing in the past four years, Neil?" asked Grace.

"She's worked for the Food Standards Authority, guv," said Neil. "It's an interesting story. Janet was between jobs and had just left the Post Office on Moredon Road. She could see two large lorries outside the Jade Garden. An argument was attracting the attention of a few passers-by on her side of the street, and Janet hurried to join them. In one lorry, an elderly Chinese man sat in the passenger seat while two white men were shouting at the Chinese driver."

"Two firms of wholesalers arriving at the same time?" said Gus. "Did that seem fishy to Janet Archer?"

Neil did a double take.

"I give up," he said. "Do you want to tell me what Janet Archer said, guv, or shall I continue reading from my notebook?"

"Sorry, Neil," said Gus. "I apologise for stealing your thunder."

"Janet told us the first lorry, the one with the Chinese writing on the side, then drove away. The other two guys started unloading pallets from the back of their vehicle and took them into the restaurant through the side door."

"Did Janet notice where these firms were located?" asked Gus.

"The Chinese lorry came from Park Royal, guv," said Neil.

"She told us the other one was filthy and came from Hounslow," said Blessing.

"And so the mist clears," said Gus.

"Good," said Grace. "It's alright for some."

"Please continue, Neil," said Gus.

"We need to tell you something else first, guv," said Blessing. "As you can imagine, Janet had agonised over why her husband had been killed ever since the police arrived to notify her. Something about that argument outside of the Jade Garden started her thinking. So, she applied for jobs with food safety and quality, thinking it could lead her to make sense of why two wholesalers might be competing for business with the same family-owned restaurant and takeaway."

"What did she discover?" asked Grace.

"That nearly half the fish you tuck into from a food outlet like the Jade Garden isn't what's advertised," said Neil.

"The people she works with now can use DNA testing to identify fish," said Blessing. "The average customer only has their taste buds, and fish is often presented in fillet form. It's a convenient way to buy fish, but you need to be an expert to tell which fish it is after someone removes the skin, scales, fins, head, and tail."

"Could you be sure it's cod when broken up, battered, breadcrumbed, or suspended in sauce?" asked Grace. "You'd have to rely on the retailer or the restaurant owner."

"If it tastes like fish when I eat it, why does it matter?" asked Alex. "As long as it's not an endangered species or in danger of being over-fished."

"Prices," said Gus. "Grace mentioned cod, but I bet more often than not, the customer has eaten haddock."

"Exactly, guv," said Neil. "Janet Archer told us it's easier to disguise fish on the plate in a restaurant, and there's less red tape than in a supermarket or a fishmonger. The last time she took Jasmine to the Jade Garden for a meal, she noticed a few menu items containing high-end ingredients that were still competitively priced. Janet suspected the restaurant was sourcing cheaper substitutions to improve their profits."

"If it looks too good to be true, then it probably is," said Grace.

"With the numbers Janet quoted, there are plenty of other outlets doing the same thing as the Jade Garden," said Lydia. "Why should this have anything to do with Matt Archer's murder?"

"A white man in his late twenties or early thirties made a phone call to the restaurant," said Gus. "Or he did if Saul Brinkworth saw the man speaking to Lily Liang. This afternoon, Lily identified that voice as coming from the Greater

London area. Michael Liang had stuck with the same wholesalers for his produce for twenty years. But then, something caused him to switch from the company belonging to an old friend from Hong Kong to a cheaper firm. When I asked him to confirm when that was, he was evasive. Neither Adam nor Danielle jumped in to fill in the blanks."

"What about the argument Janet witnessed, guv?" asked Alex. "That was only four years ago."

"Based on the elderly Chinese man in the passenger seat, I'd bet that was Michael's friend from Hong Kong, and maybe his son, hoping to regain a customer," said Gus. "The Hounslow crew sent them packing in what sounds an aggressive manner. But, you see, Danielle Liang told us this morning that Michael said he'd done what was necessary to weather the effects of the recession in 2009 and would do so again. I'm positive Danielle is cut from the same cloth as her father."

"So," said Alex. "You think this Hounslow outfit started targeting family-owned restaurants in southern England a decade ago? They used strong-arm tactics to wrestle business out of the hands of the traditional wholesalers who'd moved here from Hong Kong forty or fifty years earlier."

"The bullying tactic doesn't sound far-fetched, guv," said Lydia. "But why did they need to murder Matt Archer?"

"To send that message we discussed earlier," said Gus. "The amount of money to be made from one fish and chip supper using cheaper ingredients is small. Multiply that by the number of outlets and the meals they serve, and the wholesaler grabbing the lion's share of the business would be rolling in it. Even if they allowed the clients a modest margin."

"The fast-food industry is worth five billion pounds a year in this country," said Blessing. "Don't look at me like that. I just Googled it."

"How do you want to play it, Gus?" asked Grace.

"Danielle met with their wholesalers yesterday," he said. "In the morning, we'll return to the Jade Garden to ask for the names of the people she deals with."

"What did I miss, Gus?" asked Grace.

"When we first read through the murder file, I noticed Danielle and Suzie were almost the same age," said Gus. "This morning, when we met her, I was struck by her attractiveness but also surprised at how much make-up she used. Danielle was turned away from you; you might have missed it, but the high-collared blouse she wore with her trouser suit shifted to reveal bite marks on her neck."

"Danielle told us she stayed in London overnight," said Grace. "We don't know whether she has a lover. Although… now I think about it."

"What was her reaction to the voice she heard this afternoon?" asked Blessing.

"Fearful," said Grace.

"Perhaps that heavy make-up was disguising bruises," said Alex.

"You said you believed Danielle Liang was cut from the same cloth as her father, guv," said Lydia. "If she had to sleep with one of those thugs from the wholesalers to keep the Jade Garden from going under, she would."

"If she's getting battered, it doesn't sound as if she's been given a choice," said Neil.

"I wonder how many places have been coerced into making this firm their sole supplier," asked Lydia.

"I passed one of their lorries on my way into the office this morning," said Gus. "We'll update our files and add the final pieces to the jigsaw in the morning. Just one thing before we start. Can one of you two jokers pick up a money box? I think a fine of a pound every time one of you makes a fish-related pun will suffice, don't you?"

"Got it, guv," said Neil and Lydia.

Epilogue

Thursday, 22 November 2018

"ONCE MORE INTO THE BREECH, GUS," said Suzie as they braved the elements and slipped and skidded to their cars.

"Drive carefully," said Gus. "I know it's too soon for the baby on board sign in the rear window, but please proceed with caution."

"Ever the police officer," said Suzie, blowing him a kiss across the frosted roof of her Golf.

Once they'd reached the main road, conditions improved, thanks to the trusty gritters. Gus dispensed with flashing his lights this morning and concentrated on keeping his distance from the car in front. He prayed the vehicle behind was doing the same.

Gus parked below the Old Police Station office at nine o'clock. Everyone else was upstairs, which was gratifying. There was plenty to do if they were to join the dots between the facts they had and the theories they discussed yesterday afternoon.

When he exited the lift, the others were hard at work. Nobody had had time to finish updating their files before going home yesterday. Gus also needed to put the finishing touches to his contribution, so he set to work.

"We'll do some digging on the wholesalers while you catch up, guv," said Alex at a quarter to ten.

"Good idea," said Gus. "I should be done by ten. It will benefit us to have the answer to our question before we ask Adam and Danielle Liang for names."

"Blessing and I will do the drinks run at ten, guv," said Lydia.

"A hot coffee will be most welcome, Lydia," said Gus.

When everyone was warming their hands around a hot mug, Alex told Gus what they'd found.

"The Hounslow outfit is owned by a character called Gabriel Rollins, guv," said Alex. "He's been in business since 2005 and has a fleet of three dozen lorries supplying the country's southern half. Rollins has a reputation as a ruthless operator, and although the firm has been investigated on several occasions, so far, Rollins has emerged unscathed. However, some of his drivers have been charged with numerous offences, including speeding, dangerous driving, and falsifying tachograph records. Surprise, surprise, a couple of his drivers are ex-cons with records that include threatening behaviour and common assault."

"How old is Rollins?" asked Gus.

"Forty-two, guv," said Alex.

"We need someone who Rollins might regard as his second-in-command," said Gus.

"James Hatch fits that bill, Gus," said Grace, "He calls

himself a Transport Manager, but he's been in and out of trouble since he was ten years old. Hatch is thirty-eight."

"I've identified the Park Royal firm that supplied the Jade Garden for years, guv," said Neil. "Francis Yeoh was the man Janet Archer saw that afternoon. He's the same age as Michael Liang and arrived in the UK three years before him. Frankie Yeoh's son, Steve, is currently running the business. I asked him if he remembered the incident, and he told me Hatch was one of the two men who threatened him and his father."

"I'll call DS Mercer," said Gus. "He can contact his counterpart in the Met and arrange for statements to be taken from the Yeoh family. The sooner we get the local detectives in the picture, the better. They'll soon be bringing Rollins and Hatch in for questioning if we do our jobs properly today."

"Why can't you have the pleasure, guv?" asked Lydia. "You've done all the work."

"It's the way of the world, Lydia," said Gus. "Anyway, this team has cracked the case wide open, not just me. So what do I always say? We solve cases others couldn't and move on. But, while we're lapping up the public's adulation, another Janet Archer is out there yearning to know who murdered her husband. The last detectives handling this case forced Janet Archer to extraordinary lengths to find the answer alone. What would have happened to Jasmine Archer if Rollins or Hatch caught wind of how deep Janet was digging and silenced her?"

"Sorry, guv," said Lydia.

"Time for Grace and me to drive to the Jade Garden," said Gus. "My money's on Rollins making the phone call while Hatch was hunkered down in the passenger seat in the Mazda. Hatch is our killer. What do you think?"

Gus waited for someone to argue with him as he donned his coat. He heard nothing, and Grace joined him by the lift.

"Days like this remind me why I joined up," she said.

They were soon heading for Wootton Bassett as a weak sun slowly thawed the frosted ground on either side of the road. As Gus entered Moredon Road, Grace's mobile phone buzzed. She listened to the message and smiled.

"That was Neil," she said. "Gabriel Rollins owned a Mazda 3 between June 2007 and March 2009."

"Gotcha," said Gus.

They arrived outside the Jade Garden and parked behind Adam Liang's Mercedes. Gus wondered which of the high-end cars on that side of the street belonged to Danielle. Grace rang the doorbell, and they waited.

Adam Liang came downstairs and opened the door.

"You had better come up to my office," he said.

Danielle was waiting for them.

"My father had no choice," she said as soon as Gus and Grace stepped into the room.

"We know about Rollins and Hatch," said Gus. "Steve Yeoh told us everything we needed to know."

"Don't you think it's time for the truth?" asked Grace.

"We had no idea what was going on when Matt Archer was killed," said Adam. "Our father kept us both in the dark, and our mother doesn't know the truth to this day. When he told us he was ready to retire, our father told Danielle and me the whole story. Gabriel Rollins wanted our wholesale business at the end of 2008 and hundreds of other restaurants and takeaways along the M4 corridor. We had been with Francis Yeoh throughout, and despite rising raw material prices, our father was content to stay loyal. He hadn't met Rollins face-to-face but constantly received phone calls badgering him to switch suppliers. Then, in January, Hatch arrived with another man with an ultimatum. Either the Jade Garden joined the dozens of other local places, getting the benefit of lower prices, or we ran the risk of going out of business. My father told Hatch he wouldn't be bullied and sent him packing. Hatch told him he would regret his decision."

"Weeks later, Rollins and Hatch visited Haydon Wick, and the phone call led to Matt Archer's death," said Grace.

Adam nodded.

"Rollins called first thing on Monday," said Danielle. "He asked if the message had been received. Our father told us he stopped trading with Francis Yeoh the same day."

"How did you feel when your father told you what had been going on?" asked Gus.

"As I told you before, Mr Freeman," said Danielle, "we had many changes to make to keep the Jade Garden relevant. We continued to trade with Rollins, and although our margins were squeezed, it wasn't a fight we could ever win."

"Who handled the negotiations with Rollins?" asked Grace.

"There were never any negotiations," said Adam. "I travelled to London, and they told me the details of the following year's deal. If you've spoken with Steve Yeoh, you've already learned Rollins makes his money by substituting high-value ingredients with cheaper and often low-grade items. He retains eighty percent of the benefit that accrues, and we must be thankful we get the balance."

"Danielle, when did you start visiting London instead of Adam?" asked Grace.

"Last year," said Danielle. "Adam told me Hatch had accompanied the driver on our latest delivery. He had a message from Rollins. The economic situation demanded a change in our percentage, which would reduce to fifteen from January 2018. We studied the books and realised it could jeopardise everything we had planned for the Jade Garden. So I offered to go to Rollins and persuade him to retain the status quo."

"Rollins doesn't sound the sort of character who would listen," said Gus. "Not if it meant money from his pocket. Did you discuss your plans with Adam?"

"What do you mean?" asked Adam. "Danielle persuaded Rollins to agree to stick to the original deal, provided we reviewed the situation monthly. This week, he's extended that deal through 2019. That's why we wanted to convey the good news to our staff after Danielle returned from London. It meant we didn't have to consider redundancies, or worse still, face closing the business."

Grace could tell Danielle was close to tears.

"Shall we go to your office, Danielle?" she asked. "I'd like to look through that contract. I'm sure Mr Freeman has further questions for your brother."

Grace saw the relief on Danielle's face. Then, when they were behind closed doors, Danielle told Grace she had known before leaving the Jade Garden for that first meeting with Rollins she would do whatever it took to save the business. Adam had no idea she had agreed to sleep with Rollins, or if he suspected, he'd never mentioned it.

"Mr Freeman noticed the heavy makeup and marks on your neck," said Grace.

"Rollins is a pig," said Danielle. "There was no alternative. Despite the obstacles, Adam and I modernised the business, and I hoped our parents would pass before this came to light."

"I'm afraid that hope has sailed, Danielle," said Grace.

"So your father is still under the assumption you're contin-uing with the same deal forced on him in 2009?"

"Yes," said Danielle. "The shame I have brought on the family will kill him."

"And you're certain Adam is unaware you've been sleeping with Rollins to protect your father's deal?"

Danielle nodded.

"I CAN ACCEPT with your parents having retired to France, they have left you to develop the business as you see fit," said Gus. "You're adamant they aren't aware of what's been going on for the past year or so?"

"No idea whatsoever," said Adam.

"Did you threaten to switch suppliers when Rollins sought to change the percentage split?" asked Gus.

"Rollins reminded me it was my good fortune that Matt Archer had died instead of me. James Hatch could return to Haydon Wick with the next delivery to remind me who was in charge."

"Was that when you decided to let Danielle take your place at the face-to-face meetings?"

"I'm not proud of what I've done," said Adam. "It's just business."

GUS CALLED Geoff Mercer to arrange for uniformed officers to attend. Geoff told Gus that Gabriel Rollins and James Hatch were in custody at Hounslow Central.

Gus and Grace left for the Old Police Station office after Adam, and Danielle Liang were taken away for further questioning.

The door chimes were silent, and a notice on the front

door informed their customers that the Jade Garden was closed until further notice.

"WE'VE GOT the final piece of the jigsaw into place, Gus," said Grace as they drove into town.

"As long as people remember we're responsible for only part of the big picture," said Gus. "Another cold case review is complete, and now two teams of detectives in Hounslow and London Road must gather enough evidence to pass a winnable case to the Crown Prosecution Service. I believe we've given them the tools to do the job."

vinci-books.com/gatheringclouds

Secrets, lies, and a brutal crime.

In the tranquil city of Salisbury, the brutal murder of adventurous couple John Crees and Mandy Howard shatters the peace. As the unsolved case haunts the community, detective Gus Freeman takes on the challenge.

Turn the page for a free preview…

Gathering Clouds: Chapter One

Monday, 26 November 2018

"Will everything be ready for me to leave at eleven?" asked Gus.

"I don't see why not," said Grace. "My work is complete; we've all had long enough to get our contributions together."

"That's us told," said Neil quietly.

"What's the latest from the Met, guv?" asked Alex.

"DS Mercer tells me Rollins and Hatch have been questioned at length, plus several of their drivers," said Gus. "As you can imagine, the prime suspects didn't admit their guilt in the first five minutes. The Yeoh family statements shook Rollins's resolve somewhat when they were introduced into the equation. Given the intimidatory tactics Hatch and his cronies adopted, I don't think he believed any of his clients would ever have the guts to speak out. But, together with what we gathered from the Jade Garden's owners, the Met are confident of a positive result, even if it takes a while."

"Matt Archer was just in the wrong place at the wrong time, guv," said Blessing.

"None of us knows what's around the corner, Blessing," said Gus.

"I wonder what's next for us?" said Lydia.

"More of the same, I hope, Lydia," said Gus. "I hate surprises."

An hour later, Gus left the office to drive to London Road and his lunchtime meeting with Kenneth Truelove, the Chief Constable. Last week's clear-skied, icy weather had been replaced by a misty grey murk that seemed to last all day. Before you knew it, what little light there was had faded, and it was time to draw the curtains for another long night.

The outskirts of town were soon behind him, and there were no annoying holdups in Seend. Barely thirty minutes after leaving the Church Street car park, he arrived at the Wiltshire Police HQ on London Road. Gus began to wonder when he found a parking space not ten yards from the main building. He made his way slowly towards the front door.

"You look weary, Mr Freeman. Did you have a busy weekend?"

Gus looked up. It was Divya Yadav, the team's favourite Hub employee.

"Why are you always so cheerful, Divya?" he asked.

"I'm doing a job I love, married to a wonderful man who had his first weekend off in months. Life is good."

"My weekend was nothing special, Divya, unlike yours," said Gus. "I was in a good mood when I left the office, though, and I bear good tidings for the boss, but somehow I sense my day won't continue in the same vein. I smell trouble."

"There's been no announcement of any kind yet," said Divya, ensuring their conversation wasn't overheard. "But you must be psychic. I was only upstairs on the mezzanine for ten minutes, and it felt like everyone was holding their breath. Very odd. I can't imagine what it could be. There have been rumours, of course, but I tend to set them aside until I receive official confirmation."

"Rumours?" asked Gus.

"The PCC isn't halfway through his four-year stint yet, and in an article in the local newspaper on Friday, he stressed he was keen to leave his mark."

"Rather than the stain left by his predecessor," said Gus. "I can see his point. But, did he indicate how he might achieve this commendable aim for a legacy?"

"He was careful not to mention names, but he did sing the praises of an Assistant Chief Constable currently working in the Northeast."

"It's not news our Chief Constable's days are numbered," said Gus.

"Only the actual number of days remains to be determined, I suppose," said Divya. "No rest for the wicked. I must go."

Divya scurried across the car park towards the Hub building, and Gus went indoors. After briefly pausing at the Reception desk to sign in, he climbed the stairs and scanned the Administration area for friendly faces.

Kassie Trotter was on the far side of the office with her new trolley. She gave Gus a wave. Kenneth Truelove's door was closed, and there was no sign of Geoff Mercer yet. Thanks to his unusually rapid journey, Gus realised he still had five minutes before the witching hour. Someone put an arm around his waist and gave him an affectionate squeeze.

Her perfume identified her without Gus having to turn around.

"It may never happen, Gus," whispered Vera Butler. "Cheer up."

"I've just spoken to Divya," said Gus. "She smells trouble too. Why is everyone so quiet? Kassie waved instead of hollering a greeting across the mezzanine. That alone would make anyone nervous."

"The PCC was waiting for Kenneth outside his office when he arrived. They've been shut in there ever since."

"Does that mean I've had a wasted journey?" asked Gus. "I brought the files on another successful case, hoping to get the boss's week off to a good start."

"Kenneth phoned me earlier to add items to the lunch order," said Vera. "I think the PCC intends to join you."

Gus spotted Geoff Mercer's office door opening.

"If I hide behind Geoff, perhaps the PCC won't realise I'm there," he said.

"Get on with you," laughed Vera. "We'll be in later with your lunch. At times like this, I remember a piece of advice my father gave me. He told me he'd always listen to what was being said, and no matter how much he didn't like the news, he'd count to ten before speaking."

"Did he ever find it useful?" asked Gus.

"Hard to tell," said Vera. "He admitted he usually hit the person before he reached ten."

Gus caught up with Geoff as he reached the Chief Constable's door.

"Can you tell me what's going on, Geoff?" he asked.

"I'm as much in the dark as everyone else," said Geoff. "I don't think it will be long before we both find out. I do have news of my own, though."

Geoff knocked before Gus could grill him, and Kenneth

invited them in. He wasn't standing by the window this morning but sat beside the PCC at his desk. Gus knew Geoff Mercer had met Stuart Midwinter before, but this was the first time he'd seen their supremo in the flesh.

Gus remembered reading that Midwinter was a year older than he was and had lived and worked in Devizes all his life. He had retired from a local solicitor's office to take up his current role. Ninety grand a year from the Home Office would encourage plenty of people to join in the fun.

Midwinter's background explained why he seemed so at ease when appearing on local television or answering questions from reporters on the steps outside this building. Smooth was the first word that came to mind. He was someone who couldn't stop themselves from getting their name and face in the media.

One of his latest photo opportunities had been after the renaming of a lane in the sleepy village a few miles from Devizes, where he lived with his wife, Tessa. Midwinter had received a letter from a single resident complaining that the name, Pepper Lane, was inappropriate as it had links to a Jamaican plantation from the eighteenth century. Nobody from the village was aware whether that was how the lane had got its name in the first place and thought the link tenuous, but residents awoke one morning to find that overnight Pepper Lane had become Green Lane, sporting a new, black and white sign.

Stuart Midwinter was interviewed that evening on BBC Points West, suited and booted, all smiles, clutching a frisky King Charles Spaniel to his chest. Gus remembered being glad he and Suzie hadn't eaten.

Today, the PCC was wearing another expensive, dark blue suit over a light blue shirt, plus a tie so noticeable it had to represent a college, club, or society Gus would never get invited to join. While studying the man who held the future of everyone in the room in his hands, he realised that he'd started to speak to him.

"My role is to be the voice of the people and hold the police to account," said Stuart Midwinter. "I'm responsible for the totality of policing, and I aim to cut crime and deliver an effective and efficient police service within the Wiltshire police force area. We've made progress in the past two years, but Kenneth and I agreed that more needs to be done, and after forty years of loyal service, it's time for him to step aside."

"Kenneth knew the appointment was only ever temporary," said Gus. "Some might say he should have had the top job earlier, but we march to a different beat these days."

"Quite," said the PCC.

"When will the change take place?" asked Geoff Mercer.

"I prefer a gradual process," said Midwinter. "It has been an enjoyable time working closely with Kenneth. We will continue to work closely together on our shared goal of making Wiltshire safer until the first of April next year. My task was to find the next Chief Constable of Wiltshire Police, and an early start has allowed me to carry out a well-planned recruitment process to get the right person to lead the force into the future."

"Applications have been invited from eligible candidates from Assistant Chief Constables and equivalent ranks," said Kenneth. "Successful applicants were shortlisted, and interviews were held by an independent panel, chaired by Mr Midwinter."

"My mission since I took office has been to work in partnership with Kenneth to make our county a safer place to live, work and visit," said the PCC. "To achieve this, we need a quality policing service which meets the needs of our communities and is trusted by our residents. So I searched for the right person to drive this ambition forward."

"We're only too aware that dedicated, ethical, operationally experienced and focused leaders are thin on the ground," said Kenneth. "Stuart believes he's found someone who can quickly earn our officers' and staff's confidence and respect - from the executive level to the frontline."

"An inspirational leader to lead Wiltshire Police into the future," said Midwinter. "They will place great emphasis on getting the basics right: ensuring our force delivers quality police investigations, improves outcomes and justice for victims, and tackles those crimes that matter most to our communities."

"The right candidate will have a proven track record of delivering high-performing services, leading organisational change and fighting crime," said Gus. "But also working closely with local authorities and partner agencies to deliver effective community safety partnerships and a policing service that our residents want - and deserve."

"You have a better grasp of the situation than I gave you credit for, Mr Freeman," said Midwinter.

"I've read the pamphlets, Mr Midwinter," said Gus, "and a photographic memory helps. So I imagine you're close to announcing the name of Kenneth's successor?"

"We both agree ACC Sylvia Robbins from Durham ticked every box on our wish list," said Midwinter. "She was by far the best candidate we saw."

"Sylvia has agreed to join us here at London Road from January the first," said Kenneth. "After what we hope will be a smooth handover, I'll retire at the end of March."

Gus looked across at Geoff Mercer.

"You're quiet, Geoff," he said.

"I was half-expecting this news," said Geoff. "As it happens, the timing couldn't have been better. Christine and I have finally sold our house and can move forward with our move to Clench Common. I don't know whether ACC Robbins will want me around for the entire handover period. I'll start the ball rolling today, and perhaps I can retire at the end of February if that's acceptable, Kenneth?"

"I see no reason to object," said Midwinter.

Kenneth Truelove raised an eyebrow. Gus wondered whether he was counting to ten.

"We'll do everything we can to accommodate you, Mercer," said Kenneth.

"Thank you, sir," said Geoff.

Gus waited for someone to speak, but all was silence.

Kenneth glanced at the clock and took the opportunity to ring Vera.

"Lunch is on its way," he said when he put the phone down. "While we're waiting, perhaps you could fill us in on the contents of that folder you're clutching, Freeman."

"Another cold case solved, sir," said Gus. "Matthew Archer, a delivery driver for the Jade Garden Restaurant in Haydon Wick, Swindon, was murdered in February 2009. We've identified his killer as James Hatch, a thug working for a London wholesaler, Gabriel Rollins. The Liang family, who owned the restaurant, were pressured into switching suppliers through intimidatory tactics employed by the firm Rollins operates. The original owner and his wife have retired to France, but their two children have continued running the restaurant and takeaway. A nasty business, sir, where the daughter has been forced to sleep with Rollins to prevent an escalation in costs that would bankrupt her and her older brother."

"Why was this chap Archer killed?" asked the PCC.

"Archer and the owner's son were both handling deliveries in 2009," said Gus. "Hatch wouldn't have known who was driving to the remote address where they chose to carry out the attack. The message to the Liang family was loud and clear. Like many other takeaways and restaurants that Rollins and his crew approached, fall in line, or else."

"Nine years ago, you say?" said the PCC. "We must be thankful the county has far fewer murders now."

"The intimidation, threats, and assault have continued until last weekend," said Gus.

"Quite. When will our people get this Hatch character before a judge and jury, Mr Freeman?"

"The Met have arrested Rollins and Hatch and are running the show now. I was tasked with discovering who killed Matthew Archer and why. Job done. DS Mercer will ensure the Met gets the necessary evidence to support the case they prepare for the Crown Prosecution Service. Rollins has a wholesale delivery business with over a hundred food outlets on his books. So I imagine there's plenty of work to be done between here and London to snare all the victims. Indeed, the crime wave might travel further west."

"A complex operation then," said Midwinter. "It might not be possible to take advantage of any successful outcome before Kenneth takes his leave."

"The wheels of justice grind extremely slowly," said Gus. "With your background, you must have had first-hand experience, sir."

"Quite. Clench Common is a popular spot, DS Mercer. Tessa and I looked at houses in that village a few years ago, but nothing came on the market within our price range."

"Christine and I wished to downsize," said Geoff. "I

don't imagine our little cottage would have been among the properties your estate agent sent you."

Gus was impressed at the speed with which Midwinter had changed the subject. He guessed it had been covered in Media Training 101. After all, Police and Crime Commissioners were politicians in all but name, with bosses sitting behind a desk in the Home Office. When was the last time a politician answered a direct question?

A knock at the door scuppered any further discussion on the justice system. Vera and Kassie entered the room after the customary indistinct invitation from the Chief Constable and quickly placed the correct food and drink order in front of the four men.

"Enjoy," said Kassie as she turned her trolley and headed soundlessly to the door. Vera smiled and winked at Gus as she walked past. Wonders will never cease, thought Gus.

Stuart Midwinter sipped his milky coffee and inspected his sandwich.

"This looks good," he said. "Egg and cress with a dash of mayonnaise."

"The firm who won the contract offers a good service at a competitive cost," said Kenneth. "I believe you'll find this works out cheaper in the long run. We don't have staff disappearing off-site on extended lunches anymore."

"You would struggle to get to a fast-food outlet, get served, and get back in thirty minutes," said Geoff Mercer. "It was doable when we allowed everyone an hour for lunch."

Gus spotted Stuart Midwinter watching Geoff devouring his bacon bap. Maybe the egg and cress didn't look so good now. Gus finished his wrap and black coffee and waited for the others.

"Where are we off to next, sir?" he asked when Kenneth stood and walked to the window.

"Mr Midwinter hasn't finished filling us in on developments," said Kenneth.

"We must constantly review how we deliver the best service to the community we serve," said Midwinter. "The buildings we occupy cost a considerable sum to maintain and operate. You will know that certain police stations have closed in recent years, and others are scheduled to follow."

Gus knew that wasn't necessarily a good thing but decided it best not to interrupt.

"I've noted several buildings that aren't making the best use of the floor space available. The Old Police Station, for instance," said Midwinter. "You currently have six people in your office on the first floor, and Kenneth tells me at least one will be moving out in 2019."

Kenneth moved back to his desk.

"Ms Logan Barre has attracted much interest around the county," said Kenneth. "Indeed, she's got fans in Dorset and Avon & Somerset. This isn't news to you, Freeman. I've warned you that you can't count on her being with you much longer."

"It doesn't mean I have to like it," said Gus. "I suppose Grace will be moving back to London Road too, or is she attracting interest here, there, and everywhere?"

"DI Packenham did impress the right people in the Met when she worked there earlier this month," said Geoff Mercer.

"I sense there's no point asking for a replacement for DS Luke Sherman," said Gus.

"It's too early to say what might happen after the first of April," said Midwinter. "However, I intend to immediately make better use of the floorspace in that old building. We spent enough refurbishing it. Freeman and his team have superior accommodation and facilities than those enjoyed at many of our police stations. Staff from my department travel around the county, and that office is close to the centre. They can be anywhere in Wiltshire within forty-five minutes."

Gus could tell the PCC had never tried negotiating the road between the Old Police Station office and London Road on a Monday morning.

"There were solid reasons for providing the Crime Review Team with an open-plan office," said Geoff Mercer. "It's played a large part in their success. I've watched the team at work; they need the right information on the walls, free-standing boards, and flipcharts. Your staff members might find the graphic crime scene photos hard to stomach. The team undertake full-scale discussions in that office and interview suspects there. The presence of personnel from an unrelated department could disrupt how they operate, raising confidentiality issues for both parties."

"I don't need to remind you we're playing for the same team, DS Mercer," said Midwinter. "If certain minor adjustments must be made, then so be it. Any screening or partitioning will be carried out at the weekend, and my people will move in on Monday. The matter is not for debate."

"So, will nine people be crammed into the office on Monday morning?" Gus asked. "Or a dozen? That will be cosy."

Kenneth cleared his throat.

"There's more?" asked Gus.

"Ms Logan Barre won't be with you next week," said Kenneth. "She's being seconded to Gablecross to cover maternity leave."

"It's temporary, Gus," said Geoff. "The person originally assigned that task was rushed to the hospital with appendicitis at the weekend, meaning Lydia will work in Swindon with Raj Sengupta until Christmas. She will rejoin the team in the New Year, when, all things being equal, the other DS will be back, fit as a fiddle."

"My day gets better and better," said Gus. "Is there anything else you want to tell me, sir?"

The Chief Constable shuffled in his seat.

"The CPS has contacted me," he said. "Ahmet Tekin has opted to plead not guilty, despite the overwhelming evidence against him. As a result, his case will be heard at Swindon Crown Court starting on Wednesday."

"The name doesn't register," said Midwinter. "Was he one of the Albanian gangsters who threatened to kill you, Freeman?"

"No, he's a Turkish barber," said Gus. "He murdered a young woman in Swindon seven years ago. Laura Mallinder's death was one of the first cold cases we handled. DS Mercer passed the relevant files to Gablecross for them to prepare the case for the CPS."

"I presume they failed to identify the killer in the first place," said Midwinter.

"That's how we were set up to operate," said Gus. "Kenneth selects a historical case that had to be abandoned due to a lack of suspects, evidence, or resources. Then, we take another look, and if we're successful this time around, we allow detectives from the original police area to get the win. The system has two benefits. First, detectives who worked on the case and have been kept awake at night fretting over what they might have missed finally get closure. Then those who screwed up can be dealt with if they're still in post."

"With some historical cases, you must encounter detectives that have retired," said Midwinter. "Little can be done in that instance, I imagine?"

"We can ensure their previously glowing reputation gets tarnished," said Gus. "We're not on a witch hunt, though, Mr Midwinter. Our prime concern is the family of the victim. Nothing will ever bring back their loved one, but when a murder remains unsolved for a decade or more, it means we've let them down."

"Quite," said Midwinter.

"Why did the CPS contact you, sir?" Gus asked Kenneth. "It's never happened before."

"You've handed them a series of winnable cases, Freeman," said the Chief Constable. "I was told to ask you to invite team members who worked on the Mallinder case to attend. They wished to show their gratitude and allow you to watch justice being done. "

"How long do they believe the case will last?" asked Gus.

"You know it's never wise to speculate, Gus," said Geoff Mercer. "There's no such thing as a typical murder trial. My best guess is that you shouldn't go backwards and forwards to Swindon for more than ten days."

"Lydia won't be available," said Gus. "That leaves my two Detective Sergeants."

"DS Hardy and DS Davis," said Kenneth. "It will be a good experience for them. Although, I imagine both have given evidence in court in the past. Seeing the whole proceedings from start to finish as a spectator will be different."

"I hope Melody Davis allows her husband to hang around for the inevitable guilty verdict," said Gus. "Their first child is due early in December. We knew Neil would be taking paternity leave in the coming weeks, but we're faced with a different scenario. So why didn't Tekin plead guilty?"

"The CPS and their legal team will discover that on Monday," said Kenneth.

"My concerns about the number of people in the office on Monday morning seem misplaced now," said Gus. "Grace and Blessing will be the only ones working."

Kenneth Truelove had another card to play.

"The emergency at Gablecross meant Ms Logan Barre would be absent for a month," he said. "I was sure you could have coped with another case before I got the call from the CPS. Once I realised three more of you could be away from your desks for a week or more, it made sense to find an assignment for DI Packenham and DC Umeh to undertake here at London Road."

"Agatha Christie," muttered Gus. "And then there were none."

"We have spoken about this before, Freeman," said Kenneth.

"I hadn't imagined it happening quite so quickly," said Gus. "What did you manage to get lined up for Grace and Blessing?"

"It was a no-brainer," said Geoff Mercer. "As soon as Kenneth told me I had two rising stars available who lived in the countryside, I suggested they supplement the team assigned to the Farm Watch initiative."

"Farm Watch is the police alert service that aims to spot and prevent rural crime," said Stuart Midwinter.

"I'm aware of the frequency with which criminals separate farmers from their vital large vehicles," said Gus. "Let alone their quad bikes. Perhaps because their daughter is a detective, the thieves have given my partner's parents' farm a miss in the past. Now those two rising detectives you mentioned are lodging at the farm; John Ferris can probably get his insurance premiums reduced."

"Quite," said the PCC. "Wiltshire has more than its fair share of farms and rural properties. There are so many opportunities for a determined criminal gang to access buildings far enough away from the main house for them not to be spotted. The free scheme sends members a message about criminal activity and advice tailored to their area. The Ferris family and others can tap into police information to help protect themselves and their property. For example, if a suspicious vehicle is spotted near a farm and reported, a message can be sent out to all farms nearby, urging them to be vigilant and check their property is safe."

"Will Grace and Blessing be touring the county?" asked Gus. He wondered whose car they would be using.

"I think we have enough addresses on our books to keep them tied up for two weeks, minimum," said Kenneth.

"We hope they can persuade more owners to join the scheme," said Geoff. "We need them to stress that under the scheme, they get crime prevention advice to ensure property and goods are secure, and a property marking scheme to make it harder for thieves to dispose of stolen goods. In addition, we'll supply them with warning signs for gates and property boundaries so criminals know the property is protected."

"We know CCTV cameras inside retail businesses and outside domestic properties can deter criminals," said the PCC. "This is a similar approach, where we do what we can to make the criminal think twice before attempting to steal a tractor, or quad bike, from farms that display the items that suggest they're security conscious."

"I'm sure you're right," said Gus. "Have I heard everything now?"

"In due course, you'll return to pick up the details of your next case, Freeman," said the Chief Constable. "I can't put a date on it, but if you need something to cheer you up, it will mean returning to your old stamping ground. A double murder in Salisbury, investigated by your colleagues at Bourne Hill nick in 2012."

"Not Spider Crees?" asked Gus.

Kenneth nodded.

"John Crees and Mandy Howard, members of the biker community."

"Why did you refer to him as Spider, Mr Freeman?" asked the PCC.

"A series of tattoos," said Gus. "On his body, face, leather jacket, and the frame of his Harley Davidson."

"You were otherwise engaged," said Geoff Mercer. "A string of sexual assaults near the college."

"Five young women were attacked as they left evening classes during September and December 2012," said Gus. "As I was tied up with that business, DI Phil Crocker led the murder investigation. His second-in-command would have been DS Bob Mears. We barely saw one another until the end of January, but they hadn't had any joy with the people John Crees ran with. They've got a code that makes omerta sound like the cub scouts' promise."

"I promise to do my best, be kind and helpful, and love our world," said Stuart Midwinter.

Gus resisted the temptation to offer a one-word response.

"All potential leads were followed," said Geoff Mercer. "Nothing was found that justified extending the investigation, and it was closed down. A previous Chief Constable dismissed it as an internal dispute among the local Hells Angels community."

"Don't worry about the Salisbury case for now, Freeman," said Kenneth. "It's been in my drawer since you returned to the fold, and it can wait until you and the team can give it your full attention."

"Understood, sir," said Gus. "Might I ask who will work in the office from next Monday?"

"Morris Beard, Rosie Allison, and Sarah Holland," said the PCC. "Morris is the Strategic Delivery Lead for Prevention and Youth. Rosie and Sarah are two passionate individuals who support Morris in delivering improvements and driving forward the partnership's work within the portfolio area."

I'm sure I'll find time between now and when we meet to discover what that meant, thought Gus. He made a mental note to ask Suzie to translate it tonight.

"I don't think we need to keep you two any longer," said the Chief Constable. "We'll keep you updated on our progress."

"It was good to meet you, Mr Freeman," said the PCC. "Keep up the good work."

Gathering Clouds: Chapter Two

Geoff and Gus left the room and headed for Geoff's office.

"I knew things were going too well this morning," said Gus once they were behind a closed door.

"Try to remember what I said, Gus," said Geoff. "It's a temporary setback. At the latest, you and your team will be back in harness in the New Year. If you play your cards right, you can wangle an office at Bourne Hill to make the best use of your time working on that double murder case. You won't be disturbed by Morris Beard and his cronies."

"You and Kenneth have the finishing line in sight," said Gus. "Mine is obscured by gathering clouds."

Geoff laughed.

"A tad dramatic," he said. "Sylvia Robbins doesn't take over the reins until the first of April. You can solve several cases before then. Enough to convince her she'd be a fool not to keep taking advantage of your experience. You might lose a team member here or there, but fresh blood will always become available. The PCC told you it was too soon to say what would happen in April. We can only be sure that Kenneth will pack his suitcase for a cruise, and I'll be helping Christine decorate our new home. Oh, and you'll be in Urchfont on paternity leave at some point in the month. There are many positives for each of us to look forward to next year."

"I'd better get back to the office," said Gus.

"If you see Kassie Trotter outside, can you check whether she was baking at the weekend? I didn't dare ask when we were in with Kenneth."

"You'll miss her cakes when you move to Clench Common," said Gus.

"Not a bit of it. I've followed Kenneth's lead," said Geoff. "Kassie says she will add me to her list for a Sunday delivery after I leave London Road."

"Good to know you've got your priorities right, Geoff," said Gus. "All you have to do now is work out how to make the order last until the following Sunday."

Gus left Geoff Mercer with a problem to solve and crossed the mezzanine to the top of the stairs. Vera and Kassie were nowhere to be seen.

"Typical," muttered Gus. "Not a sign of either of them."

He shuffled downstairs to the foyer, opened the front door, and walked the short distance to the Ford Focus. As he left the car park and drove towards the town centre, Gus spotted them returning from lunch. No doubt they had been at Vera's house for their thirty-minute escape.

Gus tried to attract their attention, but they were deep in conversation. There was nothing for it. He had to soldier on without the healing properties of a Chelsea bun or a cream horn. Forty minutes later, he parked beside Lydia's red Mini and waited for the lift to descend. It was time to face the music.

"Welcome back, guv," said Neil. "My money's on somewhere in the south of the county for our next case. Am I right?"

Gus looked around the room. He'd come to enjoy working here. A deep sigh gave the game away that everything was about to change.

"It's bad news, guv, isn't it," said Lydia.

Gus told them everything.

"I never saw that coming," said Neil.

"Which bit, Neil?" asked Alex. "The Chief Constable and DS Mercer leaving within weeks of one another, or Ahmet Tekin pleading not guilty?"

"The first two getting out while the going was good was always on the cards," said Neil. "As for the rest, it all qualifies as unexpected. I can't see how Tekin can dispute the murder weapon. It matched the wounds of the murder victim and was used by him when he attacked Theo Hickerton. He was just five yards from where I was standing. As for one of the PCC's teams moving in with us, it makes no sense. We're not exactly blessed with acres of spare space."

"It might not be too bad when the screens are in place," said Grace. "It could get crowded in the restroom, though."

"I hope they bring their own supplies of coffee and biscuits," said Neil.

"Grace and Blessing won't need to worry about that before Christmas," said Lydia. "They'll be based at London Road with a long list of farms to visit, to show them ways to keep their expensive equipment safe."

"No, it's you I feel sorry for, Lydia," said Neil. "Raj Sengupta isn't Mr Dynamite. Gablecross thought they'd got rid of him when he went to join the Met as a cybercrime team leader, but he returned within twelve months. DI Sengupta reckoned he didn't fit in in London, and they got him working on similar crimes in the West. He can do less damage that way. Raj won't stray far from the office, so you'll get plenty of exercise if there's any fetching and carrying to be done."

"I need to get a floor plan of Gablecross," said Lydia. "That building is a rabbit warren."

"Did the Chief Constable hint at what we'd be doing later in the month, or the New Year, guv?" asked Alex.

"Neil backed the right horse," said Gus. "We're off to Bourne Hill police station for a double murder on my old patch in 2012. I don't imagine that will be something to look forward to. A biker gang was involved, not a friendly bunch of people who go for a spin at the weekends. The sort that has amusing phrases attached to them."

"Three can keep a secret if two are dead, d'you mean, guv?" asked Alex.

"That's one of them," said Gus. "Another favourite is we don't conform, so the police harass us."

"When I was working in my old job, I witnessed several occasions where the local club staged positive demonstrations to convince the public they belonged to the ninety-nine percent," said Alex. "They'd make a big show of turning up at the hospital with toys for the kids at Christmas; that sort of thing."

"Why ninety-nine percent?" asked Blessing.

"For decades, there were stories about bikers being responsible for all manner of violent behaviour," said Gus. "Before I joined the police, the Rockers in the Fifties got a bad reputation. It harks back to the 'we don't conform' idea. For their part, official motorcycle organisations would stress that ninety-nine percent of riders were law-abiding, solid citizens. Only one percent were intent on causing trouble."

"That backfired," said Alex. "The one's intent on causing trouble adopted the one percent as a badge. As a result, you often see the one percent patch sewn onto their clothing."

"I remember the cavalcade of bikers who always arrived first at the war memorial in Wootton Bassett when bodies were being repatriated from Afghanistan," said Neil. "That always felt genuine. It goes to show you never can tell."

"Whether you think of them as gangs or motorcycle clubs, they're far more complex an organisation than you could ever imagine," said Gus. "As for the charitable exercises and the cavalcades, don't forget the rogue element is a tiny percentage."

"I can't imagine you in a grubby leather jacket, Alex," said Blessing.

"I never rode without a full set of leathers, Blessing," said Alex. "If my accident had occurred in the Fifties when helmets weren't compulsory, I wouldn't have stood a chance. Despite the protection that my leathers gave me, my injuries were extensive."

"All that trauma is behind you now, thank goodness," said Lydia.

"I've got you to thank for that," said Alex.

"I read there are around two dozen chartered motorcycle clubs in this country," said Gus. "You can't mistake the uniform - leather jackets that have seen better days and powerful motorcycles. The club usually has a meeting place where members can enjoy a party with loud music. These gangs don't often hit the news headlines. The Hells Angels, the biggest motorcycle club in the world, steadfastly maintain that, first and foremost, they're just a motorcycle club."

"You sound as if you had dealings with them, guv," said Neil.

"I wasn't involved in the double murder investigation, Neil," said Gus. "That pleasure fell to DI Crocker and DS Mears. I didn't bump into them often during the two months after the bodies were discovered, but when I did, Phil Crocker told me that they hadn't felt safe since."

"What do you mean, guv?" asked Neil. "Were they threatened?"

"It wasn't subtle, Neil," said Gus. "Phil Crocker told me fifteen to twenty bikes would ride past their houses, day and night, while they tried to gather evidence. There was little they could do. There were no phone calls or death threats in the post. If they asked traffic cops to find an excuse to pull a patched biker over, they never carried any weapons. They could issue a few fines for minor offences, but it didn't deter the intimidation. A decade before this double murder, Phil Crocker had seen reports from Scandinavia where motorcycle gangs not only had access to machine guns, hand grenades, and car bombs but were prone to using them. He was scared."

"I remember a TV report after an attack in Copenhagen, guv," said Alex. "That was a clash between two gangs. They weren't targeting the police with that rocket launcher."

"Not on that occasion, Alex," said Gus. "However, the Salisbury bikers allegedly involved in the murder were a law unto themselves. They had bought a house on the outskirts, close to the ring road, in 2002. It was an end terrace property. Nothing special, just a three-bedroom, one-bathroom family home. Within twelve months, the next-door neighbours moved out."

"They'd had enough of the partying and loud music," said Blessing.

"Motorbikes roaring up and down the street without

regard for other people," said Grace. "Did the council do anything?"

"There wasn't much they could do," said Gus. "The neighbours never complained. It was private property, not social housing. Nobody asked where the money came from, but the gang members bought the vacant property and knocked through the walls downstairs and upstairs to convert the place into a clubhouse. Phil Crocker told me that people on the street reckoned the building had a fitted bar and a full-sized snooker table on the ground floor."

"Why didn't the police raid the clubhouse?" asked Neil.

"No laws were broken," said Gus, "and nobody ever complained about what was happening."

"They were too scared," said Lydia. "Do gang members still live at that address?"

"I don't have that information," said Gus. "The boss told me the case file would stay in his drawer until we could give it our full attention."

"No wonder you said this case wasn't something to look forward to, guv," said Neil. "A pity we handed back those stab vests we borrowed at Burnham-on-Sea. We might need them."

"Forewarned is forearmed, Neil," said Gus. "We'll ensure we carry out interviews at Bourne Hill police station. Then, if uniformed officers have to escort our guests from their homes, they can take the necessary precautions."

"And the risks," said Grace. "I feel safer already."

"Is there anything we need to do before we leave this evening, guv?" asked Lydia.

"We have squatters' rights to this end of the office," said Gus. "I suggest you move your desks closer to mine. Don't give the people the PCC is sending here at the weekend any ideas. If there's a space at the far end of the room under the clock, they will use it. It's human nature."

At five o'clock, everyone took a last look around the office and travelled in the lift to the ground floor.

"Enjoy your day off, guv," said Neil when they reached their cars. "What time shall I pick you up on Wednesday morning?"

"Eight o'clock?" said Gus. "What about Alex?"

"I'll be taking him with me, guv," said Lydia. "I can drop him at the Crown Court building in Islington Street on my way to Gablecross."

"Of course," said Gus. "Good luck tomorrow, Lydia. Try not to fall out with Raj Sengupta. Although, be warned that he'll try the patience of a saint."

"Nothing to worry about then, guv," said Lydia. "I'm no saint."

Lydia's red Mini soon reversed out and shot towards the entrance. Neil wasn't far behind them. Gus waited for Blessing Umeh to ease her Nissan Micra out of the parking bay as Grace stood and watched.

"Don't forget your wellington boots, Grace," he called. "I know the ground will be frost-hardened at this time of year, but items left behind by farmyard animals can play havoc with your shoes."

Grace gave him a rueful smile.

"You didn't say much about what you feel about these upcoming arrangements, Gus," she said as she joined him by his car.

"It is what it is, Grace," said Gus. "Geoff Mercer tells me it's temporary. However, we both know what the powers-that-be are like. The PCC is responsible for how the Wiltshire force operates, and he's keen for Sylvia Robbins to move in next week. He's got an agenda, and she will want to make a name for herself as soon as possible. We can only hope any final decisions aren't made until Kenneth has closed the door on his office at the end of March. I don't see any of you having anything to fear from what happens after that date. Rumours will soon start spreading on what the future holds for the Crime Review Team, but if my services are no longer required, I'll be the only real casualty. If there's a good time to be put out of a job, then April is the month I'd choose. I can work on my allotment until Suzie has the baby, and then I'm well-placed to let her get back to work as soon as she's ready."

"You've got it all worked out, haven't you?" said Grace.

"Pretty much," said Gus. "This job was always going to end in tears."

Grab your copy…
vinci-books.com/gatheringclouds

About the Author

Ted Tayler is the international bestselling indie author of The Freeman Files and The Phoenix series. Ted lives in the English west country, where his stories are based. He was born in 1945 and has been married to Lynne since 1971. They have three children and four grandchildren.

His thought-provoking mysteries appeal to readers of Sally Rigby, Joy Ellis, Pauline Rowson, and Faith Martin. His action-packed thrillers are a must for fans of Mark Dawson and J. C. Ryan.

Gus Freeman's cold case investigations are carried out with reasoned deduction rather than bursts of frantic action. In each of the twenty-four books, unsolved murder is accompanied by romance, humor, and country life. The core message in the twelve Phoenix novels is that criminals should pay for their crimes. Unfortunately, the current system fails to deliver the correct punishment, so Phoenix helps redress the balance.

Acknowledgments

The love and support of my family; without them, this would have been impossible.

www.ingramcontent.com/pod-product-compliance
Lightning Source LLC
Chambersburg PA
CBHW011425010726
47494CB00011B/2511